Where the hell had this come from?

Jack frowned at the high-heeled pump he held in his hand. Suddenly he felt a prickling at the back of his neck, as if someone else were in the room... watching him. He turned his head.

A woman he had never seen before was standing in the doorway of his cabin bedroom, wearing only a robe. On her head was a towel wrapped like a turban. The robe was wide open, revealing well-rounded breasts, smooth white skin and long shapely legs.

Jack swallowed. The woman's pink lips were parted but she said nothing. She looked as shocked as he felt. After what seemed an eternity, he cleared his throat.

"Cinderella?" he said softly, holding out the shoe. "I think I found your slipper."

ABOUT THE AUTHOR

Before penning her first romance, Kay Wilding was a
copywriter for an advertising agency, a free-lance
writer and an editor for a trade-magazine publisher.
She lives in Atlanta, Georgia, with her husband and
their daughter and son.

Kay loves books—all kinds, but especially romances—
crossword puzzles, her water-aerobics class and movies
that make her laugh and/or cry.

Books by Kay Wilding

KAY WILDING

GOING OVERBOARD

Harlequin Books

TORONTO • NEW YORK • LONDON
AMSTERDAM • PARIS • SYDNEY • HAMBURG
STOCKHOLM • ATHENS • TOKYO • MILAN
MADRID • WARSAW • BUDAPEST • AUCKLAND

To a real-life Frances—my best friend

Published November 1992

ISBN 0-373-16463-7

GOING OVERBOARD

Prologue

The will was a surprise.

Frances Lanier had known it existed, of course. Anybody who knew her father even casually knew about his will. He'd had it drawn up more than twenty years ago, shortly after his wife died, although nobody in the family knew exactly what it contained, as it had been updated. The surprise came when its contents were made known following his death. Frances was as shocked as anybody to learn that she was her father's prime beneficiary.

Thinking about it, however, Frances decided it made sense. After all, she was the one who'd taken care of him for the last thirteen years of his life, nursing him through stroke after stroke, from the time she was seventeen and fresh out of high school.

Besides, as she and her sister Juli and her brother Howie all knew, the estate wouldn't amount to much. There was the family home in a working class neighborhood in Charlotte, but both the home and the neighborhood were on the seedy side. There might be a little cash left from the sale of Howard Lanier's junkyard business, but Frances knew there wouldn't be much because both she and her father had been living off the proceeds of the sale of the junkyard for years. Maybe *nothing* was left, she thought with a sinking feeling.

Richard Morrison, her father's old friend and longtime lawyer, had handled the sale, along with all of Howard Lanier's personal and financial affairs. He had set up a special account for Frances's use, depositing money for household expenses into it, and telling Frances to come to him if she ever needed more, which she hadn't. Now she wondered whether she might have ended up owing *him* money.

The sound of Richard Morrison's voice distracted Frances from her musings. She sat up straighter in her chair, trying to concentrate on what the lawyer was saying, something about the accumulated cash value of their father's estate, the actual amount she would inherit. Her mind registered disconnected phrases—inheritance taxes...write-offs...stock investments...Treasury notes, and a couple of other things she couldn't decipher because Mr. Morrison had a tendency to mumble. It was all a bunch of mumbo jumbo to her anyway. With mild surprise, Frances saw her brother suddenly jump to his feet.

"What?" Howie shouted.

Richard Morrison pushed his glasses up higher on his nose and looked at a piece of paper he held in his hand. "About nine-eighty or ninety," he said. "That's roughly what Frances will inherit."

"That can't be!" Howie said, shouting again.

Frances frowned, embarrassed by her brother's outburst. Even though Howie was a lawyer, too, that didn't give him the right to be rude to Mr. Morrison. She wondered what he was so excited about in the first place. Nine hundred and eighty or ninety dollars sounded good to her. Fantastic, in fact. It meant she didn't owe Mr. Morrison money, after all.

"I assure you my figures are accurate," Mr. Morrison said, removing his glasses to glare at Howie.

"I didn't mean to insinuate..." Howie said, backing down.

Frances saw the small, slightly smug smile that touched Mr. Morrison's lips before he quickly suppressed it. She wondered what it meant.

"That's after taxes and legal fees, of course," Mr. Morrison continued, "but it doesn't reflect the current quarterly interest on investments. The amount Frances will receive *could* run as high as a million, but I quoted the lower figure to be on the safe side."

"What did you say?" Juli screeched, jumping up from the sofa, too.

Frances blinked. She opened her mouth to speak, but nothing came out. She watched Mr. Morrison, who suddenly turned to her and winked! There was no mistaking the smirk on his face this time.

"I said," he replied slowly and distinctly, "that Frances will inherit close to one million dollars, after taxes."

"You mean," Juli said, her voice at a hysterical pitch, "that our father had *that* much money? And he left all of it to Frances?"

"You realize, of course," Howie said, his manner more controlled this time, "that if our father failed to mention his other two children in his will, we can probably have it declared invalid in about two seconds flat."

"Your father and I discussed that point," Richard Morrison said. "And he decided to leave both you and your other sister a bequest."

"How much did he leave us?" Juli asked.

Frances watched from her chair, still unable to move or speak, while Mr. Morrison carefully donned his glasses, then read directly from her father's will. "To my daughter Julianna, who first shortened her name to Julia and now calls herself Juli, and to my son Howard Junior, who goes by the name of Howie for no good reason that comes to my mind, I leave...only my best wishes, because that's all I ever received from them.''

"That's not..." Howie began, but Richard Morrison held up his hand for silence.

"There's more," Mr. Morrison said, and proceeded to read from the will again. "My good friend and competent attorney, however, advises me that I should include a monetary bequest in order to make this will binding, so I'm leaving both Juli and Howie a dollar each. I figure the two of them can pass the buck for the rest of their lives, just as they've been doing so far.''

Frances held her breath, watching as Mr. Morrison slowly removed his glasses, inserted them into his glass case, and put the case into the pocket of his coat. A stunned silence fell over the living room. Then everybody started talking at once.

"Frances."

At the sound of her name she looked up and saw her brother's wife. "Lisa," Frances said, smiling her pleasure. Her sister-in-law was her favorite person in the entire family, more like a sister to her than her own sister was.

Frances held up her hand and Lisa took it. "My sister-in-law, the heiress. I can't believe it. Wow! A million bucks!''

"I still can't believe it, either," Frances said. "I keep wondering if there hasn't been some mistake. Maybe Pops didn't really mean for me to have *all* the money.''

Lisa shook her head. "There has been no mistake," she stated emphatically. "And justice is served.''

Frances glanced at her brother and sister in the middle of a heated argument with Richard Morrison. "I doubt that either Juli or Howie will agree with you on that assessment.''

"Not to worry," Lisa said. "Howie was taken by surprise and he hates surprises, especially unpleasant ones, but

I know my husband. He'll come around. I'll make sure he does."

"And then there's Juli," Frances said with a sigh.

"She'll be after you to share your inheritance, that's for sure. But you can deal with her."

"You know me better than that, Lisa. I've never been able to stand up to Juli."

Lisa frowned. "Then maybe you should get away from her for awhile. Take a vacation."

"A vacation?" Frances repeated, as if it were a foreign word. It was, in a way, and it was something she'd never considered. "To where?"

"Who cares? Just make sure it's a long one. Isn't there some place you've always wanted to go…something you'd like to do?"

A vacation. Frances considered the idea. "Well," she said after a few moments, "I used to enjoy 'The Love Boat' on TV. I used to think it might be nice to take a cruise someday."

"That's perfect!" Lisa said, slapping her own forehead. "I should have thought of it myself. Some friends of ours went on one last year and had a fabulous time. It's just what you need, Frances. The crew takes care of everything, pampering you like crazy. You won't even need to think if you don't want to."

The idea sounded appealing but… "What about Howie and Juli?"

"Don't worry. The vultures will still be here when you return. The thing is … you'll be different by then."

Frances giggled, already caught up in Lisa's wild scheme and beginning to enjoy it. "How will I be different?"

"You'll be relaxed, confident …"

"Me? Confident?"

"You bet. Because it will have sunk in on you by then that you have money. Money means power and that, in turn, breeds confidence. I'm not sure I'll be able to bear being around you by the time you get back, what with all the money and power and confidence you'll have . . . not to mention, the rich, handsome lover you'll meet on the boat.''

Frances laughed. "You're crazy, you know that?"

"Sure I am," Lisa agreed. "Now. Forget about me, forget about your money-grabbing brother and sister . . . and go sail into the sunset. Have some fun for a change!"

JACKSON SHERROD KNEW it was going to be a bad day as soon as he stepped out of the private elevator to his penthouse office suite and saw the young, pretty receptionist staring at him from wide lavender eyes that were close to tears or panic, or both.

"Mr. Sherrod!" she exclaimed. "I didn't know you were here."

"I wasn't, but I am now," he said, stating the obvious and hoping she wouldn't start crying. At the moment he didn't think he could cope with a woman in tears on top of everything else.

"Mr. Armstrong has been looking for you. I think something *terrible* has happened."

Martin Armstrong had been with Jack from the very beginning, almost ten years ago, and had been with his father before that. Discretion was one of the traits Jack valued most in his top aide, that and loyalty, and he considered ignoring the receptionist's overreactive remark, but immediately changed his mind. The company *was* involved in delicate negotiations right now, and it was possible that because of the pressure, Martin had inadvertently let something slip without knowing he'd done so.

"I'm sure it's nothing serious, Ms. Burke," Jack said, giving her his most sincere smile. "But thank you for your concern. And your diligence."

Before she could respond, he quickly walked away, heading for the safety of his private office. Closing the door behind him, he took a deep breath and then went to his desk where he punched out the code numbers that would connect him directly with Martin Armstrong.

"Martin. You were looking for me?"

"Since early this morning."

"What happened?"

"I'm not sure. Yet. But I think there's been a leak about our, um, project."

"Damn!" Jack exclaimed. "Do you know who? Or where?"

"No. But I'm working on it. And there's more. Are you in your office?"

"Yes."

"Don't move until I get there."

Jack slowly replaced the phone in its cradle. He closed his eyes for a moment, then opened them and walked over to the window wall in his office, looking down at the unobstructed view of the river below. His father had had such a view as this from his office window, Jack remembered with a sudden sharp pain.

His father's office had looked down on Boston Harbor, though, and his was in New York. And Jack was going to succeed where his father had failed. *No,* he corrected himself, *my father didn't fail. He had his company—a company that had been in the Sherrod family for generations—stolen away from him.*

Now, Jack was going to get his father's company back. And he was going to take over the conglomerate that had stolen it from his father in the first place. He considered it to be *due interest,* and he was determined not to rest until that interest had been paid in full.

Hearing a knock at his door, Jack said, "Come in."

Martin Armstrong entered the office and closed the door behind him. "First Fidelity is calling in our loan," he said without preamble. "As soon as word gets out on the street, our other creditors will probably do the same."

It took a moment for the words to sink in and when they finally did Jack shouted, "Damnation! They can't do that!"

"They already have. So calm down."

"Calm down? Calm down when everything I've worked for—and everything you've worked for, too, Martin—*for almost ten years,* is going down the tubes?"

"It hasn't come to that. At least, not yet."

"And what about the Japanese? Has somebody leaked our situation to them, too? Is that why they're dragging their feet on this?"

"I don't think so," Martin said, rubbing the back of his neck. "I'd say they were proceeding at their normal, deliberate pace so far. They're very meticulous, you know. That's one of the reasons they're so successful."

Jack took a deep breath. "So what do you suggest we do now?"

"Well...we could abandon our takeover plans, at least for the moment. We could lay low for awhile and regroup our forces."

"You know I don't want to lose all we've built up, Martin, no more than you do. But I hate the idea of giving up now...when we're so close. I can almost smell the sweat of fear coming from those crooks who stole my father's company."

Martin nodded. "I can understand that. I loved your father, too, Jack. He was the finest man I ever met."

Jack sighed. "So what are our options, aside from giving up? Do you have any other suggestions?"

Martin rubbed the back of his neck while he thought. "I do have one idea," he said at last. "But you won't like it."

"Try me."

"You could go on a vacation to someplace remote. Very remote, where our creditors can't find you."

"A vacation?" Jack repeated incredulously. "Are you crazy?"

"I told you that you wouldn't like it. But it's what a lot of leaders do at a time of crisis."

"Hide?"

"Hell, yes! The enemy can't attack you if they can't find you."

Jack shook his head. "I still don't like it. It seems to me that taking time off is the *last* thing I should be doing right now."

"Look at it this way. You'll be gone, and I'll make sure nobody knows where you are or how to get in touch with you. It'll buy us time...plenty of time for the Japanese to make up their minds. I can stall our creditors until they do." Martin took a deep breath and expelled it. "It's the best idea I've been able to come up with, but you might have a better plan."

"You know I don't."

"So...?"

Jack shrugged in resignation. "I'll do it. What kind of vacation did you have in mind for me?"

"Don't make it sound like a death sentence," Martin said with a little laugh in which Jack detected a note of relief. "I was thinking you might go on a long cruise. You might actually enjoy it."

"I doubt that. But a cruise sounds like a good place to hide out for awhile. I'll call some of my friends who have yachts and..."

"Absolutely not! With that kind of visibility, you'd be tracked down immediately."

Jack frowned. "Then what do you suggest?"

"I was thinking more along the lines of you traveling under an assumed name...on one of those 'Love Boat' kind of cruises."

"I can't think of anything worse."

"Yes, you can." Martin waited for a long moment. "And nobody would think to look for you on a fun-filled vacation voyage like that."

Jack raked his fingers through his hair while he considered the idea. "I suppose you're right," he said at last. "Will you book me a stateroom on such a vessel... please?"

"Where would you like to go?"

"Does it matter?" Jack shrugged. "Just make sure it's a long cruise, so we can give the Japanese all the time they need to make up their minds."

Chapter One

Frances clenched her teeth, fighting a rising panic as her fellow passengers swept her along the gangplank leading to their cruise ship, *American Dreamer*. As far as she was concerned, the dream was rapidly turning into a nightmare.

She'd started out this morning with such great expectations, too. After much thought—not to mention poring through hundreds of brochures—she'd finally decided on this particular cruise. It would take her from Montreal to Quebec and via the Gulf of St. Lawrence to St. John, along the eastern seaboard to Miami, then through the Panama Canal to Los Angeles and return. She had been looking forward to this as the trip of a lifetime.

But what a disastrous beginning!

She wondered what would go wrong next. Her early-morning flight out of Charlotte had been delayed, which caused her to miss her connecting flight to Montreal. The next available flight had been booked solid and she'd waited on standby for hours, finally managing to grab the last seat.

That flight had been late arriving in Montreal, and she'd spent a fortune getting from the airport to the boat dock after being told that a taxi was the only way she'd be able to reach *American Dreamer* before it sailed without her.

Maybe she should have *let* it sail without her, Frances thought, using the rumpled sleeve of her suit jacket to wipe away the sweat that had formed on her brow. Maybe all the trouble she'd had today was an omen.

But it was too late to turn back now. Even if she wanted to, there was no way she could escape the surge of the crowd carrying her along to board the cruise ship. She suddenly felt claustrophobic on top of everything else. The last time she'd been in a crowd as large as this had been at her high school graduation, where she and her classmates had lined up beside the stage waiting to receive their diplomas.

She'd been nervous then, too, and there'd been a lot of pushing and shoving for position, the same way there was now. The difference was that she'd known all those people; they were her classmates, boys and girls she'd known all her life, whereas these people were total strangers. Frantic strangers.

She wondered why they were in such a rush. When she'd finally checked in at the dock after her helter-skelter ride from the airport in a taxi from hell, she'd found out that the ship wasn't scheduled to leave port until eleven o'clock tonight, almost an hour from now. Surely these passengers must have received the same information.

Frances let out a yelp as a man who must have weighed three hundred pounds elbowed her aside, then stepped on her foot as he passed. He never looked back. She sighed. Then she sighed again, with relief this time, as she finally stepped inside the ship and the crowd around her began to spread out.

Her relief lasted for only a moment, the length of time it took her to realize that she had no idea which way to go to find her stateroom. And she really needed to find her stateroom. She was almost desperate to get to it—to finally escape from the masses of strangers who'd surrounded her since early this morning, and to recuperate from what had been one of the most harrowing days of her life.

Frances moved over to one side, trying to get out of the way of the main crush of people, and dug around in her purse until she found her ticket. She also had a key to her stateroom and a floor plan of the boat, somewhere. But where? She tried to remember what she'd done with them.

She saw a white-uniformed young man approaching her at a rapid pace—almost a run—and decided to ask him for directions. "Could you—"

"Sorry, ma'am. If you have a problem, see the purser," he said over his shoulder as he rushed past her.

Sure, she thought. *As if I have any idea who the purser is... or where to find him.*

She saw another white-uniformed blur rushing toward her. "Excuse me," she said, grabbing his sleeve before he could get past. "Would you direct me to my room?"

The harried-looking young man tried to pull away, but Frances held on tight and waved her ticket in front of his face. Sighing as if in resignation, he glanced at her ticket. "Two decks up, ma'am. The escalator's on your right."

She relaxed her grasp and he was gone before she had a chance to thank him. Oh, well. She headed for the escalator. The next deck up wasn't quite as crowded as the one she'd just left, and the second deck up seemed positively deserted by comparison. Frances breathed a sigh of relief and stepped off the escalator, where another young man in a white uniform immediately stepped forward to meet her. This one didn't seem to be hurried or harried in the least; in fact, he was smiling.

"Welcome aboard *American Dreamer,* ma'am. May I be of assistance?"

"Thank you," she said, returning his smile. "I'm looking for my room. It's number two, two—"

"Just follow me," he interrupted, his smile broadening. "It's right this way."

Well! Frances thought, starting to relax. Maybe this was where the pampering began. She could certainly use a little pampering after the day she'd had. She followed the young man down the corridor, where he stopped beside an open door.

"Here we are," he said cheerfully, holding out his arm to motion Frances inside the room, where a white-uniformed young woman was placing a huge basket of fruit on the glass-topped coffee table in front of the sofa.

Sofa? Frances hadn't realized that her stateroom would be large enough to have a sofa. Then, looking past the sofa to sliding glass doors on the other side of the room, she caught her breath. "A patio?" she whispered.

"The open promenade, ma'am. The lounge chairs will be in place before you wake up in the morning. We always re-move them at night, of course."

"Of course," she agreed automatically. At that point, she would have agreed with anything the young man said. She was enthralled by the room, and was beginning to be-lieve it was worth the outrageous sum she'd paid for it, al-though she'd fought Lisa tooth and toenail to get something cheaper. Thank heavens Lisa had won the battle!

The nice young man insisted on showing her the entire suite, pointing out every convenience from the wet bar and TV to the complimentary terry-cloth robe in the bathroom and the Jacuzzi in the tub. "Is there anything you need?" he asked when he finally finished.

"Well . . ." she said, almost embarrassed to bring up the subject after he'd been so nice and had taken such pains to show her around, "I don't see my luggage here. I mean . . ."

He frowned. "Were you late checking in at the dock?"

"Yes," she admitted.

"That's it, then," he said, breaking into another broad smile. "It should be here any moment. But if you have any trouble—any trouble at all . . ." He handed her his card. "Call me. Day or night."

"Thank you." She looked at the card he'd given her. "Dave."

"My pleasure," he said, heading for the door. She halfway expected him to salute, but he gave her another blinding smile instead. "Don't forget." Then he was gone, closing the cabin door behind him.

Frances took a deep breath, let it out with a whoosh, and looked round her stateroom. "Alone at last," she said, kicking off her high-heeled pumps because her feet were killing her, especially the one that the fat man had stepped on. She'd already planned what she was going to do next— spend a long, relaxing time in the Jacuzzi, something she'd been wanting to do for years, since she'd first seen one advertised on TV. After that, assuming her luggage had arrived by then, she might get dressed and go up to the bon voyage party that was scheduled to take place on the bridge.

Or she might not.

Maybe she'd make herself comfortable in the plush terry-cloth robe hanging on the knob inside the bathroom door instead. And there was also the yummy-looking basket of fresh fruit waiting on the coffee table, begging to be eaten. She just might have herself a dandy time right here, by herself. The idea of facing another big group of people tonight wasn't all that appealing, anyway.

But she could decide later what she wanted to do. She went over and closed the drapes at the sliding glass doors after first making sure they were locked. Then she padded across to the bathroom, remembering at the last moment to lock it behind her, too, in case her luggage arrived while she was in the Jacuzzi.

"JUST PUT MY BAGS in the bedroom," Jack told the steward as they entered his suite.

"Shall I unpack them, sir?"

"Don't bother. I'll have them taken care of later. Right now I need to make an important phone call," Jack replied, the tone of his voice making it clear that he wanted privacy.

He'd been rushed all day, barely making the last call for boarding *American Dreamer*, and on the flight up from New York he'd remembered a couple of points he needed to discuss with Martin right away. He waited until the steward returned from depositing his luggage in the bedroom.

"You've been very helpful," Jack said, shaking the steward's hand and slipping him a hefty tip. "Thank you."

"If there's anything you need—"

"I'll let you know. Good night."

After the man left, Jack removed his jacket, dropping it onto the back of a chair. He loosened his tie and unbuttoned the top button of his shirt. Then he went to the telephone and punched the number for the ship's operator.

"Damn!" he muttered in frustration as he replaced the receiver a few moments later. All the ship-to-shore lines were busy at the moment, the operator had said apologetically, but she would call him back as soon as one became available. He raked his fingers through his hair. Then, spotting the wet bar in the corner, he walked over to inspect its contents. He nodded with satisfaction when he found a bottle of Scotch malt whiskey, and mixed himself a Glenfiddich with water.

"Cheers," he said aloud, lifting his glass toward his reflection in the mirror above the bar. He took a deep gulp of the whiskey. "And bon voyage," he added, taking another drink.

Then it hit him...like a ton of bricks, as the old cliché went. What was he going to do—what the *hell* was he going to do—with himself on this damn boat? For days. Weeks. And possibly even longer. He closed his eyes, blotting out the tortured reflection of himself in the mirror, and took another gulp of whiskey.

Then he freshened his drink and took it over to the sofa, where he sat down beside the phone. Sighing, he stretched his legs out under the coffee table...and encountered something with the tip of one toe. He couldn't see what it was because of the basket of fruit blocking his view. He leaned over to one side but still couldn't see. He put down his drink and slid to his knees beside the sofa, feeling under the table with one hand and finally pulling out...a woman's shoe?

Jack stood up, frowning at the high-heeled pump he held in his hand. Where the hell had this come from?

He was still looking at the shoe, still frowning, when he suddenly felt a prickling at the back of his neck. It was as if someone else were in the room...watching him. He turned his head and saw her.

She was standing in the doorway leading from the bedroom, wearing only a terry-cloth robe and a towel wrapped around her head like a turban. The reason he was positive that was all she was wearing was because the terry-cloth robe was wide open, revealing two well-rounded breasts with erect, pink-tipped nipples, a smooth, white, softly-feminine stomach and a thatch of dark hair perched atop the inverted V where her long legs met above her shapely thighs.

Jack swallowed. The woman's pink lips were parted but she said nothing. She simply stared at him, looking as shocked, startled, speechless as he felt.

After what seemed an eternity, he cleared his throat. "Cinderella?" he said softly, holding out the shoe. "I think I found your slipper."

She screamed.

OH, DEAR LORD, Frances thought. *Just when I thought nothing worse could happen to me today, it has.*

She saw the man—the intruder—drop her shoe onto the floor, and frantically tried to clutch the terry-cloth robe closed as he rushed toward her. *Too late!*

He was already on her, holding her pressed tightly against him with one arm while he covered her mouth with his other hand, smothering her screams. She shook her head from side to side, trying to break free from his painful grasp. That only seemed to incite him—or excite him—causing him to increase the pressure of his hand and arm.

"Stop it!" he said in a fierce whisper. "Don't make me hurt you."

Don't make me hurt you? Did that mean he didn't plan to kill her? Or harm her in . . . other ways? Frances tried to think clearly, to think at all. But how could she think when this stranger—possibly a rapist or a serial killer—was holding her the way he was, almost squeezing the breath out of her.

Don't panic! she told herself. *But be realistic.* Of course he intended to hurt her. Otherwise, why had he stolen into her room while she was in the tub?

She bit his hand. Hard. As much of it as she was able to sink her teeth into.

"Damn!" he exclaimed, removing his hand from her mouth and relaxing his grip for a moment.

A moment was all it took for her to extricate herself from his arm around her shoulders. She started for the door but had taken only a couple of steps when she felt his fingers close around her arm, pulling her back.

"Let me go!" she shrieked, scratching at his hand with her fingernails.

"Stop it!" he shouted.

"*You* stop it!" she shouted back at him, making a swipe at his face this time, then watching with horror as she saw she'd drawn blood.

"Why, you..." he muttered, struggling to grab her hand before she could take another swipe at him.

Panic-stricken as she was, she was conscious of the fact that he was breathing as fast and hard as she was. *I've done it now,* she thought. *He'll kill me for sure.*

With nothing more to lose, she drew back her bare foot and kicked his shin, then gasped with pain. "Oh!" she exclaimed, wondering if she'd broken something.

"What are you trying to do? Kill us both?" he asked, reaching again to try to capture her free hand.

She turned away and pulled her arm behind her just as he reached, and he ended up capturing her breast with his big hand instead. Frances hadn't realized until then that her robe must have reopened while they were struggling. She screamed again.

The man jerked his hand away from her breast and clamped it over her mouth. "I'm sorry," he said. "Excuse me. I didn't mean to... that is... Dammit! Calm down. I told you I wasn't going to hurt you!"

You just did! she tried to say. Her words, even to her own ears, came out sounding like, "Hmn hunx hnh!"

"Why do you insist on making a big racket?" he asked. "What the hell is wrong with you?"

In a few choice words, she told him what was wrong with *him.* "Mmghmn mhx pmnm cmhm!"

"I don't understand a word you're saying," he said with a frown. "But don't get your hopes up. I have no intention of making the same mistake twice by relaxing my hold on you."

She was extremely conscious of the hold he had on her, crushing her bare breasts—including the one that still smarted from his grabbing it so roughly a moment ago— against the front of his white shirt. She gritted her teeth, wishing she had his hand between them again.

"But we do need to talk this over," he continued.

She managed to extricate one of her arms, and immediately started flailing her fist against his back. It might not do him much harm, but it sure did her a lot of good to show him how she felt.

"And we need . . . to do it . . . rationally," he said, recapturing her arm and holding it, along with her other arm, behind her back. When he had her even more firmly in his grasp again, he gave a deep sigh, then frowned at her. "Why are you so damned skittish?"

"Hmm?" she said, wondering who wouldn't be skittish in such a situation.

"Is that all you can say?"

She nodded her head vigorously.

"I can see your point. If I let you go, will you promise not to scream again?"

Never! she thought, shaking her head from side to side.

"That's what I thought," he said. "Still, we do need to talk. Maybe I can ask you questions that you can answer yes or no. What do you think of that idea?"

She started to tell him exactly what she thought of him *and* his idea, but realized he wouldn't be able to understand her. She growled instead.

"Why did you scream the way you did when we first saw each other?" he asked, ignoring her growl. "Was it because I startled you?"

She nodded.

"I'm sorry. In my defense, I'll have to say that you surprised me, too."

Frances blinked. He was beginning to sound sane. Rational. Or was it simply that she was starting to lose *her* mind?

"And," he continued, "at the risk of sounding less than a gentleman, I have to remind you that you were in my room, dressed the way you were... or weren't..."

Frances caught her breath. Was *this* the way rapists operated these days? Mortifying you with their words before they... before... And what was it he'd said? That she was in *his* room? That didn't make any sense at all.

"So naturally I assumed... I mean I knew... why you were here."

What? she wondered. What was he suggesting?

"But hey. I'm not going to turn you in, if that's what you're worried about. I know you working girls have to make a living. So why don't I just turn you loose? You can get dressed and go to your own room... and we'll both forget the whole thing. What do you say?"

What was *he* saying? That he thought she was a... a... hooker? She tried to think... rationally, as he'd suggested. Maybe he did think she was a hooker. Or maybe he didn't. Maybe he was using that accusation to throw her off guard... so she wouldn't turn *him* in to the authorities after he'd gone. That, in turn, might mean that he didn't intend to harm her, after all, as he'd said.

And if that was the case, her best move would be to go along with his suggestion. But only long enough to get away from him. After that, she'd have him behind bars so fast he'd think a tornado had hit him.

"Hmm," Frances said, nodding her head to show him she agreed with his suggestion.

"But can I trust you?"

She nodded more vigorously.

"I'm not so sure," he said, frowning.

Damn you! she said. It came out sounding like, "Dnhn hnu!"

"What was that?" he asked, his mouth quirking up at the corners in something that looked suspiciously like a sarcastic grin.

She narrowed her eyes, glaring at him.

"Still . . . I can always muzzle you again if you go off the deep end and start yelling. Besides that, we all need to have a little faith in our fellow human beings sometime. Don't you think so?"

Frances didn't trust herself to give any kind of reaction, so she kept quiet and still, watching him.

He took a deep breath. "I'm going to release you on the count of three. One . . . two . . ." He abruptly released her and jumped back a couple of steps. "Three! There. You're free to go."

Frances immediately pulled the robe tight around her and looped the belt around her waist. Then she looped the belt another time, tying a knot. She wondered what her next move should be . . . and also what he planned to do. She no longer believed he meant to harm her, but still couldn't understand what his game was.

"There's still something I don't understand," he said. "What exactly *is* your game?"

"What?"

"Was it your plan to come in here and undress, then scream bloody murder, hoping to extort money from me?"

Frances didn't believe what she was hearing. "You bastard!" she whispered through clenched teeth.

"Okay. So maybe that was a bad guess. But why *did* you come into my room, take off all your clothes, and then act like a frightened virgin when I appeared? I never heard of a scam like that."

"In the first place," Frances said, clenching her fists and drawing herself up to her full five-foot, four-inch height, "I didn't come into your room. You came into mine. And..."

"What?"

"You heard me. Here I was, having a bath in the privacy of my own room, and when I came out I found a drunken intruder. So I screamed. It's what anybody—any sane person—would do under the circumstances."

"I am *not* an intruder. And I'm not drunk."

"You smell like a distillery!"

"I had one drink..."

"Sure."

"And that has nothing to do with any of this! You're trying to cloud the issue."

"Okay, I'll get back to the issue. When I came out of the bathroom, you *grabbed* me ... manhandled me..."

"So *that's* it!" he shouted.

Frances was confused. "What?"

"*That's* the way you plan to extort money from me. By claiming I manhandled you. But I'll tell you now—*babe*—you won't get away with it. I'll fight you to the highest court in the land before I'll pay you a penny!"

Frances shook her head. "I ... think we've lost communication here somewhere." Maybe he *was* crazy. Or maybe she was. "If you'll leave quietly, right now, we'll forget the whole thing."

"That's exactly what I told you!" he shouted. "Only a few minutes ago!"

"Okay," she said, trying to make her voice sound soothing. She didn't want to agitate him anymore at this stage, when they finally might be getting close to a solution. "I agree with you."

"Fine," he said, raking his fingers through his hair. "So leave ... quietly, I hope."

"Not me. You."

"What?"

"You're the one who has to leave," Frances said, trying to keep her voice calm so she wouldn't upset him again, but firm at the same time. "This is my room."

He shook his head. "No. This is *my* room."

Frances opened her mouth to speak, but couldn't think of anything to say, so she merely shook her head.

"It *is!*" he insisted.

"No."

"Dammit!" He looked around the room, almost frantically it seemed to Frances, and finally raced over to a chair, where he picked up a jacket—probably his—and started searching through the pockets. "Here it is!" he shouted, holding up what looked like a boarding pass. "My ticket!"

He thrust the ticket directly in front of her eyes, so Frances had no choice except to look at it. "It says you're in room P-22," she said. "So?"

He grabbed her wrist, none too gently, and pulled her over to the door to the corridor, flinging it open, then pointing to the numbers emblazoned on the outside. P-22. "So?" he said triumphantly.

Her room number was 222, not P-22, Frances thought with a sinking feeling. Then she remembered the harried crewman who'd given her directions in the lobby after only a momentary glance at her ticket . . . and the attendant upstairs who'd cut her off before she could add the final "two" to her stateroom number.

"Oh, no," she said.

Chapter Two

Jack watched the woman, waiting for her to continue. After a long moment, she did.

"I think I owe you an apology," she muttered in a small voice.

"Then you admit—"

"No! I'm not who—I mean *what*—you think I am. I'm a paying passenger... paying my own way, is what I meant to say. It's just...I seem to have gotten into the wrong room by mistake."

Jack frowned, uncertain whether or not to believe her.

"I don't blame you for being skeptical," she said, correctly interpreting his frown. "I would be, too, under the circumstances." She attempted a laugh, which caught in her throat. "But it's true. I promise."

She seemed frightened and unsure of herself, like a small child. Jack felt a quick surge of sympathy, but stopped himself short of expressing it because he still wasn't sure about her. She could be a really good actress as well as an experienced con artist.

"How did you get into my room in the first place?" he asked. "Did your key fit my—?"

"No! The door was open. An attendant was delivering fruit." She gestured toward the bowl of fruit on the coffee table.

"So you simply walked in and made yourself at home?"

"Of course not!" she said, a flush creeping into her cheeks. "Another attendant escorted me inside."

"Into the wrong room?"

"I . . . I think it happened because he cut me off before I could give him my entire room number. And I never got a look at the number on the door until a few seconds ago. I think what caused the whole thing in the first place was that another attendant down in the lobby told me to come up to this floor and the second attendant naturally assumed I belonged here. But I don't blame him—the first attendant, that is—because everything was so confused in the lobby with people rushing every which way and. . ." She was blushing furiously now. "I know it all sounds farfetched."

It did. At least, the part of it that Jack had been able to make out from her jumbled rush of words. The thing was— her story was too disorganized and ridiculous *not* to be true. He also was convinced she wasn't a con artist. He doubted that even the most experienced professional could fake a blush such as the one she wore so prettily on her cheeks.

"I believe you," he said, holding up both his hands in surrender.

"Just like that?"

"Yes. Why? Do you think I should *not* believe you?"

"No! I mean... I don't think many people *would* on the basis of what I just told you."

Jack was beginning to enjoy this. "Do you *want* me not to believe you?"

"Certainly not! I want you *to*...and you just told me that you *did*. And I think I'd better get myself out of here while the getting's good," she added, "before I get myself into more trouble than I already have."

He grinned. "That's a terrific exit line but . . ."

"But what?"

"Are you absolutely positive you want to go to your own cabin—which I assume is on another floor—dressed only in a terry-cloth robe and turban? Not that it's not a fetching outfit," he added. In truth, she looked delectable in the outfit, he thought, remembering vividly the sight of her with the robe wide open.

She grimaced. "I forgot."

"I assume you were wearing some other clothes when you first came into my cabin by mistake..."

She didn't even bother replying to that.

"What I'm trying to say—Cinderella—is that I'd be honored to have you make use of my humble abode once more in order to change...if you'd like."

She looked at him with narrowed eyes. "I don't want to press my luck. You've been really nice to me everything considered and..."

"You think I might revert back to my drunken intruder self and jump you?"

"Now you're making fun of me."

"No, I was merely teasing you. There's a big difference."

She didn't say anything for a long moment. Then she nodded. "In that case, *may* I use your bathroom one last time while I change clothes?"

Jack resisted the temptation to deliver a double entendre or something equally smart-mouthed. Instead, he bowed from the waist and made an elaborate, sweeping gesture with his arm. "Be my guest."

She giggled.

"What? You've never had anyone bow to you before?"

"Not in recent memory."

"That's a pity," he said, still teasing her. Then he suddenly realized he'd meant what he said. He was intrigued by the wistfulness he'd seen—or imagined he'd seen—in her warm brown eyes. For a fleeting moment, he had the eerie sensation that the two of them were kindred spirits.

The jarring ring of the telephone shattered the spell. Jack blinked, and remembered the telephone call he'd placed to Martin, the call that had seemed so urgent only a short while ago. He glanced at the telephone, then quickly back to her, catching her off guard.

He knew he wasn't imagining the wistfulness he saw in her eyes this time. It mirrored his own feelings. Exactly.

"I, uh... I'm expecting this call. It's a business associate."

"Oh, I'm sorry. I didn't mean to..."

"You didn't," he said quickly, trying to reassure her. "And the call won't take long. I should be finished by the time you are. I mean... with dressing and all."

"Don't hurry because of me."

"I won't." Jack knew he wasn't making much sense, torn as he was between the incessant ringing of the telephone and trying to tell the woman... what? What *was* he trying to tell her?

"I'd like to talk to you some more," he blurted.

"About what?"

"Nothing in particular. I mean... just talk. Maybe we could have a drink..."

"I don't think so," she said, shaking her head.

"Look. I have to answer the damn telephone..."

"Then answer it."

"But..." he began, and stopped in frustration. "Don't leave until after we've talked," he said brusquely. "Okay?"

She shrugged, scooped up her shoes from the floor, and headed for the bathroom. Jack watched her for a moment, then ran to answer the phone.

"Why did it take you so long to answer?" Martin said. "And why are you calling me tonight in the first place? We only said good-bye a couple of hours ago."

Jack ignored Martin's comments and went directly to the reason he'd called. "I think I've figured out who leaked the information on our project," he said, turning to face the wall and keeping his voice low, so the fascinating woman in his bathroom wouldn't hear what he was saying, in case she returned before he finished.

"Who?" Martin asked.

"Ms. Burke."

"The receptionist on the executive floor?"

"None other. Our new, eager, lovely receptionist."

"I don't see how that could be," Martin said. "We got her from our usual source, and I'm sure they checked her thoroughly. I just can't believe—"

"I know we don't have any concrete evidence—so far—but I can feel it in my bones. Humor me on this one, Martin, and have her desk checked from top to bottom before she comes in tomorrow."

"What are we looking for?"

"Anything that would tie her to the bad guys... but especially for sophisticated monitoring equipment. Something that would allow her to tap into the direct private line between your office and mine."

"If we found such a device," Martin said slowly, "that would explain a lot... like how they seemed to know what we were going to do before we'd even made a move."

"Yeah."

"Okay. I'll handle it first thing. But before we hang up, there are a couple of things I need to discuss with you."

"Now?" Jack asked with dismay, thinking about the woman in his bathroom and wanting to end the conversation with Martin.

"Certainly now. Why do you ask? Are you in a rush or something?"

"No," Jack lied. "Although there *is* a big bon voyage party taking place on the bridge, and they sort of expect everybody to show up. I thought I might look in on it for a few minutes.'' That was another lie. He had no intention of going to the party, not when he had something—someone—much more interesting right here in his own cabin.

"That's great!" Martin said. "I'm glad you're getting into the spirit of things. And don't worry. This'll only take a minute.''

Martin was true to his word. But when Jack hung up the phone only a short time later and looked around the stateroom, he was immediately struck with a sense of loneliness—almost bordering on desolation—and knew in his heart that the woman was already gone.

She was.

And he didn't even know her name.

FRANCES FINALLY FOUND cabin 222 and found that her key fit the lock to open the door. She still wasn't completely convinced. She made a quick but thorough search of the single room and bathroom—noting the presence of her own luggage—before closing and locking the door behind her.

Then she made a more leisurely inspection of her quarters—the stateroom that would be her home during the long voyage ahead. The cruise would last seventy-four days and would take her to places she'd dreamed about all her life...exotic ports in Canada, the Caribbean and Mexico...not to mention historic cities along the eastern seaboard and a passage through the Panama Canal. She should be thrilled to death.

And she had been. Until tonight.

She tried to push the thought from her mind and concentrate on her inspection. The cabin had a serviceable bathroom with tub and shower, but no terry-cloth robe. It had a single bed, dresser, color TV, radio and a sitting area with two chairs on each side of a large picture window.

There was even a basket of fresh fruit on the table between the chairs.

It was a nice room—very nice—and Frances would have been delighted with it if only... *Damn!*

She still couldn't believe she'd done what she'd done.

Being stupid enough to go to the wrong room in the first place was bad enough. And then after that, she'd flounced out of the bathroom practically naked, feeling as wickedly wanton as she must have looked. And when she'd met *him*—him staring at her, seeing all of her there was to see, his dark eyes darkening even more while he thought his dark thoughts—she'd gone completely to pieces.

All of that was embarrassing enough, but there was worse, Frances remembered, clenching her eyes closed. Even *after* she'd learned she was in the wrong room, even after she'd learned that he'd thought she was a professional hooker... even after all of that... she'd ended up laughing and giggling. *Flirting* with the man, for heaven's sake!

It was only after she was dressing in his bathroom while he was talking on the telephone that she'd recognized the full extent of her folly. Her actions—especially those near the end of their encounter—must have confirmed his original opinion of her. In spite of what he'd said earlier, he once again—or *still*—thought she was a hooker. That was why he'd invited her to have a drink with him after he finished his phone call... why he'd insisted that she wait for him.

How humiliating!

Thank heavens she'd recognized the situation for what it was in time, she thought as she opened her eyes again. She'd finished dressing in record time, then waited by the bedroom door until she'd heard his voice, and stolen silently away while he was still talking, only daring to breathe again when she was safely on the escalator two floors down.

Thinking about the whole episode in retrospect, Frances saw one glimmer of sunlight—the fact that she'd probably never have to face the man again. The ship was so big that the chances they'd accidentally encounter each other were almost nil... and she certainly had no intention of ever going anywhere close to his deck. With that comforting thought, she unpacked her bags, took another bath—a shower this time—ate an apple and went to bed.

After her exhausting day she went right to sleep, but was wide awake again within hours, drenched with perspiration and feeling as if every nerve in her body was exposed. Sitting up in bed, Frances pressed her palms against her temples, trying to forget the lingering horrors of her nightmare.

"There she is!" the handsome dark-haired stranger whose cabin she'd invaded had called out in her dream. "You can tell what she is by looking at her!"

Frances, completely naked, had frantically tried to cover herself with her bare arms while onlookers stood by and jeered. "We know what you are!" they'd chanted.

"No!" Frances had protested, starting to cry.

"Arrest her!" the handsome stranger had demanded.

"No," she'd protested again and again but—in her dream—nobody had believed her.

And what would happen if she *did* meet the stranger again? What if he tried to track her down? She tried to remember whether she'd mentioned her room number to him. *No,* she decided. At least she thought not. She hoped not. He *might* remember that two of the numbers to her cabin were "two-two," but that wouldn't do him any good. There must be more than a hundred cabins on this deck, all of them beginning with the same numbers.

And he probably wouldn't even try to find her in the first place. But what if they should meet accidentally? The ship was big—as she'd rationalized to herself earlier—but there was always the possibility...

She was still worrying about the possibilities while she watched dawn slowly creep up over the horizon.

She skipped breakfast, eating a banana from the fruit basket instead. She thought about skipping lunch, too, but the insistent growling of her stomach reminded her that she couldn't hide out in her cabin forever. Not that she didn't want to.

Okay, she finally said to herself. *Enough is enough. This is ridiculous.* It was time for her to go out and confront her problem head-on, face-to-face if need be, and spit in his eye, too, if that proved necessary. Keeping that in mind, she squared her shoulders and went to lunch.

Wearing a disguise.

In truth, she hadn't started out actually *planning* to disguise herself. Searching through her closet for something to wear, and looking at her clothes with a dispassionate eye—as if from the view of the stranger she'd met last night—she'd come to the conclusion that the wardrobe she'd brought on the cruise wasn't as bad as she'd thought it might be. It was worse.

All her dresses were hopelessly outdated and none of them fit. She'd bought them either by phone or mail-order and none of them had ever looked the same on her as they did on the models in the photos. In addition to that, she must have lost more weight than she'd realized during her father's final illness.

I should have listened to Lisa and bought new clothes for the trip, she realized. But she hadn't.

Sighing with resignation, she put on a cotton print granny dress that almost swept the floor and only touched her at the shoulders. There was one consolation, she thought, eyeing herself in the mirror. If she happened to meet the stranger again, he wouldn't be able to recognize her by the shape of her body. *Or by my eyes,* she added, donning dark-tinted sunglasses as soon as she realized the advantage of her attire.

Then, walking down the corridor on her way to the escalator, she passed the beauty parlor and saw a selection of wigs on display. *Perfect!* she thought, detouring into the shop where an operator tried to dissuade her by pointing out that the wigs were cheap ones—"fun" wigs for costume parties and such.

"That's okay," Frances said, selecting a brown one similar to her own hair...except the wig had long bangs that came all the way down to her sunglasses. "I'm only wearing it for fun."

What's the point in taking unnecessary chances? she rationalized as she stepped aboard the escalator. Pushing her dark sunglasses up higher on her nose and gathering the full skirt of the granny dress around her so it wouldn't get caught in the machinery, Frances confidently made her way toward the dining room.

Her confidence slipped a bit when the maître d' stopped her before she could slink over to a little table in a corner, as she'd intended. And it completely deserted her when the man informed her that she was assigned to permanent seating for the length of the voyage at a table for eight.

Frances felt herself starting to sweat. Even though it would be nice not to have to look for a place to sit every time she came in to eat, the flip side of the coin was terrifying. She'd be expected to make conversation with seven people—total strangers—three times a day, day after day, week after week. Could she do it? Of course not. The bulk of her conversation for the past thirteen years had been with her father, who'd barely been able to answer her back much of that time.

Trailing along behind the waiter who was leading the way to her table, Frances wondered if she could get away with pretending she couldn't hear. Or speak. Or both.

Four people—four strange faces—were already seated at the table watching while the waiter pulled out her chair and Frances sat down. She swallowed and readjusted her dark glasses, feeling four sets of eyes trained on her.

"Hello," said the attractive, white-haired woman seated across from Frances. "We're so relieved to have you join us."

Frances blinked, not knowing how to respond to the strange comment.

"The four of us were the only ones at the table for breakfast this morning," the woman explained. "We were beginning to think the rest of you had deserted us," she added, gesturing to the three empty seats at the table.

"I, uh, overslept," Frances lied when the woman paused as if waiting for an explanation of her absence.

The woman nodded, accepting the lie. "I imagine the party last night went on until the wee hours."

Party? Then Frances remembered the big bon voyage party she hadn't attended. "Oh . . . yes," she mumbled.

"Did you have a good time?"

Frances didn't know what to say. "It was . . . nice," she finally replied, cursing herself for sounding so awkward . . . for *being* so awkward.

Why had she chosen to take this stupid cruise in the first place? Shouldn't she have known beforehand that she'd be thrown into close contact with strangers . . . and that she was totally unequipped to deal with them? What had she expected? That she'd suddenly, miraculously turn into a social butterfly able to make charming conversation with everyone she met?

Stupid. Stupid. Stupid.

"I'm Evangeline Curtis," the white-haired woman said with a smile. "But you can call me Angie. All my friends do. And this is my husband, Lionel," she added, gesturing toward the handsome white-haired man seated to her left at the head of the table.

Frances exchanged nods with Lionel, who had the brightest blue eyes she'd ever seen. Frances guessed he was in his early seventies and his wife was about the same age. They made an extraordinarily attractive couple.

"And the two ladies sitting beside you are Mavis and Maxine McSwain," Angie said.

Frances turned to face the two middle-aged women. "You're sisters?" she asked, making another awkward stab at conversation.

"Cousins," the woman beside Frances replied. "I'm Maxine." She had a pleasantly-rounded face and body to match, while her cousin Mavis was much thinner and more angular, at least from what Frances could see of her.

"And I'll bet you're Leo," Maxine added with a satisfied smile.

Leo? "Uh, no. I'm Frances Lanier."

Maxine laughed raucously. Her cousin Mavis shook her head. "Don't pay any attention to her, Frances. She's always trying to show off like that. And she was talking about your sign, not your name."

"Oh. You mean my astrological sign?"

"Yes," Mavis replied, shooting a look of scorn at her cousin. "We're both licensed professional astrologers. And Maxine *thinks* she can tell a person's sign by their facial features and the shape of their body, but she almost never gets it right."

"That's not true!" Maxine protested. "I was right about Lionel being an Aries only this morning."

"A lucky guess," Mavis commented, pursing her lips.

"Don't look now," Evangeline Curtis said in a loud stage whisper, interrupting the cousins' bickering. "But I think our other three missing tablemates are headed this way."

Everybody stopped talking and turned to look. Frances saw the maître d' himself coming toward their table, with two men and a woman following him. The woman was tall and striking. Her alabaster skin was contrasted by jet black, shoulder-length hair and fire-engine red coloring at her lips and fingernails. The same vivid colors were repeated in the dress that clung to her model's figure.

Cruise clothes was the phrase that leapt immediately into Frances's mind. The things she should have bought but hadn't.

The man walking beside the striking-looking woman was of medium height and build, with regular features and stylishly groomed sandy colored hair. He was rather nice-looking in his navy blazer and gray slacks, although Frances thought that the ascot he had on was a bit much.

Shifting her gaze to the tall man walking behind the others, she caught her breath and held it. Her heart stopped beating, too, for all she knew.

It couldn't be.

Please, don't let it be.

But it was.

Him. The Man. The same man whose room she'd invaded last night, the one who'd seen her naked as a jaybird. The man she'd hoped never to see again in her entire life.

He was coming closer to the table, getting nearer with every stride of his long legs. She picked up a menu and tried to hide behind it, although she knew it was a futile gesture. He'd be here soon, and she couldn't hide behind the menu forever. Obviously, through some cruel twist of fate, he was assigned to the very same dining table where she'd be eating . . . or not eating.

For the entire length of the cruise.

Frances peeked over the top of the menu. It was him, all right. Even if she hadn't recognized his dark eyes and gorgeous black hair, she'd have known him immediately by the angry red scratch she'd made along the cheek of his handsome face. She shifted her gaze to his left hand. Sure enough, another scratch was visible. That was the one she'd made when she was trying to claw his hand away from her bare breast.

Remembering *that,* she felt her cheeks growing hot, blazing with mortification.

She pretended to study the menu, but was acutely conscious of the maître d' seating the woman, and of the two men taking their chairs. *He* was here. Right here. Sitting diagonally across the table from her.

He hadn't seen her yet. But he would. Soon. She could only pray that he wouldn't recognize her.

Chapter Three

Jack glanced at the woman sitting diagonally across the table from him. She was half-hidden behind the menu, the same as she'd been for most of the time he'd been sitting here. She'd lowered it briefly when everyone introduced themselves, then immediately retreated behind her shield again. The menu hid the bottom half of her face, while long bangs and dark glasses effectively concealed the top half. And the baggy dress she had on hid most of her body as well. He had only the vaguest idea what she looked like, and couldn't begin to guess her age. Not that it mattered.

He swiveled around in his seat, sweeping the dining room with his gaze, hoping to catch a glimpse of the intriguing woman who'd invaded his room last night. He was sure he'd be able to recognize her immediately if he saw her, even from a distance, but so far he hadn't had any luck. Nor did he this time.

Turning back around, he caught the woman across the table looking at him. She immediately ducked behind her menu again, holding it in such a way that it hid her entire face this time. Jack kept his smile to himself.

Frances Lanier. Wasn't that the name she'd murmured when everyone at the table introduced themselves earlier? *Timid Mouse* suited her better, he decided. Dismissing her from his mind, he turned his attention to the other passengers at the table. The two middle-aged spinsters seated beside Frances seemed harmless enough, although their prying questions about birth dates, times and places were a nuisance. He hoped they wouldn't try to delve too deeply into his private affairs because if they did, he'd have to cut them off. That, in turn, would only call attention to himself, something he wanted to avoid in his persona of Jack Smith, the alias he'd chosen for the cruise.

Jack looked at the older couple—thc Curtises. He'd liked them on sight, probably because they reminded him a little of his own father and mother as they would have been if his father were still alive.

Then there were Arthur Fortuna and his sister, Sharon Lane, whom Jack had met while they were waiting in line for their seating assignments. In the brief span they'd talked, Jack had learned more about Art than he'd ever want to know in a lifetime. The man was pushy, self-centered and conceited beyond belief. According to Art— evidently a "regular" on cruises such as this—"Women fall all over you if you're an unattached male, especially if you can dance. You *do* dance, don't you Jack?"

"Not in recent memory," Jack had replied, repeating the phrase that his mystery woman had said the night before.

"Too bad," Art had said, shaking his head. "Still... you're a nice enough looking guy. You shouldn't have any trouble... if you know what I mean."

Yeah, Art, I know what you mean. Exactly, Jack thought, remembering the episode with distaste.

He also remembered that all the time the two of them were talking, Art's sister had been watching them. Watching *him,* Jack had thought at the time. Sizing him up. Measuring him, the way a female barracuda might measure her prey.

Is it worth it? Jack wondered now. He agreed with Martin's reasoning that it was in the best interest of the company if he hid out for a while, but could he really survive being cooped up on this boat—in the company of these people—for what seemed to be looming as an eternity?

"So, Jack. What do you do for a living?" Art asked.

"I'm in sales," he replied quickly, already prepared for that particular question.

"*Sales?*" Sharon repeated, her tone of voice suggesting that the occupation was slightly lower on the social scale than being a professional snake charmer.

"Yes," Jack said cheerfully. "Furniture." The answer was in the general vicinity of the truth. His father's company had been in the business of manufacturing fine furniture for more than a century and if Jack could regain the company from the thieves who'd stolen it—which he had every intention of doing—the tradition would continue and he *would* be selling furniture.

"Nothing wrong with that," Art stated emphatically. "You might even be able to say that *I'm* in sales...in a sense."

"For heaven's sake, Art," his sister corrected him. "You're an investment banker."

"I said *in a sense.* I sell money, or the use of it," he explained condescendingly to Jack. "And I'm out to turn a profit, just like you are, even though we *do* operate on different levels."

You jerk, Jack thought, fervently hoping that Art's company wasn't one of the ones that had sold *him* its money.

"I'm a vice-president with First Fidelity," Art added, "so I'm not down in the trenches the way you are."

It figured.

Jack kept a carefully controlled smile on his face. First Fidelity *was* one of his creditors, the first one to call in his loan. And with the way his luck had been going lately, it also figured that he'd be assigned to permanent seating on this so-called pleasure cruise with an obnoxious employee of that firm.

"I think that being in sales of *any* kind is a challenging, worthwhile profession."

Jack jerked his head around so quickly that he almost got a crick in his neck. Had it really been Frances Lanier—the Timid Mouse herself—who had spoken? It must have been her, he decided. She had even put down her menu and was glaring at Art from behind her dark glasses. And there was something vaguely familiar about her voice. Jack tried to place it.

"As a matter of fact," Frances continued, "one of our most admirable presidents of modern times was a salesman. Harry Truman sold men's clothing."

"Don't tell me, let me guess," Art said, grinning. "The little lady is a Democrat."

Sharon, who was sitting beside Jack, giggled as she leaned closer to whisper in his ear. "I can't believe it," she said. "The Timid Mouse can actually talk."

Frances had heard what Sharon said. Jack knew it in his bones, even before he saw the slow flush creep up her cheeks and saw her search for her menu again, not realizing that the waiter had already taken it away while she was speaking. *Poor, dear Timid Mouse!*

"Actually," Jack began, coming to her defense the same way she'd tried to defend his profession moments ago, "both Republican and Democratic historians tend to support what Frances said. Harry Truman is already recognized in academic circles as our most effective president of this century. *Public* accolade is always many years later in coming, of course...what with public opinion being constantly manipulated by the media, et cetera."

Jack had made that up, all of it, but thought it sounded pretty good. He tried to catch Frances's attention, to no avail. She seemed to be fascinated by the design in the white damask tablecloth. Jack sighed. At least, he'd succeeded in silencing Art Fortuna and his witchy sister . . . for the moment.

He swiveled around in his chair again to look for his mystery woman of the night before.

HE STILL DOESN'T KNOW who I am. He doesn't recognize me with my clothes on.

At first, Frances had felt a deep, overwhelming relief that The Man—Jack Smith, she corrected herself—didn't know her and expose her as soon as he saw her. Then for some unfathomable reason, she'd started to feel hurt—angry, even—that he *hadn't* recognized her.

Which was really stupid.

It was almost as stupid as her watching his hands all during lunch had been. What she'd really wanted to do was study his face . . . his dark hair, with one unruly lock that kept falling onto his forehead and he kept pushing back . . . his nose, straight, almost aristocratic . . . the shadow of a beard on his cheeks and the mark her fingernails had made on one of them . . . the firm, sensual fullness of his lips.

She didn't dare risk having him catch her watching him, of course, so she'd kept her head down and surreptitiously studied his hands instead. They were large hands, strong and utterly masculine, but graceful at the same time. She saw the way his fingers curled around his fork and could almost feel them curling around her breast again, as they'd done last night. She watched him lift a knife to cut his meat, and remembered the strength of his hands holding her wrists, pulling her close against his chest . . . his broad, hard chest . . .

Lunch was finally over. At last. It seemed to Frances that they'd been sitting at the table for hours. She muttered a quick goodbye to Maxine sitting beside her, and to Angie

Curtis across the table, and got up to leave, not daring to look at the other passengers. At *him.*

She knew she'd been tense all during lunch, but hadn't realized exactly *how* tense until she started to relax in the corridor outside the dining room. Her knees felt like melting Jell-O. She took a deep breath and wiped her sweaty palms on the skirt of her granny dress.

"Frances. Wait up."

Oh, no. She'd know that voice anywhere. She started walking faster, hoping her weak legs wouldn't collapse and send her sprawling on the floor.

She should have known her stride was no match for his long legs. He was beside her in mere seconds.

"Hi," Jack Smith said. "I called out to you a moment ago, but I guess you didn't hear me."

"I guess."

"I wanted to thank you."

"Thank me?" she repeated.

"Yes. For saying what you did to Art about sales being a worthwhile profession. It was nice of you to come to my defense that way."

He smiled, and his teeth were the whitest she'd ever seen. She swallowed. "I didn't say it because of you."

"Oh."

Frances was surprised at the sudden vulnerability she saw in his dark eyes. Then he blinked and it was gone. "I mean . . . it wasn't entirely because of you," she amended, wondering why she bothered, why she cared whether she'd punctured his ego. "My father was a salesman, too."

All that was true but it wasn't all of the truth. Frances hesitated. She didn't want to reveal her personal life to Jack Smith—*him* of all people—but she also refused to misrepresent her background.

"He ran a junkyard," she finally said. "He worked hard all his life, as long as he was able to work, selling stuff that other people didn't want or couldn't bother with anymore.''

She stood up straighter and squared her shoulders. "And I couldn't let that man get away with suggesting there was anything to be ashamed of in what my father did.''

Jack Smith looked at her for a long moment . . . so long that she started to get sweaty palms again. Then he nodded. "You were completely right to say what you did. And I'm sure your father would be proud of you.''

Frances let out the breath she'd been holding.

Jack Smith smiled at her again, a smile so warm that it made her feel as if she were being patted on the head for being such a good girl. Then he frowned. "Please forgive me,'' he said, "but a moment ago—when you were so impassioned—your voice reminded me of someone. Have we ever met before?''

She caught another breath. "No.''

"Are you sure?''

"Positive,'' Frances replied, walking faster while she cursed herself for the fool she was. She should never have told Jack Smith anything about her personal life . . . or anything about anything, for that matter. She should stay as far away from him as possible, and keep her mouth shut during the times she was forced to be around him.

She started walking even faster, hoping he'd take the hint and go away but feeling almost certain he wouldn't. He didn't. He increased his stride to match hers . . . even when she speeded up still more, until both of them were almost running along the corridor and people were standing aside to watch.

"Are you in a rush to get someplace?'' he asked after a moment, his voice slightly breathless.

"Yes. I . . . I remembered something I have to do.'' *I have to get away from you.*

Frances spied the escalators directly ahead and felt like doing a tap dance for joy. At last she could escape his dark, knowing gaze—his prying questions—and retreat to the safety of her cabin. "I guess this is where we part company," she said, stopping beside the escalator well.

"I'm going down to the Pacific Deck," Jack said.

The Pacific Deck! Her deck? "Is...uh...that where your cabin is?" Frances asked, knowing it wasn't.

"No, but I have a friend whom I *think* is on that deck, although I'm not sure of the exact room number. I thought I'd go down and wait around for awhile and maybe catch a glimpse of...my friend."

He's looking for me! Frances realized with something close to panic. *Or at least for the naked woman he found in his room last night, who isn't me at all—the me I've known for thirty years.*

"I see," Frances said, thankful that her voice didn't quiver, and wondering where she could go now that her own cabin, her private sanctuary, was forbidden to her because it was under siege by Jack Smith.

"Which way are you headed?"

"The other way," she replied grimly, thinking she might as well take a walk around the deck until he got tired of waiting for a woman who didn't exist.

"Well, see you at dinner," Jack said cheerily.

"Yeah," Frances said. *That's something to look forward to,* she thought morosely as she headed for the up escalator.

SO MUCH FOR THAT great idea, Jack thought after skulking around on the Pacific Deck for almost two hours, waiting in vain for his mystery woman to show up. He finally gave up when one of the deck stewards approached him for the third time—still courteous, to be sure—but also quietly insistent and obviously suspicious.

And no wonder.

He'd be suspicious under the same circumstances, Jack decided, walking along the corridor toward the escalator. *But where could she be?*

He'd been so certain that she was on the Pacific Deck because of the "two-two" numbers of his cabin, which she'd entered by mistake. Maybe. But—if she wasn't lying—she could be on the Atlantic Deck, in cabin "one-two-two", or on the Mediterranean Deck, in cabin "three-two-two"... or wherever, even on this Pacific Deck, where the hundreds of cabins *all* began with the numbers "two-two."

The possibilities boggled the mind.

And why was he going to all this trouble in the first place?

Was he *that* attracted to her?

He had to admit that a great deal of his attraction to her probably came as a direct result of being so bored on this confounded ship. Her face was pretty enough, but no more so than hundreds of women he'd met. Her body, however...

Ah, her body was a work of art—perfectly smooth, unblemished skin that felt even softer than it looked, curves in all the places curves should be—and the most beautiful breasts he'd ever seen in his life. Closing his eyes, he could almost see them again—full, proud and erect—with magnificently developed pink nipples that cried out to be touched, suckled. He could imagine her holding a babe in her arms, doing just that... or holding *him* in her arms in the same manner...

Jack opened his eyes, and saw a familiar figure getting off the escalator a few steps away. "Frances? What are *you* doing on this deck?"

She jerked her head around, obviously surprised to see him. Then she frowned. "I might ask you the same question."

"As I told you earlier, I was visiting a friend."

"So you did. I guess you found her."

"Her?"

"Or him. Whoever."

"No. As a matter of fact, I didn't find my friend."

"Then why are you still down here?"

"I'm persistent, okay?" he said irritably. "And you never did answer my question about what you're doing on this deck."

He saw her frown again, then sigh. "I live here. I mean . . . my cabin's on this deck."

"But . . . a little while ago . . . you went *up*."

"Yes. I took a walk."

"For two *hours?*"

"The same length of time you've been down here looking for your friend," she pointed out. "It must be a really good friend for you to wait so long."

"I . . ." Jack began, about to defend himself. He stopped just short of saying something that would make him appear even more foolish than he already felt. "I must have missed my, uh, friend somehow," he said instead. "I'll try again another time."

"May I make a suggestion?" Frances asked sweetly . . . too sweetly by far, Jack thought.

"I suppose."

"Why don't you check with the purser before you come down here the next time? I'm sure he'll be able to give you the exact cabin number of your . . . friend. That should make it a lot easier for you to find her or him."

Damn! If he didn't know better, Jack would almost have sworn that Frances *knew* he didn't know the name of his mystery woman. "Good idea," he said, forcing a smile. "Well . . . I guess I'll be on my way . . ."

"Goodbye."

"But say...could I get a glass of water from you before I leave?"

"What?"

"That smoked fish we had at lunch made me thirsty," Jack explained.

"Then why don't you go to your own cabin to get some water?"

"Because my cabin is three decks up. And didn't you say that you live right around here somewhere?"

"Well...yes, but..."

A sudden light began to glimmer in the back of his mind. "Surely you're not afraid of me, Frances."

"Of course not!" The flush that crept into her cheeks below the dark glasses made a lie of her words.

"I mean...we *are* tablemates on this voyage—this long, long voyage," he said, having a hard time keeping his grin to himself. Frances—the Timid Mouse—actually thought he was interested in her! The idea that he might be attracted to such a dowdy, timid, inept temptress as Frances was one that could only take place in her own mind, he thought, rubbing his hand across his mouth to smother his smile.

But it was a little sad, too, he thought suddenly.

"I assure you my intentions are honorable," he said, softening his voice. "I only want a glass of water. I had nothing else in mind."

"I didn't think you did!" she exclaimed. "It's just...my cabin is in such a mess and..."

"I won't look around. I promise."

Frances stared at him for several seconds before she abruptly turned and started walking briskly down the corridor, the same corridor where he'd been skulking around for two hours. "Come along, if you're *that* thirsty," she tossed at him over her shoulder.

Jack followed her without another word.

She stopped in front of a door after only a few steps and fumbled around in her shoulder-strap purse, obviously searching for the key to her cabin. Extracting it, she opened the door. Jack frowned. Was it his imagination or had her fingers been shaking?

If so, she was even more nervous than he'd thought. He followed her into the room and purposefully left the door ajar so she wouldn't think he was after anything more than a drink of water. Also, with the door open, he'd be able to see anyone who happened to stroll down the corridor past the room.

He hadn't been lying to Frances when he told her he was persistent. He still hadn't given up on finding his mystery woman today.

"I suppose you'll want ice in your water," Frances said.

"Please." Looking around for the first time, Jack noticed that the room was neat—as he'd expected—and though comfortable, wasn't luxurious like his suite. Instead of a fully stocked wet bar, there was a tray on the dresser with a carafe, glasses and ice bucket. "I mean . . . if you *have* ice," he corrected himself.

"I used to, but it's probably melted by now," she said.

Jack wondered about the tone of her voice—it was almost accusing. *Accusing him?* And if so, accusing him of what? He watched silently while she walked over to the dresser and lifted the lid to the ice bucket.

"It's full," she said with surprise.

"The steward probably came in and refilled it while you were out for your walk."

Frances frowned and reached for tongs to ladle ice cubes into a glass. "I'm not sure I like that," she said.

"What? Having a steward come in to give you fresh ice?"

"Having someone come into my room while I'm not here, period," she replied, pouring water into the glass before bringing it over to him.

"It's the way service is *supposed* to be done, Frances," he said gently, accepting the glass. "And sometimes," he added, thinking of the unexpected but lovely visitor in his room the night before, "having someone come into your room while you're not there . . . can have quite pleasant results."

"You mean like the steward leaving fresh ice?"

More like meeting the most provocative woman you've ever encountered, he thought. "Something like that . . . but not quite."

"Then what exactly?"

For the second time that day, Jack had the uneasy sensation that Frances knew more about him than he'd intended to tell her. But it must be his imagination.

"Never mind," he said with the smile he used during business negotiations, the smile that revealed nothing.

"I'm serious," she said, frowning again. "You can't make a provocative statement like that, and then simply leave it hanging in the air."

She *was* serious.

He hesitated. "There are some things a gentleman never discusses."

Frances peered at him intently from behind her dark glasses. "In other words, you're trying to evade the question," she said accusingly.

"I am not!"

"Then tell me—what pleasant results have you found waiting for you in *your* room? Lately. A woman?"

"That's none of your business."

"A man?"

"Don't be ridiculous!"

"Then it *was* a woman!"

"I didn't say that!"

"You didn't have to."

Was she deliberately trying to provoke him? "Do you always wear dark glasses?" he asked, changing the subject.

"Are you going to answer my question?" she countered.

"I thought you'd already decided on the answer yourself."

"That was just a guess. Are you confirming it?"

"No. *Do* you wear dark glasses all the time? Or only when you're trying to hide your eyes from me?" he added, teasing her a little because of the way she'd reacted to his simple request for a glass of water.

"Don't be ridiculous!" she said, almost shouting as she repeated the words he'd said to her only moments before.

Jack raised his eyebrows, thinking he must have struck a nerve.

"And don't flatter yourself," she added in a more normal tone. "I wear dark glasses because my eyes are light-sensitive."

"So much so that you need them in here?" he asked, glancing around the shadowed room illuminated only by the faint reflection of the late-afternoon sun coming through the windows.

"Yes. Do you always ask so many personal questions?"

"Not always," he replied, thinking that there was more to Frances—The Timid Mouse—than he'd originally thought. Or was it simply that he was already so bored on this damned boat that he was clutching at straws…reading things that weren't there?

"And do you make a habit of asking people for water and then not drinking it?" she asked pointedly.

Jack glanced down at the full glass of water he held clutched in his hand. "The conversation was so interesting that I forgot about it," he replied sheepishly.

Frances made no response to that remark, and he didn't blame her.

He lifted the glass and gulped down its entire contents. "Ah, wonderful," he said, holding out the empty glass to her. "May I have another?"

For a long moment, he thought she wasn't going to take the glass. Finally she did. He watched her carry it over to her dresser and pour more water from the carafe, not bothering to add extra ice this time.

She wants me out of here, he suddenly realized. The idea came as a shock. He really had been thirsty when he invited himself to her room for a glass of water, but he'd also wanted to show her he appreciated her coming to his defense at lunch. He'd thought he might reciprocate . . . boost her confidence by paying a little attention to her. What was wrong with that?

Plenty! he had a feeling Frances would say. *How dare you be so presumptuous!*

And she'd be right.

It *was* presumptuous of him to assume that she needed his protection or wanted his attention. His earlier idea— that she was acting skittish because she was shy and thought he was interested in her—seemed equally off-base.

She simply wanted to be rid of him. Nothing more and nothing less. What a sublime ego he'd had to imagine anything more than that!

Was he as bad as Art Fortuna?

Jack took the glass of water Frances held out to him. For the first time in a long time, he felt uncertain about what to do next in the presence of a woman.

He wasn't thirsty anymore, not in the least, but he took the water and drank it all. Then he murmured his thanks and made a hasty exit.

Chapter Four

Frances squirmed uncomfortably in her seat at the dining table. The wig was hot, making her scalp itch underneath it. Her feet hurt from the hours of walking she'd done in her dress shoes that afternoon. And Maxine McSwain kept asking her all sorts of personal questions about when and where she was born.

None of those things was the main cause of her discomfort, however. She glanced at the empty seat diagonally across the table from her.

Where was he?

It wasn't as if she wanted to see him—far from it—but she was becoming edgier by the moment wondering what he'd say to her, if anything, when he finally showed up. If he did show up.

"I wasn't so far off base, after all," Maxine said to Frances, holding up a spiral notepad where she'd been scribbling. "Your sun sign is Cancer rather than Leo, but you're so close to the cusp that you have many Leo characteristics."

"Is that good or bad?" Frances asked, keeping her voice pitched low and hoping that Art Fortuna and his sister Sharon Lane couldn't hear what they were discussing. She didn't like those two, not a whit, and trusted them even less.

"Neither," Mavis McSwain answered for her cousin. "It's simply Maxine's way of trying to prove that she's never wrong."

Maxine ignored her. "I'll need to refer to my charts to get the position of *all* your houses. I'll have them for you by tomorrow."

"Please don't go to any trouble..."

"I love doing it," Maxine assured her with a wave of her hand.

Waiters took away their dishes from the appetizer course and served the soup. *Maybe he isn't coming.*

Could she be that lucky?

More likely, he'd make a dramatic late appearance and denounce her for what she was—an ill-mannered, ill-tempered, devious woman. And she was. All of that and more.

First, she'd deliberately tried to provoke him this afternoon by asking leading questions about his "friend" whom he was trying to find on her deck. She'd continued questioning him even though she knew full well that he couldn't possibly have found the woman...and even though she knew she was treading on dangerous territory. Still, she hadn't been able to resist the temptation.

Why had she done it? Was it because she'd come completely unglued when she finally returned from her walk and found him still skulking around, forcing her to admit she lived on the same deck as his naked visitor of the night before? Maybe she'd automatically attacked him in self-defense...so he wouldn't suspect that she was the woman he was searching for. Maybe. Or maybe it was something more than that, some reason or emotion she didn't quite understand.

And what about him? Was it normal for a man to hang around for hours looking for a woman he'd met only once? Even though that meeting had been intense—and even though he'd explained that he was persistent—wasn't there something sinister about his behavior? Or was that the way men usually reacted? She honestly didn't know.

The last date she'd had with a man—a boy, actually— had been when she was eighteen years old, more than twelve years ago. That had involved so much preparation and trouble trying to arrange for someone to sit with her father...and the date itself had been so dull and anticlimactic...that she hadn't bothered trying to do it again for a long time, and by then the few male friends she still had had stopped calling.

With that kind of experience, how was she supposed to know how to deal with a mature, sophisticated man—a man so drop-dead handsome that her heart beat faster simply being in the same room with him?

Like now, she thought, looking up and seeing him making his way toward their dining table.

"There's Jack Smith," Maxine whispered to Frances. "Isn't he the most gorgeous male specimen you've seen in years?"

"I hadn't noticed," Frances lied, thinking that tonight—dressed in a black tuxedo that fit him perfectly—he looked especially tall and handsome, better than a movie star.

Maxine raised a skeptical eyebrow. "It's probably because you can't see properly with those dark glasses you wear all the time."

"My eyes are light-sensitive," Frances said, once again repeating the lie she'd told Jack.

"Well trust me," Maxine said. "He *is* gorgeous. And he'd probably make a good match for you," she added.

"*What?*"

"I can't be sure until I've completed both your charts, but he's a Scorpio, which is compatible with Cancer, and he's thirty-five, which is just about right for you..."

"He's not interested in me!" Frances whispered fiercely, rushing her words because the object of their conversation was getting closer by the moment.

"Don't be too sure of that," Maxine said with an enigmatic smile.

"I *am* sure! Positive."

"You must not have seen the way he was looking at you at lunch."

"I..." Frances cut off her protest because Jack Smith was already at their table, taking his seat as he apologized to everyone in general for being late because of a last-minute phone call.

He'd had a phone call last night, too, Frances remembered. That particular one had probably saved her from... no telling what.

"You're looking well tonight, Frances," he added now without skipping a beat. "Fully recovered from that long walk this afternoon, I see."

Frances felt an elbow dig into her ribs and was almost sure she heard Maxine snicker as well. *Damn him! What was he up to now?* He was obviously trying to pay her back for this afternoon—to get even—but how far would he go?

She wished she could crawl into a hole and hide from him and from the curious stares of the other passengers at the table. She supposed it was too much to hope that the *American Dreamer* would suddenly hit an iceberg in the St. Lawrence in the middle of October.

THAT'S RIGHT, FRANCES. Squirm. The way you made me squirm this afternoon, Jack thought with satisfaction.

She'd really had him going for awhile there, making him feel like a lecher... even comparing himself with Art Fortuna, for heaven's sake!

He *wasn't* an Art Fortuna, nowhere close to it, as he'd known all along and finally remembered when he was thinking rationally in the privacy of his cabin. It was only Frances's own insecurity—and her perverse reaction to him because of it—that had made him consider the idea.

"You and Frances went for a long walk this afternoon?" Sharon Lane asked Jack. He could hear the surprise—the incredulity—in her voice.

See, Frances? he wanted to say. *Other women don't consider me a masher or a monster. Far from it.*

Sharon doesn't count, he could imagine Frances responding with a sneer. *She's as bad as her brother.*

"No. Frances went for a walk alone," Jack said, looking directly at her across the table. He deliberately paused for a moment before delivering the telling blow. "I had a couple of drinks with her afterward... in her cabin."

He heard a woman gasp, but it took him a moment to realize it hadn't been Frances who'd done it. It was Sharon.

Frances was glaring at him from behind her dark glasses.

He glared back at her, telling her with his eyes that he could be as underhanded as she could. All he'd ever tried to do was be kind to her, and she'd thrown his kindness back in his face.

Who did she think she was? A sex goddess with men knocking themselves out in hot pursuit of her?

Jack knew he was overreacting to the situation between Frances and himself. But he was beginning to realize that he'd probably never find his lovely mystery woman of the night before, and he was bored to distraction. Already. And the boat had been under way for less than twenty-four hours.

He was clutching at straws for something to do, something to distract him. Anything. Anyone.

"There's a great dance band playing in the Vegas Lounge tonight, Jack," Art Fortuna said. "Sharon and I plan to go up there after dinner. Would you care to join us?" he asked, pointedly ignoring the other people at their table.

Jack's first instinct was to immediately refuse Art's invitation, but then he had another idea, a really wicked one at that. "What do *you* think, Frances?" he asked, staring directly at her and managing to catch her looking at him for a change. "Shall we go dancing tonight?"

"I don't dance," she replied in a firm, steady voice after only a moment's hesitation.

He felt a surge of admiration for her, and nodded his head to acknowledge her victory in this minor skirmish. But the war wasn't over yet; it was only beginning.

So beware, Frances. Whatever game you're playing, I won't let you get away with it. I'm determined to be your friend on this damned voyage. Whether you like it or not.

HIS EYES WERE TELLING her something, although Frances wasn't sure what it was. Or maybe she didn't want to know. She did know that there was a *dare* in there somewhere. Definitely a dare.

Why? What was he daring her to do... or not do?

She really wasn't up to this—playing mind games and eye games with a man like him. She simply wasn't equipped to deal with it.

And why was he doing it in the first place?

She was positive he hadn't guessed that she was the woman he was searching for—the nearly naked woman he'd found in his room last night. And in that case, why would someone as handsome and worldly as he was be interested in a plain, dowdy nobody like her?

A timid mouse was what Sharon Lane had called her. Frances knew she wasn't a timid mouse, but could understand how she'd appear to be that way to a stranger... especially one who kept her constantly off base the way Jack Smith did.

So how could he possibly be interested in her?

He couldn't. Wouldn't. Unless he had an ulterior motive. Could he possibly have found out about the money she'd inherited? He'd said he was a salesman, but could it be himself he was selling? Was he a fortune hunter?

Whatever his reasons for paying attention to her—and embarrassing her in the process—she wanted nothing more to do with him. At all. Let him play his little games with somebody else.

Stewards removed the dishes from their soup course, which she'd barely touched, and served the salad. Another waiter offered Jack a menu from which to choose his entrée, but he shook his head. "I don't want to delay the others because I was late," Jack said. "Bring me whatever you have that's already cooked."

That was nice. Really nice, Frances thought, sneaking a quick glance at him before turning her attention to Angie Curtis seated next to him and directly across the table from her.

"If you're not interested in dancing," Angie said, "we'd be delighted to have you join us, Frances. Lionel and I plan to go up to the Polaris Room for the early floor show right after dinner. Mavis and Maxine are coming, too."

Frances hesitated. The floor show sounded fun, something she'd enjoy, and she was already beginning to feel comfortable with the other four people who'd make up the party. But what if... She glanced in Jack Smith's direction and just as quickly looked away. He was talking to Art and Sharon, probably discussing their plans for dancing tonight.

Confident that he wasn't listening to her conversation with Angie, Frances nodded. "I'd like that. Thank you for asking me."

Dinner was delicious, the best food Frances had ever eaten, although she was too nervous to enjoy it properly.

She kept expecting Jack Smith to say or do something to embarrass her again.

He didn't. And that only made her more nervous.

Frances breathed a sigh of relief when Jack was the first one to leave the table after the meal was finished. She'd been wondering whether she should excuse herself and go to her cabin, then sneak up to meet the others at the Polaris Room later. Now that he was gone, she didn't have to bother trying to conceal her plans, so she accompanied the rest of her party upstairs.

The Polaris Room was big but not huge, opulent but not overpowering. Frances liked it because it reminded her of the really nice nightclubs she'd seen depicted in TV movies. She half expected Fred Astaire and Ginger Rogers to come out dancing at any moment.

As soon as the Curtis party was seated at a choice table close to the stage, a waiter came by for their drink orders. After much indecision, Frances finally decided on a Dreamer Deluxe, the house specialty, which the waiter described as a concoction of rums and tropical fruits "...something along the lines of a frozen daiquiri, but far superior to anything you've ever tasted."

The waiter was absolutely right, Frances decided after her first sip. "This is heavenly!" she exclaimed.

Mavis, Maxine and Angie, who'd also ordered Dreamer Deluxes, agreed with the assessment. Lionel was skeptical. "It's probably extremely potent as well," he cautioned, "especially if you're not accustomed to alcoholic beverages."

Frances definitely wasn't accustomed to alcohol, so she decided to drink slowly. The houselights blinked a couple of times and the orchestra started warming up. Frances felt a surge of excitement that started in her toes and spread all the way through her body. She'd never seen a live show before—a professional one at that, with several performers whose names she recognized from TV.

The only problem was, she'd barely be able to see them with these dark glasses she had to wear all the time in order to hide from Jack Smith. Maybe after the show started and everyone was concentrating on it, she'd take a chance and remove them.

"Hello, there."

Or maybe she wouldn't remove them, Frances thought, grimacing as she recognized the distinct masculine voice behind her.

"Jack," Lionel said, getting to his feet and extending his hand.

Frances didn't move her head but she could see the two men shaking hands out of the corner of her eye. What was *he* doing here? Deliberately trying to spoil her evening? Probably.

"I thought you were out dancing the night away," Lionel said.

So did I, Frances silently agreed. *And why aren't you?*

"I changed my mind," Jack said.

"In that case, would you care to join us?" Lionel asked.

No, Lionel! Frances silently screamed. *Don't be polite to him. He might take you up on your offer simply in order to make me miserable.*

"I'd be delighted," Jack replied. "Do you suppose we can get the waiter to bring us an extra chair?"

No! No! she thought.

"No problem," Lionel said, signaling to the waiter, who produced another chair in a matter of seconds.

"I'll just scoot in here between Frances and Maxine," Jack said. "Is that okay with you two?"

Maxine giggled. Frances didn't trust herself to speak so she took another sip of her drink and kept quiet.

"I'll have a Scotch and water," Jack told the waiter, then glanced around the table. "Anybody ready for a refill?"

Angie and Lionel declined. Frances was surprised when she looked at her glass and found it almost empty. She remembered Lionel's warning about the drink being potent, but figured she'd be safe in ordering one more, especially since Mavis and Maxine were doing the same thing. Besides, she probably would drink very little during the show. She ordered another Dreamer Deluxe.

Then she made the mistake of looking directly at him. She hadn't realized before that they were sitting so close to each other at the small table, a table much too small for six people, especially if he was one of the six and was sitting next to her. She could almost feel the masculine heat of him, coming at her through his clothes and her own.

It was only her imagination, of course, but she suddenly *did* feel warm...probably because of the way he was looking at her, an enigmatic expression in his dark eyes. Unable to help herself, she lowered her own gaze to his mouth, full and wide, dangerously sexy. She swallowed. And breathed a sigh of relief when Lionel said something to Jack, distracting his attention away from her.

"What's in that thing all you women are drinking?" Jack asked a few minutes later when the waiter served fresh drinks.

"Tropical fruits and rum," Maxine replied. "Want a sip?"

He sipped from Maxine's glass. "*Lots* of rum," he said with an exaggerated shudder. "You'd be wise to drink it slowly," he added to Frances.

By way of reply, she defiantly lifted her glass and took a deep swallow. Jack raised an eyebrow, but said nothing. Then the houselights dimmed.

The show started with the orchestra doing a rousing medley of Broadway show tunes. Frances watched with delight when half a dozen dancers pranced onstage a few moments later and broke into a snappy, high-stepping routine. She'd seen similar shows on TV, of course, but this was so much better...actually being here, right in the middle of all the color and excitement.

She applauded enthusiastically when the number ended.

"Is this the first time you've seen a live show?" Jack asked.

Turning her head in his direction, she saw that he wasn't being derisive, as she might have expected. Instead, there was an understanding smile on his face. She nodded.

"I still remember the first one I saw...and how thrilled I was," he said wistfully. "I guess it's something you never forget."

Surprised that he'd shared the personal revelation with her, Frances didn't know what to say. She took a sip of her drink. More dancers came back onstage, along with several singers she recognized from television, and the Broadway revue continued. While she watched the show this time, however, Frances was more conscious of the man sitting beside her than what was happening onstage.

Taking a surreptitious look at him out of the corner of her eye, she saw the angry red scar along his cheek, the scar she'd made when she lashed out at him with her fingernails last night. *Had it really been only that short a time they'd known each other?* It seemed much longer.

She wondered how she'd react—knowing him as she did now—if they were put in the same situation they'd been last night. Would she still want to lash out at him? Maybe. At times he really was the most infuriating man.

But maybe before she lashed out at him—or after—it would be fantastically exciting to explore that dangerously sexy mouth of his...

The idea came as a surprise. A shock. Even though her mind was clouded by rum and tropical fruits.

Or maybe it was *because* her mind was clouded.

Whatever.

And of course she'd never actually *do* anything about it. Would she?

And even if she would, he wouldn't. He wasn't interested in dull, dowdy Frances Lanier. He was interested in the mysterious woman he'd found nearly naked in his room last night.

The woman who also happened to be dull, dowdy Frances Lanier.

She wondered what his reaction would be if he found out the two of them were one and the same. She snickered at the thought.

"What?" Jack asked.

"Beg pardon?"

"I wondered what you were laughing about."

"Oh. Just a crazy idea I had. You wouldn't be interested." That struck her as extremely funny and she snickered again.

His dark brows furrowed in a frown. "Are you all right?"

"Certainly. And don't lecture me again about drinking slowly."

"I won't. It's too late for that," he said pointedly, looking at her glass.

She had no choice but to look, too. The glass was empty. "It was delicious," she said, being careful to enunciate every word clearly. "I didn't want it to melt."

"It didn't."

She had another impulse to laugh, but thought it best to suppress it. She turned her attention back to the show instead, but it suddenly turned blurry, almost as if the TV needed fixing. She tried closing one eye and that helped, but only for a little while.

She closed that eye and opened the other one, and that only made things blurrier than they'd ever been. She closed both eyes.

A mistake.

The room, the ship, the entire world, whirled around at a dizzying speed. She immediately opened her eyes and the dizziness didn't go away. She blinked once, twice, a third time, but nothing seemed to help.

"Frances?"

That sounded like Jack's voice, except it was very far away and she'd thought he was sitting right beside her. At least he had been the last time she looked in his direction.

She closed one eye and looked in his direction again. Yes. That was him, all right. Peering at her. Frowning again.

"Why are you frowning at me?" Her words sounded a little strange, even to her.

"I'm frowning because I'm concerned about you. *Are* you all right?"

She started to tell him that she was, but suddenly realized that she wasn't. At all. She shook her head. Another mistake. On top of the dizziness, she felt a sudden wave of nausea.

She was vaguely aware of Jack standing up abruptly, pulling some bills from his pocket and leaving them on the table.

"Frances isn't feeling well," he said in that strange, faraway voice of his. "I'm going to take her for a walk on deck."

She started to protest that she'd be okay in a minute if he'd only leave her alone, but felt herself being pulled to her feet by the firm grasp of his hand on her arm. "Do you need any help?" Lionel asked.

"No," Jack replied. "I'll see that she gets to her cabin safely."

Again, Frances wanted to protest his cavalier treatment, but she was too tired to do it right now. Maybe in a minute or two, when she regained her strength . . .

She allowed herself to be pulled—literally—from the supper club. Then Jack opened a door, pulled her through it, and she felt a fierce gust of wind hit her body, a gust so strong that it almost pushed her back inside.

She stopped in her tracks. "No."

"Yes," Jack insisted, ignoring her protest. "You ignored my warning before, but now I'm going to take care of you . . . whether you want it or not."

He forced her to accompany him along the deck, half pulling her until she realized the futility of her protests and gradually fell into step beside him, with her hand still held firmly by his, both hands nestled in the crook of his arm.

She didn't want to take a deep breath but finally was forced to because he'd increased their pace. She was relieved that the deep breath didn't make her dizzy or sick this time. She took another. Then another.

At last she dared to take a glance in his direction . . . and caught her breath again at the sight of his profile in outline against the midnight sky. *God, he was beautiful.*

He was also silent. And determined. His chin could have been chiseled in stone. "I'm going to take care of you whether you want it or not," he'd said.

She smiled, lowering her chin so he wouldn't see it in case he looked her way, which he probably wouldn't do anyway. He was only doing this—taking care of her—out of kindness. Nothing else. But as long as he was being silent, she could *pretend* that something else was involved, and he wouldn't dispute it.

She started pretending.

They were lovers, but something had kept them apart for years. Not an invalid father, which was too close for comfort for her, or a wife who didn't understand him, which

*would make it shabby for both of them...but something
else. What? He'd been in the military? Yes. He was a much-
decorated veteran, a real hero, who'd finally returned to her
after serving his country. Now the two of them were on this
wonderful cruise, free to explore their love in ways they'd
never done before...*

"Are you feeling better?"

"Yes," she admitted, finding herself embarrassed, as if
he could read her mind and know the fantasy she'd been
having about him, about them. "A little."

"Do you think we should make one more turn around
the deck?" he asked solicitously, although she thought she
heard impatience in his voice.

"I think *I* should," she replied. "But I'm feeling much
better now and there's no reason for you to bother yourself," she added. "I'm perfectly capable of..."

"Nonsense! Of course, I'll accompany you."

He didn't want to, she knew, but had insisted on it as a
matter of courtesy, which was an even nicer thing for him
to do. She smiled her thanks and tried to make it up to him
by walking as fast as she could on their last turn around the
deck. She stopped dead in her tracks, however, when the
full moon made a sudden, blazing appearance on the horizon.

"Oh, my!" she said.

Jack stopped walking, too. "I agree," he said, releasing
her hand and draping his arm around her shoulders. "Oh,
my."

Frances didn't know whether the sudden staccato beating of her heart was brought on by the awesome show na-
ture was staging, or by the feel of his arm around her
shoulders. She didn't move, and barely breathed, while the
two of them watched the moon silently make its way upward through the heavens, finally taking its place among
the stars.

At last she sighed. "That was..."

"Heavenly."

She nodded. Then she sighed again. "I'm feeling much better now. Thank you for...everything."

"You're welcome. But I have to confess that I had nothing to do with the moon's spectacular performance tonight."

She laughed—a little nervously, because his arm was still draped around her shoulders. He probably wasn't even aware of it; it was probably the kind of thing he did all the time.

"I really am feeling better now, so..."

He removed his arm and her shoulders felt naked, cold. "I'll see you to your cabin."

"That's not—"

"Yes it is."

Jack walked Frances to her cabin, took the key from her suddenly lifeless hands, and opened the door. Then he leaned over to poke his head inside the room and look around. "Everything seems in order," he said, straightening again.

"I'm sure it is," she agreed. Neither of them moved. Frances wondered what she should do next. Thank him?

"Don't bother thanking me," he said, helping her over the awkward moment. "I'll send you an itemized bill."

She smiled with relief. "I suppose you're expecting a hefty tip as well."

"You bet." He grinned. "Good night, Frances."

He was gone before she had a chance to respond. She went into her cabin, locked the door behind her and kicked off her shoes. Her poor feet would probably never recover from all the walking she'd done lately in high heels, something she was totally unaccustomed to wearing.

The next thing to go was the dark glasses, followed closely by the wig, which she hated already after only one day. Could she survive wearing it the entire cruise? What other choice did she have?

Her scalp was itching like crazy, so she gave her hair a vigorous brushing, then tied it back from her face with a ribbon before starting for the shower. She'd taken only a couple of steps toward the bathroom when she heard a knock on her cabin door.

She frowned. Somebody must have the wrong cabin. The only people she knew aboard the ship were the people at her dining table and none of them would be knocking on her door at this time of night. *With the possible exception of Jack,* she thought. But he'd only left a few minutes ago, so it wouldn't be him.

The knock sounded again. She debated whether to respond or to ignore it. If she ignored it, maybe whoever it was would realize they had the wrong room and go away. She tiptoed over to the door and pressed her ear against it. She didn't hear a sound.

Then the knock came again, louder than before, startling her and almost causing her to jump out of her skin. "Who is it?" she whispered angrily.

"Room service."

"I didn't order room service."

"A gentleman told me to bring you some aspirin."

Frances hadn't realized she'd been holding her breath until she suddenly let it out with a long sigh of relief. *Jack* must have ordered the aspirin for her! How really nice of him. Thoughtful. Considerate.

She smiled. Then she threw back the deadbolt and opened the door. Her smile vanished immediately.

"Jack! What on earth...?" she began. She stopped when she saw the expression on his face.

Then she remembered. She wasn't wearing the wig. Or the dark glasses. All her protection was gone. And he was staring at her. She tried to close the door. His foot stopped it.

"It's *you!*" he exclaimed.

"No it isn't!"

Chapter Five

"It was you all along!" Jack said.

"No—"

"It was! You, pretending to be whoever it was you were pretending to be."

"I'm not pretending! This is who I am—Frances Lanier."

"Sure. And I'm Art Fortuna."

"What?"

"Never mind. Do you deny that you were in my room last night?"

"No. But—"

"Then why were you wearing that ridiculous disguise today?"

"It wasn't all that ridiculous...."

"Not ridiculous? Dark glasses and a wig with bangs down to your elbows?"

"Well..."

"Not to mention outlandish dresses that my grandmother would have thrown away years ago."

"These are *my* dresses!" she protested, angered by his words even though she knew there was a measure of truth in his assessment. "They're the clothes I *always* wear."

"You weren't wearing them last night."

"I wasn't wearing anything last night!"

"You had on my terry-cloth robe..."

"Which you immediately tore off me!"

"That's not precisely true."

"It's true enough!"

"What was I supposed to do...with you yelling and screaming the way you were?"

"I was screaming because I thought—"

"And you were wrong. Right?"

Damn him! "I apologized for the mix-up last night. I thought we had it all settled."

"So did I, until you sneaked away while my back was turned."

"I didn't *sneak* away."

"Okay. You left. Without a word."

"You were still talking on the telephone. How do you know I left without saying anything?"

"Did you say anything?"

"No," she admitted reluctantly. "But you wouldn't have heard me if I had."

"It was a business call. Important business."

"Hey, you don't have to explain that to me. I'm not the one making all the fuss."

"But you *are* the one who left. And then went to all kind of trouble to make sure I didn't recognize you today."

That was true. And Frances couldn't immediately come up with a snappy response to it. Besides, she was suddenly feeling tired.

"Listen," Jack said. "We're going to wake up all your neighbors if we stand here like this much longer. Is it all right if I come inside?"

"I don't see that it's necessary. We've said about all there is, haven't we?"

"Not me. I've barely begun. And I'm not leaving until I get some answers."

She could tell he meant it. Sighing in resignation, she stepped back and opened the door wider, motioning him to come inside. She closed the door and squared her shoulders before turning around to face him.

"You don't have to act as if you're facing a firing squad," he commented.

"The guillotine, then?"

"Not that either."

Was it her imagination or had his stern expression relaxed slightly?

"So tell me, Frances. Why *did* you wear a disguise in order to hide from me?"

It was her imagination, she decided. His expression was more daunting than ever. "It's a little hard to explain," she said.

"Try."

"Because I didn't want you to know who I was. Okay?"

"You mean you didn't want me to know that you were the same woman I met in my room last night?"

"Yes."

"Why not?"

"Because I was embarrassed."

"But we'd already cleared up the misunderstanding. At least, I thought we had."

"I thought so, too. But then you invited me to stay for a drink and . . ."

"And what?"

She was starting to feel trapped. Panicky. "Do we have to keep on with this?"

"We don't *have* to do anything . . . except share a dining table on this cruise. I thought we'd both be more comfortable if we got everything straightened out between us now."

He was right, of course. She took a deep breath. "While I was dressing, it occurred to me that you'd invited me to stay for a drink but that you were probably expecting something more."

He stared to speak, stopped, then started again. "I wasn't expecting us to share anything more than a drink, Frances. That's the truth."

She believed him. Which only made her actions since last night all the more embarrassing.

"I'm sorry if my behavior led you to believe otherwise," he said. "That was inexcusable of me."

"Don't blame yourself! *I* was the one who got the wrong idea. My imagination probably ran away with me because you'd seen me... You know."

"Without much clothing?"

"Yes," she replied, forcing herself to look him straight in the eyes.

"And no man had ever seen you...that way before?" he guessed correctly.

"Is that important?" she asked, wishing he'd stop asking her these probing questions.

"I think it is."

"No," she said, lifting her chin defiantly. "No man had ever seen me nude before." She stood stiffly, waiting for him to do his worst—she only hoped it was a snide comment or a double entendre rather than outright laughter— but he didn't say anything for a long time.

"I think that explains a lot," he finally said softly. And then, surprisingly, he added, "I'm sorry, Frances."

She didn't know what to say.

"As I said, it explains a lot... but not everything."

"What else is there?"

"This afternoon, when we met down here by the escalator after your walk, I thought you acted rather..."

She relaxed a little when she saw him searching for the right word, and even managed a slight smile. "Strangely?" she suggested.

"More like defensive, I thought."

"I was. The only reason I took the walk in the first place was because you'd told me you were coming down here to search for your 'friend.' "

"Whom you knew very well I wouldn't find."

"Yes. And then when I finally returned after hours of walking in uncomfortable shoes, and found you *still* on my deck, I came completely unglued."

"Why did that upset you?"

"I didn't want you to know that I lived on this deck, too. I thought it might make you suspect that I was the woman you were trying to find."

"You needn't have worried. I wouldn't have suspected you in a million years."

"Because you wouldn't recognize me with my clothes on?" Frances asked, bristling.

"Because your disguise was that good. And don't try to put words in my mouth, and then get angry because of something *you* said."

"I wasn't—"

"No?" he interrupted, raising an eyebrow.

"Maybe a little." Frances wondered how he was able to read her so well after only the short time they'd known each other. "How did you happen to come back to my cabin tonight?" she asked, changing the subject.

"Thanks for reminding me. I'd almost forgotten," he said, reaching into his pocket and pulling out a tin of aspirin. He took her hand, placed the medicine in her palm, then folded her fingers around it.

"I really *did* bring you some aspirin," he said with a grin. "I thought you might need them."

Frances grimaced.

"What's the matter?" he asked.

"Nothing much—just one more reason for me to be embarrassed. First you find me naked in your room, and then you see me drunk. I guess you're wondering what I'll do next."

"Eagerly," he said with a wicked grin. "I'm looking forward to it."

"Don't hold your breath. You wouldn't know it from the way I've acted on the cruise so far, but I'm probably the most conservative person you'll ever meet."

"Now I *am* disappointed."

"I'm serious."

"So am I. I thought I'd found somebody to play with on the cruise."

"*Play* with?"

"You know. Like a buddy—somebody to do things with."

She shook her head. "You're talking to the wrong person."

"I think not."

"It's true. I'm not exactly a timid mouse like Sharon called me, but—"

"I knew you heard that witch. But she doesn't know you like I do."

"You don't know me, either. I'm much closer to Sharon's perception of me than yours."

"I don't buy that . . . any of it."

"I promise you it's the truth."

"No. It might be your opinion at the moment, but I'll make you change your mind."

She narrowed her eyes. "How? What do you intend doing?"

"I'm not sure yet," he admitted. "But I'll think of something."

"It'll be a waste of time."

He rolled his eyes. "Time is what I have too much of at the moment."

"You mean you're bored?" she asked incredulously.

"Aren't you?"

"Heavens, no! There's so much to see and do aboard ship...and we'll be stopping at interesting places along the way. I don't see how you could possibly be bored."

"It's possible, believe me."

"In that case, why are you taking the cruise in the first place?"

"It's a long story," he said. Then he grinned, revealing his beautiful white teeth again. "And one day soon I'll bore you, too, by telling you the whole thing. Okay?"

"Okay. But I don't think I'd be bored."

His grin disappeared and he studied her seriously. "Maybe we can help each other on this trip, Frances."

"What do you mean?"

"Maybe I can teach you how to stop thinking of yourself as a timid mouse, and maybe you can teach me how not to be bored."

She was sure he didn't intend it, but his words and especially the way he was looking at her made her feel more like a timid mouse than ever. "I...I'm not sure those things can be taught."

"We'll see." He looked at his wristwatch. "In the meantime, you're probably tired. And anxious for me to leave so you can get to sleep."

She *was* tired, but had no desire to call a halt to the most fascinating conversation she'd had with a man in her entire life, and was certain she'd probably still be awake rehashing the entire thing until the sun came up. She couldn't tell him that, of course—any of it—so she merely shrugged.

"I'll say good night again, then," Jack said. "Will I see you in the morning? I mean, will you be at our table for breakfast?"

Our table, he had said. She nodded. "Yes. If I don't get another all-out attack of embarrassment beforehand."

He took her hand and held it, along with the tin of aspirin, between both of his. "Look at it this way. I've seen all of you there is to see—almost. And according to you, I've seen you on your very worst behavior. So what's left to be embarrassed about?"

She had to laugh. "I'll probably think of something."

"Don't. Just take two aspirin and see me in the morning."

"Yes, Doctor."

"Good." Still holding her hand, he pulled her closer and kissed her lightly on the forehead. Then he released her hands and stepped back. "Will you be wearing your disguise?"

"I doubt it."

"In case you change your mind, remember that I'll track you down anyway. I need someone to play with on this voyage. And you're *it*."

"Yes, Doctor." ·

JACK MADE IT A POINT to get up early the next morning, and was the first person at their dining table for breakfast. He ordered coffee, telling the waiter that he'd wait until later to eat, and settled back to wait for Frances. He half-expected her not to show up, or to come in her disguise if she did show up.

She surprised him. Sort of.

She made her appearance at the dining table not long after Angie and Lionel arrived, and she wasn't wearing her dark glasses or the wig with the long bangs. But she had on a dress that was almost as god-awful as the ones she'd been wearing when she was hiding herself from him.

Thinking back, he remembered something she'd said to him the night before. "These are my dresses ... the ones I always wear."

Why? he wondered.

Why was she deliberately hiding that spectacular body of hers? Was she going out of her way to make herself appear as unattractive as possible?

"Good morning, Frances," he said, getting up from his chair as she took her place at the table.

"You look different this morning, Frances," Angie Curtis said. "How are you feeling?"

Frances glanced at Jack. "I already told Angie that you seemed fine last night after we walked around the deck a couple of times," he said.

He saw the quick, grateful, almost shy look she shot him. "I *am* feeling fine," she replied to Angie. "Thanks to Jack."

By damn it! He felt almost shy himself. And unexpectedly pleased. "My pleasure," he said.

"Have you done something different with your hair?" Angie persisted.

"Well . . . I'm not wearing my wig today."

"That's it!" Angie exclaimed. "Your own hair is much more attractive, Frances . . . beautiful, in fact. You should forget about the wig."

Jack managed to keep a straight face by not looking in Frances's direction. He agreed with Angie about her hair, though. It was a rich, lustrous brown with reddish highlights, worn in a straight, simple bob that brushed her shoulders.

Breakfast aboard the *American Dreamer* was more informal than other meals, and passengers were encouraged to eat at their leisure without formalities, so Jack ordered his food when Frances did. Mavis and Maxine arrived while they were waiting for their orders to be served.

"My goodness!" Maxine said to Frances. "I never expected to see you at breakfast this morning."

"Why not?" Frances asked.

"Well...you were feeling poorly the last time we were together. You know, the Dreamer Deluxes and all..."

"The Dreamer Deluxes *were* all," Frances said.

"And where are your dark glasses?" Maxine asked.

"Oh." Frances appeared flustered for a moment before she recovered. "I've been taking some new medicine and my eyes are much better now. I don't think I'll have to wear the dark glasses as much anymore."

Jack put his napkin to his mouth to hide his amusement.

"And how are you feeling this morning, Maxine?" Frances said. "You had as many Dreamer Deluxes as I did."

Jack looked at her again with admiration. She was doing great. What's more, she seemed to be enjoying herself. *Way to go, Frances.*

"I feel like death warmed over," Maxine admitted. "And I had *more* than you did. I ordered another one after you left."

"I warned her not to do it," Mavis said. "But she never listens to me."

"That's not true," Maxine said. She proceeded to enumerate the reasons why it wasn't.

While Frances listened to the quibbling cousins, Jack took the opportunity to study Frances without her disguise. She wasn't a great beauty, he decided, but she also wasn't anywhere close to the low opinion she seemed to have of herself.

Wholesome.

That was the single word he'd use if he were asked to describe Frances. As Angie had pointed out, her hair was beautiful...and he was sure it would smell as clean as it looked. Her mouth was wide and generous; her nose straight, slightly upturned at the tip, and her intelligent eyes were the same warm brown shade as her hair.

Everything about Frances seemed to fit together. Jack found himself smiling his approval. *I enjoy simply looking at her,* he realized with a slight jolt of surprise.

Except for the dreadful clothes she wore.

He'd been wondering what the two of them should do today, and now it came to him. The boat was docked until six o'clock this afternoon, so he'd suggest that they make use of the opportunity to explore Quebec City. Then, along with their sightseeing, he'd gently steer her into one of the city's better dress shops.

He'd have to be careful, though. And subtle. Even though he was determined to help her improve her wardrobe, he didn't want to hurt her feelings.

While he was eating breakfast, Jack planned his strategy.

He timed his departure from the dining room to coincide with Frances's. Catching up with her in the corridor, he put his plan into action. "What do you think about the two of us exploring Quebec today?"

"The province or the city?"

He made a face.

"Bad joke?" she asked.

"Very."

"I like your idea, though. The only problem is that I've decided to buy some new clothes while we're here, and you might not enjoy shopping."

"I wouldn't mind," Jack replied, trying to hide his surprise and elation.

"Okay. I'll need to go to my cabin and pick up a couple of things first."

They agreed to meet in the ship's reception lobby in half an hour. Jack used the time to make a hasty phone call to New York. "Martin? I'm sorry we got cut off before we finished talking yesterday. You were just telling me that Ms. Burke turned out to be the spy we were looking for."

"That's right. You were completely on target, Jack. Our lovely young receptionist confessed everything after we confronted her with the evidence we had against her."

"What evidence did you find?"

"Primarily a state-of-the-art monitoring device hidden in her desk . . . as you suspected."

"Did she give you a reason for betraying us the way she did?"

"Money," Martin replied. "Lots of money."

Martin named the amount and Jack whistled. "The bad guys are really serious."

"Of course they are," Martin agreed. "They'll resort to anything in order to stop us."

"How much ammunition do you think Ms. Burke supplied them before we found her out?"

"It's hard to say. We'll know more in a couple of days. In the meantime, I called an emergency meeting of the executive committee and informed them. We terminated Ms. Burke without references, of course, but decided not to try to prosecute her."

"I agree with that decision," Jack said. "She's already done all the damage she can do . . . and going public with something like this would only endanger our position more."

"Yes. So . . . I guess that brings you up-to-date on what's going on here."

"Not quite."

Martin laughed. "No, we haven't heard anything from the Japanese. I admire your restraint in not asking sooner."

"It was hard."

"I *promise* I'll let you know the instant I hear something, Jack . . . good or bad."

"Day or night?"

"Whenever. In the meantime, how are things aboard the cruise ship?"

"Boring," Jack replied automatically. Then he realized that it wasn't completely true; he was actually looking forward to spending the day sightseeing and shopping for new clothes with Frances. But wasn't the fact that he was anticipating something as mundane as shopping a sign of boredom, too?

"I'm sorry to hear that."

"Not as sorry as I am."

"I was hoping you'd be able to relax and have some fun for a change."

"I didn't come on this trip for *fun,*" Jack reminded his associate.

"In addition to the other reasons, of course. But it's not a crime to have fun..."

"And I had my share of it... for *years,* if you'll think back on it."

"And that was years ago!" Martin said. "When you were just a kid."

"But I kept it up, even after I was married...and supposedly was a mature adult."

"Dammit, Jack! You can't keep blaming yourself for—"

"Yes I can." He heard Martin take a deep breath and expel it, obviously trying to calm himself. Jack tried to calm down, too. There was no point in arguing with Martin about the distant past...especially not now, when they had so many more pressing things to worry about.

Chapter Six

"Well...what do you think?" Jack asked.

"What?" Frances blinked, feeling her cheeks grow hot because she'd been caught admiring the outline of his profile against the azure sky. Then she realized that he was referring to her opinion of the scenery, not himself.

"It's, uh..." She groped frantically for words to describe her impression of Canada's oldest city, wishing he hadn't thrown her off guard the way he had. She didn't want him to think she didn't appreciate Quebec's distinctive flavor...or that she was too dull-witted to *have* an opinion. Actually, she adored the city, with its narrow streets and sweeping promenade above the river.

"It's lovely," she said, mentally chastising herself for not being able to come up with a better description than that. "And exciting. For the first time I feel that I'm really in a foreign country."

"Montreal didn't make you feel that way?"

"I didn't actually see Montreal," she admitted. "It was after dark when I arrived, and the taxi driver who took me from the airport to the boat dock drove like a maniac, so I kept my eyes closed most of the way. I *did* enjoy hearing all the people speaking French."

What a stupid thing to say, she thought, telling herself to stop babbling.

Jack smiled.

"Do you speak French?" she asked, trying to shift attention away from herself.

"Some. I spent a year in Paris."

"Really?"

"It was while I was in college," he said. "So long ago that I've forgotten a lot of what I learned."

Frances was impressed. He'd spent an entire *year* in Paris. Until now, the farthest she'd ever been from home was the Panhandle of Florida. "Have you been back since then?"

"Only a few times . . . short business trips, mostly."

She wondered what kind of furniture he sold that took him to Paris. They started walking again. After a few minutes Frances dared to shift her attention away from the sparkling split-level city spread out around them and take another quick glance at the man walking beside her. He was wearing a sedate blue blazer and casual slacks today, but she'd seen the admiring looks women gave him as they passed on the street.

And no wonder. He was gorgeous. For the umpteenth time she wondered why he'd chosen her, of all people aboard their cruise ship, to be his so-called "buddy."

"Don't question things so much, Frances," she could imagine Lisa saying. *"Simply enjoy them."*

She decided she'd try to do exactly that . . . except she couldn't help feeling as if she'd just stepped out of a fairy tale . . . or perhaps she was still in it. The weather contributed to the overall dreamlike effect—it was about as perfect as a day could be, cool and crisp, with a blue sky that was only enhanced by high, fleecy clouds.

They walked for miles through the Upper Town and the Lower Town, and stopped for lunch at a delightful café with red-checked tablecloths and candles in empty wine bottles colorfully coated with the drippings of other candles. Jack ordered their food in what sounded like perfect French to Frances.

"Have you done much traveling?" he asked, taking a sip of wine while they waited for their food to arrive.

"Me? Heavens, no. This is the first trip I've taken in...years." She considered telling him about her father and the reason why she hadn't done any traveling, but decided that was too personal. Besides, she was sure he wouldn't be interested in the story of her life. It was much too boring.

"That's a pity," Jack said. "I mean, you seemed to enjoy sightseeing so much this morning. It's a shame you haven't been able to do more of it."

He seemed to be waiting for her to say something but she didn't know what to say, so she kept quiet, wishing with all her heart that she was more adept at casual conversation. She started tracing her finger around the red check squares in the tablecloth.

"I suppose it's because you've been caught up in your work or something."

Glancing up in surprise, she saw him watching her intently, as if he really *was* interested, and wasn't merely making idle talk. "Well . . . yes. In a way," she said.

"What way is that?"

"You really want to know? I mean . . . you're not just being polite?"

"I wasn't being polite. I was being nosy as hell. And if you want to tell me to mind my own business, I'll understand."

"No. I mean...I wasn't trying to *hide* anything. It's just that I thought you'd find it boring."

"Boring? Why do you think I've been asking you all these questions?"

"What questions? You haven't—"

"Frances," he said, placing his hand over hers. "Let's start all over again."

She swallowed, acutely aware of his hand covering hers. His was warm. Hers wasn't. His was steady. She was sure hers would be shaking if he weren't holding it in place.

She nodded her agreement.

"The two of us have decided to become friends, and friends have the right to ask each other personal questions, right?"

"I—"

"Right?"

She nodded again.

"I'll begin," Jack said with exaggerated formality. "Frances... since you enjoy travel so much... why is this the first trip you've taken in years?"

Frances always giggled when she was nervous or embarrassed. She did it again now.

"Frances..." he cautioned.

"I've been taking care of my father," she blurted, wanting to get it out in the open quickly.

"What?" he asked.

"For the past thirteen years. Since he had his first stroke."

"And you nursed him... all that time?"

She nodded again. "Until he died."

"When was that?"

"A little more than a month ago."

"Thirteen years," Jack said quietly. "My God. *Thirteen years!*" he repeated.

"Don't make it sound worse than it was," Frances said, wondering whom or what she was trying to defend. "Pop was able to take care of himself a lot, especially during the early years. Until he had some more strokes."

"And after that?"

"Not much," she admitted.

"Did you have anyone to help you? Your mother maybe?"

"She died years ago. But Lisa was a godsend. She—"

"Who's Lisa?"

"My sister-in-law."

"And that would make her ... your brother's wife?"

"Yes."

"Where was your brother all those thirteen years you were taking care of your father?"

She felt her cheeks burning again. "Don't be so quick to criticize people. You don't know—"

"That's right. I don't know. And I wasn't criticizing; I merely asked a question."

"You ..." she began, then stopped and started again. "He was in college and law school. Then he was working trying to build up a law practice in order to support his wife and family. What's wrong with that?"

"Nothing! It's admirable, in fact. Completely admirable. Assuming that he already had this wife and family when your father was first stricken and you were saddled with the responsibility of taking care of him when you were ... what? Fourteen or fifteen years old?"

"Seventeen," she replied, trying to pull her hand away from his. He didn't let go.

"Seventeen," Jack repeated. "And was that the case, Frances?"

"You know it wasn't."

"I *don't* know. Not unless you tell me."

She sighed deeply. "No, it wasn't the case. Howie married Lisa while he was in law school, several years after Pop had his first stroke."

Neither of them spoke for a long time. Frances took several deep breaths while she tried to regain her composure...which had been shaky at best to begin with. She was starting to feel a little better when Jack hit her with another salvo.

"Do you have any other brothers or sisters?"

Frances closed her eyes. *Here we go again.*

She opened her eyes. ''Yes. I have a sister,'' she said belligerently. ''Why do you ask?''

''Hey,'' he said, obviously trying to feign innocence. ''I thought we agreed that friends have the right to ask each other questions.''

''I don't remember agreeing to that. And I'm not even sure we *are* friends.''

''Frances.''

If she hadn't been so upset, she might have laughed at his exaggerated attempt to appear hurt. ''My brother and sister were both in college when Pop had his first stroke. It was the summer after I'd just graduated from high school.

''My sister Juli said she should make the decisions since she was the oldest. She decided that she and Howie should finish college first, and then take care of Pop while I went to school. It sounded okay to me . . . except Howie and Juli both got married while they were still in college. And they both had families of their own not long after that.''

Frances looked directly at Jack and lifted her chin. ''Juli is three years older than I am. And she looks five years younger than I do. And does that answer all your questions?''

She waited for him to say something but he didn't. Not for a long time. Instead, he rubbed the top of her hand with his fingers, almost absentmindedly.

''Frances,'' he finally said, lifting his head and capturing her gaze with his. ''As one friend to another . . . may I say something to you?''

''I guess,'' she replied uncertainly. ''What is it?''

''Your family stinks.''

FOR A LONG, AGONIZING moment, Jack thought he'd gone too far. Then Frances laughed.

''That's what Lisa says, too.''

"Your sister-in-law?"

She nodded. "She's on my side."

"Thank God somebody is."

"It wasn't as bad as all that."

"It wasn't? Caring for an invalid father... for thirteen years... and it wasn't that bad?"

"I already told you—Pop was able to do a lot for himself during the early years."

"I remember. And Lisa helped you as much as she could later on. How much was that?"

"A lot! She brought dinner over to us at least once or twice a week. And she sat with Pop while I went out shopping, or simply to give me some time off for myself..."

Jack suddenly found it hard to breathe as the extent of Frances's bondage—her captivity for *thirteen years*—finally sank in on him, penetrating his thick skull.

She wouldn't have been able to shop for groceries—to buy food for her father and herself—if it hadn't been for her sister-in-law.

She wouldn't have been able to shop for clothes.

Or go to a movie.

She wouldn't have been able to go for a simple walk around the block.

Inhaling the first sweet smell of spring blossoms.

Seeing the first glorious burst of autumn color.

Feeling the first snowflakes of winter falling on her face.

None of that.

And he suddenly understood, too, why no man before him had ever seen her naked.

She was a thirty-year-old virgin.

Because she wouldn't have been able to go out on a date.

Hell! She probably couldn't even go to the bathroom without leaving the door open... listening in case her invalid father needed her!

Jack cleared his throat. "You must have found it difficult to shop for clothes...what with so little time to—"

"Jack."

"What?"

"It was *impossible* for me to shop for clothes. That's why
I dress in things your grandmother would have thrown
away years ago, as you so aptly put it."

He winced. "I shouldn't have said that."

"It's true. I've been buying from mail order catalogs for
years now...and nothing ever seems to fit right...or it's
out of style by the time I get it...or both."

"We'll remedy that today."

She nodded. "As soon as we finish lunch. But are you
sure you want to come along? I thought men were supposed to find that kind of thing..."

"Boring? Not this man. Not with you," Jack said, hoping to make her feel better. Then he realized he meant it. He
took another sip of his wine, wondering what *that* meant.

Their lunch was served and they made small talk while
they ate. Or rather, Jack made small talk. Frances said little, mainly responding to direct questions, but Jack didn't
mistake her lack of response for antagonism this time. He
thought he had more of an insight into what she was feeling now.

Or maybe he didn't.

When the check came, Frances insisted on sharing it.

"No. Please," he said. "I wanted this to be my treat."

"Why?"

He couldn't think of a reason...at least, not one he could
tell her.

"I thought you said we were friends," she said. "Buddies. Do you make it a habit of buying your buddies
lunch?"

He didn't have an answer to that, either. "I'll take care
of it and you can pay me your half later, then," he said,

sighing in resignation. "I have to put it on my credit card anyway. I forgot to get some cash before we left the ship, and I didn't bring my checkbook with me."

Jack gave the waiter his credit card and then turned to Frances. "What sort of clothes did you plan to buy today?"

"At this point, almost anything would be an improvement, don't you think?"

Jack wasn't about to respond to *that* loaded question, so he merely smiled.

"Actually, I was thinking I should look for something to wear in balmy weather," Frances said. "Even though it's cool here in Quebec, we'll be in warmer climates for most of the cruise, so..."

"I agree," he said, picturing Frances's fabulous body draped in some sort of soft, clinging material...maybe with one shoulder exposed. "And don't forget about a bathing suit."

"Thanks for reminding me."

"Sir?"

Jack looked up and saw their waiter standing beside the table. "Yes?"

"I'm sorry, sir," the man said, shifting from one foot to another, "but this credit card isn't working."

"Not working?"

"There's probably some trouble with our computer but...do you have another card?"

Jack frowned as he reached into his pocket and then handed the waiter another card.

"What do you suppose the trouble is?" Frances asked.

"I have no earthly idea. Probably a computer glitch, like the man said."

The waiter was back in only a matter of minutes. "I'm sorry, sir," he said with obvious embarrassment. "This card isn't working, either."

"What the..." Jack began angrily. He stopped. After all, this wasn't the waiter's fault. "Here," he said, reaching into his pocket again and pulling out his entire credit card portfolio. "Take them all!"

The waiter snatched up the cards and scurried away.

Jack looked at Frances, but she quickly averted her gaze. "Hey, there's no reason for *you* to be embarrassed," he said. "I'm not."

"You're not?"

"Hell, no! I'm furious. And I'd like to know exactly what's going on here." Frances fell silent—no surprise there—and Jack was no longer in the mood to make small talk by himself so he impatiently drummed his fingers on the table while he waited for the waiter to return.

As soon as he saw the man, Jack knew that the news wasn't good. "No?" he asked anyway.

"I'm afraid not, sir."

"*None* of them work?"

"No, sir."

"*Why the hell not?*"

"Beg pardon?"

"I mean," Jack said slowly and evenly, "you keep telling me that my credit cards 'don't work.' What does that *mean?* Exactly."

"It, uh, means that they've been declined. Denied. Our computer won't accept them in lieu of payment."

Jack thought about protesting but realized the futility of it. Besides, there was no point in embarrassing the waiter or Frances more than they already were.

"Well, Frances, I guess you get the check, after all. And you'll have to spring for most of my share, too. I only have a few dollars with me."

"No problem," she said, digging around in her purse.

"I'll pay you back later."

"Don't worry about it."

Jack *did* worry about it, though. Had his enemies somehow gained access to his credit accounts? Most of them were corporate accounts in the first place. Were they trying to sabotage him through them?

Jack saw Frances fumble around with a credit card of her own—starting to extract it from her purse, then quickly pushing it back inside and taking out cash instead.

"YOU DON'T HAVE *ANYTHING* that's lightweight?" Frances asked the salesclerk in frustration.

"Not until December," the clerk answered. "That's when our new spring line will start coming in. In the meantime . . ." The woman shrugged.

Frances looked at Jack. He shrugged, too.

Frances sighed, shaking her head. This was the fourth store they'd visited—the best ones in town, according to Jack—and all of them were stocked with heavy winter garments. What were people supposed to do if they needed something to wear *now?* Stay inside and forget about it . . . and wait for winter to arrive?

And when it *did* arrive—in December when the weather was frigid—what were they supposed to do when they found the stores filled with lightweight spring clothes? It didn't make sense.

"I guess this just isn't my day," Frances said to Jack in the taxi on their way back to the boat.

"Nor mine."

That was the first reference he'd made to the scene with the credit cards in the restaurant. Frances hadn't mentioned it, either. And even though Jack had said he wasn't embarrassed, she didn't see how he could help but be. Anyone would be. She knew *she* was . . . still.

She wished she could think of something to say to make him feel better. She tried but couldn't.

"I meant to tell you earlier, though," he said. "That suit you have on today isn't bad at all. In fact, it's quite becoming."

"Thank you," she said, feeling her cheeks grow warm at the compliment. "Lisa helped me pick it out to wear to my father's funeral." She'd also worn it the day she boarded the ship, the night she wound up in his room by mistake. But of course he hadn't seen her with her clothes on then. She'd sneaked out of his room as soon as she finished dressing.

"You should wear it . . . at least until the ship docks in South Florida. We'll be able to outfit you in proper cruise clothes there."

"That's two weeks away," she pointed out. "I can't wear this suit for two whole weeks."

"Why not? It's dark blue . . . and the ship has overnight cleaning service."

"Jack," she said, shaking her head. "Women simply don't *do* that."

"How do you know? I thought you'd been living a sheltered life."

"Not *that* sheltered."

"How sheltered, then?" he asked, taking her hand in his. Again. For the second or third . . . or was it the fourth? . . . time that day. She was sure he didn't mean anything by it; he probably did it all the time. But she didn't.

That was why her heart started racing like crazy and she found it hard to breathe every time he touched her.

Wasn't it?

"How did you keep up with what was going on in the outside world during all those years you spent caring for your father, Frances?" Jack said, rephrasing his question.

"Books and magazines," she replied, looking away from the sight of their two hands—hers clasped firmly in his, both of them resting intimately on his gray flannel-clad thigh. "Radio and TV, of course," she continued. "And movies. Lots of movies."

"Old movies on TV?" he asked.

"Yes, but new ones too. We bought a VCR a few years back."

He frowned. "But how—"

"Mobile movies."

"What are they? I never heard of them," he said, shaking his head.

"It's probably because you've been sheltered," she teased. She was surprised when he didn't react in a similar vein.

"You could be right," he said thoughtfully. "I've been working hard for the past few years."

"Oh. Well . . . the mobile movie company sends you a catalogue with capsule reviews of all their titles. Then you order what you want by phone and they deliver it to your door."

"Sounds ideal for your situation . . . or at least for what your situation used to be. And how did you get your books?"

"Book club."

"Faithfully delivered to your door by mail each month."

"Right."

"It seems to me," he said, giving her hand a quick little squeeze, "that you did an excellent job of coping with your situation, Frances. I can't believe that many people would have handled it as well."

"Thank you," she murmured again, outrageously pleased by his compliment.

The taxi pulled to a stop at the boat dock and Frances saw Jack reach for his wallet, then wince. "Oops," he said. "I forgot."

"It's my turn anyway," she said, handing the driver money. "You paid for the taxi on the way into town."

Jack didn't say anything.

"I really enjoyed the day," she said when they were in-side the boat, about to take their respective escalators down and up. "Thank you for playing tour guide. I wouldn't have seen half as much without you to show me where to go." She'd been rehearsing that little speech for ages and thought it had come off rather well.

"You're welcome. But don't forget—you wouldn't have spent half as much money if I hadn't been along, either."

She didn't know what to say, and looked away in em-barrassment.

"Hey, I was only teasing," Jack said after a moment.

Gathering up her courage, she turned back to him again. Sure enough, he was grinning.

"I wanted to see if your cheeks still turned that fantastic shade of pink when you're embarrassed about something. They do."

"That's..." she began angrily. "You're—"

"I know. And I apologize. But I've already told you that *you* shouldn't be embarrassed by what happened with the credit cards today. If anyone should, it's me. And I'm not."

She still wasn't sure she believed him.

"Believe me," he said. "I'm not embarrassed. But I *am* angry. Mad as hell, in fact. And I'm also going to find out what's going on, so I'll say goodbye now."

He lifted his index finger, kissed it, then pressed the kiss to her lips. "See you later."

He was gone before she could reply. Not that she could think of anything to say.

Frances went to her own cabin, where she kicked off her shoes and went to the bathroom to wash her face because she still felt warm. Looking at her reflection in the mirror above the lavatory, she saw that her cheeks *were* flushed.

"A fantastic shade of pink," was what Jack had called them. She smiled. Then she lifted her hand and touched her index finger to her lips, to the exact spot Jack had touched when he gave her his kiss.

She smiled again.

Where was he?

"Do you know where Jack is?" Sharon Lane asked, looking directly at Frances and echoing her own question.

"Uh, no," Frances mumbled. "Why do you ask?" *Why ask me?* is what she'd meant to say, but she was so nervous that it came out jumbled. Dinner was almost over and he still hadn't made an appearance at their dining table. He'd said that he was going to find out what had caused the mix-up with the credit cards today, and maybe what he'd discovered was really bad news. And maybe he was embarrassed about his credit being refused, after all, which she still halfway suspected was the case, although he continued to deny it.

"I *asked* because Jack and I had discussed doing something together later on tonight," Sharon said coldly, her tone of voice making it clear that none of this was Frances's business in the first place. "And I asked *you* because I saw the two of you returning to the ship this afternoon and I assumed you might know what had happened to him."

Sharon looked directly at her, daring her to deny that she knew where Jack was.

"Not me," Frances said, denying it. She felt proud of herself for sounding so forceful...so woman-of-the-world. She wished Jack had been there to hear her.

And thinking about him, her woman-of-the-world confidence evaporated. Jack and Sharon were planning to get together later tonight. Frances swallowed, feeling slightly ill.

But that was ridiculous. She had no reason to feel as she did, because she had no claim on him. None at all.

What's more, Sharon was the kind of woman she'd imagined Jack would want to be with. Well-dressed. Confident. Sophisticated. Almost as beautiful as he was.

Except he hadn't been with Sharon last night or today. Instead, he'd chosen to be with her.

Again she asked herself—*why?*

An aberration? Kindness on his part? Either of those reasons—or any other explanation she could come up with—was unacceptable to her.

Not that it mattered now. He'd finally seen the light, come to his senses, or whatever cliché applied. He'd made plans to be with Sharon tonight. The woman he should have been with in the first place.

Frances made it through dinner and excused herself immediately afterward. She headed straight for her cabin. Once inside, she kicked off her shoes, took off the blue suit she'd worn again tonight because Jack had said it looked good on her, and went directly to the shower.

A good place to wash away guilt, she thought, stepping into the stream of hot water and feeling it beat against her bare body, cascading over her, touching her in places no man ever had, places no man had ever even seen . . . except Jack.

Forget about Jack, she told herself, reaching for the knob and turning the stream of water up higher, hotter. *He was nice to you. And that's all he ever intended. It's only your own fault that you read more into it than that.*

When the water had finally washed away her jealous feelings about Jack—or any feelings at all, for that matter—Frances readjusted the temperature gradually until the water ran cold. After bearing that as long as she could, she turned off the water, stepped out of the shower, and briskly toweled herself dry.

"That's better," she said aloud, pulling on a pair of her father's old cotton pajamas and rolling up the sleeves and legs. She felt more in control of herself now. She was Frances again—sane, sensible Frances—not some foolish spinster entertaining romantic, schoolgirlish notions.

She brushed the tangles out of her hair, leaving it free to air dry, and brushed her teeth. She was just reaching for the remote control to turn on the TV when she heard a knock at her door.

She froze in her tracks.

It couldn't be. It absolutely couldn't.

She tiptoed over to the door, not making a sound. She listened for a moment, but didn't hear anything. Then there was another knock.

She took a deep breath. "Who is it?"

"Room service."

She closed her eyes, and immediately opened them again. "Jack?"

"Yes. Open up and let me show you what I've brought you."

Chapter Seven

"What are you doing here at this time of night?" she asked, opening the door a scant two inches...barely enough to peer out at him.

"This time of night?" Jack repeated. "It's only ten o'clock. And I'm here because I brought you goodies. Well...actually, some of the goodies are for both of us. I missed dinner tonight."

"I noticed."

"So how about letting me in? I'm starving."

"Aren't you supposed to be someplace else?" she asked, thinking about the plans he'd made with Sharon.

"Someplace else?" He frowned. "No, I don't think so." He shook his head. "I'm positive I'm not. Why do you ask?"

Well. Frances wasn't sure what the situation was—what had or had not happened between Jack and Sharon. *And don't go reading too much into it,* she cautioned herself. Still, she couldn't help feeling that a dark cloud had suddenly lifted from over her little part of the world.

"No special reason," she said, opening the door wider. "What on earth is that?" she asked, spying a serving cart laden to overflowing with a wine cooler, glasses, covered dishes...and something that looked suspiciously like...

"A boom box?" she asked incredulously.

"And cassette tapes to go along with it," Jack said, pushing the cart into her room. "I thought we'd do a little dancing after supper."

"I don't—"

"I remember what you said last night. So I'll teach you to dance...unless you have some serious religious objections or something. Do you?"

"Of course not."

"It's a deal, then."

"If *you* like dancing so much," she said, thinking about Sharon again, "why don't you—"

"I didn't say I liked it."

"Then—"

"But that doesn't mean I don't know *how*." Jack wheeled the serving cart to a spot in one corner of her room—the room she'd considered quite spacious until now, when it seemed to be shrinking by the moment. His presence filled it. And filled her, too. With something close to joy.

"Actually, I'm told that I'm quite a good dancer," he said. "But you can make up your mind after our lesson. In the meantime..."

Jack placed the boom box and tapes on Frances's dresser. Then he removed the silver lids covering the food on the serving cart, revealing an array of cheeses and wafers, three kinds of caviar, plump strawberries and raspberries. Finally, he took a bottle of champagne from the wine cooler where it had been chilling.

Frances's eyes widened. "This must have cost a fortune," she said.

"Only a small one," Jack said with a grin as he popped the cork on the champagne. "But I'm back in the chips again. I even have money to reimburse you for lunch."

"You mean you're able to use your credit cards again?"

"Well-l, no, not exactly. But I found out what the trouble was, so don't worry about it. Drink up," he said, pouring a glass of champagne and handing it to her.

She took the champagne but didn't drink it.

"Is something wrong? It's vintage champagne."

"I know. I saw the label."

"Then ... ?"

"I'm not sure I should touch alcohol again. I mean, after last night and those Dreamer Deluxes."

Jack laughed, shaking his head. "Those Dreamer Deluxes were loaded with rum, Frances, enough to make an experienced sailor drunk. This is different. Trust me."

She *did* trust him. And then again, she didn't.

He'd said that the glitch with his credit cards was cleared up. But that he couldn't use them.

Yet—as he'd phrased it—he was "back in the chips again."

Where had the money come from?

Suddenly...almost from out of nowhere...she remembered that their cruise ship had a complete gambling casino. Was that where he'd suddenly acquired all this money?

Was he a gambler, either professional or amateur?

That could explain where he'd been during dinner...and during *all* the hours since the two of them had said goodbye after returning from sight-seeing. It could explain a lot of things. Such as the business trips he took to France. It wasn't furniture business he went for; it was gambling business. She wasn't sure whether or not Paris had gambling casinos, but she'd read all about Monte Carlo and places like that, within easy distance of Paris.

She could picture him, tall and handsome in his tuxedo, strolling through a posh gaming salon on the Riviera. Women would turn to look at him, of course—and men, too—the women with admiration and the men with envy.

"Frances."

The sound of his voice brought her out of her daydream. She was startled to see him standing so close to her, close enough to...

"Drink your champagne before it loses its bubbles," he said, taking her hand in his and guiding the glass to her mouth.

She took a swallow and choked on it. While she was coughing and wanting to die with embarrassment, Jack took the glass from her hand and put it on the serving cart. Then he hit her on the back a couple of times.

"I don't think there's any danger of the champagne losing its bubbles anytime soon," she finally managed to say when the coughing subsided.

"I'm really sorry. It's all my fault, almost forcing you to..."

"You didn't force me to do anything. I shouldn't have taken such a big sip, that's all."

"Have you never had champagne before?"

"Not the expensive kind, like this." He was looking so concerned that Frances wanted to do something to make him feel better. "I'm ready to try it again," she said, reaching for her glass.

"You don't have to—"

"I want to. But I'll be more careful this time." She took a tiny sip, feeling him watching her intently. "It's good," she said. "Really good," she added, exaggerating. Her reward was seeing the immense relief on his expressive face.

She smiled at him and took another sip.

"It'll be even better with caviar," Jack said, turning to the serving cart. "Which kind would you like?"

"I have no earthly idea," she admitted truthfully.

"This is my favorite," he said, spreading a cracker liberally with tiny black fish eggs. He placed the cracker on a cocktail napkin and handed it to her. "See what you think."

She had no choice except to accept his offering.

She'd expected him to prepare himself a wafer with caviar but instead—to her dismay—he stood there watching and waiting for her to eat the one he'd handed her. Gathering her courage, she took a small bite.

"Well, what do you think?" Jack asked after a moment.

"Mmm," she said, nodding her head to pretend approval while she tried not to think about what was in her mouth.

Surely he'd turn away now. He didn't. Finally, she was forced to swallow. She immediately took another drink of champagne, a bigger one this time, and was surprised that it tasted better than it had before. Of course, anything would be an improvement after the caviar.

Jack mercifully turned his attention to the serving cart then and Frances tried frantically to think of a way to dispose of the remainder of her cracker and caviar. She couldn't throw it in the trash without him finding out, and she didn't want to hurt his feelings. She might pretend to drop it but if she did that, he'd probably insist on preparing her another.

There was only one way.

Gathering her courage, she popped the rest of it in her mouth, took a couple of quick chomps, then washed everything down with a big swig of champagne. Her eyes were watering by the time she finished, but at last the thing was gone. Forever.

And by the time Jack turned back around, she was smiling. Mainly with relief.

"Do you want me to spread you another wafer with caviar? Or maybe you'd like to try a different variety," he said, gesturing toward a mound of plump pink fish eggs.

Frances suppressed her shudder. "No thanks. They served a huge dinner in the dining room tonight." That was true, but Frances wasn't about to admit that she'd been concerned about Jack's absence and as a result had barely touched her food. For one thing, she didn't want him to know that particular truth. And for another thing, he might insist that she have some more caviar if he *did* know it.

After Jack finished his supper, he looked at Frances again and raised one black brow. "Ready to dance?" he asked.

She wasn't. And probably never would be. "Are you sure you want to go through with this? And what's the point of it anyway?"

"I'm sure. And the point is... you're going to become a fantastic dancer. Then, when we get you outfitted in those fabulous cruise clothes in Miami, you're going to be the reigning belle of the entire *American Dreamer* cruise ship."

"Why on earth would I want to be that?"

"Because..." he began, then hesitated. "Because it's what every woman wants."

"To be the belle of the *American Dreamer?*"

"Or whatever circle she moves in."

"Why?"

"I don't *know* why! But that's the way it is. You'll just have to trust me on this one, Frances."

He'd said it again. *Trust me.* And she did. Most of the time. She sighed. "Okay, I'll give it a go. But I think you've taken on a really big job for yourself, trying to teach me to dance. It's a waste of time."

AFTER ABOUT FIFTEEN minutes of trying to guide Frances's ramrod-straight, stiff body around the cabin room, Jack agreed with her. He *was* wasting his time. He'd never danced with a woman as rigid as she was.

He couldn't figure it out. She seemed to be *trying* to follow his lead—almost painfully so—but . . . And then it hit him.

The reason she was so stiff was that she was embarrassed because she wasn't wearing a bra.

He'd known she didn't have one on immediately, of course, the moment he'd come into her cabin and seen her dressed for bed. He'd wondered at the time why she didn't seem embarrassed, but then had realized she must think her braless state was hidden by the men's oversized pajamas she wore. She was totally unaware of the enticing picture she presented to his practiced male eye.

But then, when they started to dance and he placed his hand on the warm, firm flesh of her back, she must have realized that he would notice the smoothness...the lack of any straps whatsover. With that realization, she must have tensed immediately. And the longer they tried to dance, the more tense she became.

Reluctantly, with an inward sigh of regret, Jack did what had to be done. He stopped dancing. ''This isn't working,'' he said.

''I told you—''

''I think the problem is that you're so much shorter than I am without your shoes.''

''What?''

''Will you do me a favor, Frances? Will you put on your high heels? And of course you'll need stockings; otherwise, you'd develop blisters. Do you want me to wait outside while you change?''

''I have a better idea. Why don't we just forget about the whole thing.''

''Absolutely not.''

She rolled her eyes. ''It'll take me a few minutes.''

''I don't mind waiting.''

''I have to find my darn shoes first.''

"I think I saw them over by the bed. Do you really hate wearing them that much?"

"Oh, no, not at all. And I'd probably enjoy the Chinese water torture, too."

He laughed and went over to pick up her shoes. "Here you are, Cinderella," he said, holding them out to her. Their gazes met, held. He could tell she was remembering the first time they saw each other, the same as he was. And she didn't scream this time. Instead, her eyes were warm, her lips slightly parted. He could see the rapid rise and fall of her breasts underneath the man's pajama top she wore.

He found himself holding his breath.

"Thank you," she said after an eternity, breaking the spell as she took the shoes from his hand.

"I'll be just outside the door," he said, surprised at the huskiness in his voice. "Let me know when you're ready."

She nodded. Jack hesitated a moment longer, then left the room, closing the door behind him. He took a deep breath, wondering what had just happened inside Frances's room. *Something* had, although he wasn't sure exactly what it was.

It probably had something to do with hormones—probably both his and hers—he decided, searching for an explanation.

He'd been driving himself relentlessly in business for years now, leaving little time for other pleasures and pursuits. And for the past several months, he'd almost lived a hermit's existence.

Then to suddenly find himself at sea—literally—with nothing to occupy his mind . . . and just as suddenly finding Frances, whom he'd first believed to be a seductive siren but who turned out to be an inexperienced lamb instead . . .

All that combined had thrown him off kilter. Yes. That was it. A reasonable explanation.

In addition to that, he'd probably been a little giddy with relief tonight after discovering that it wasn't his business enemies who were responsible for the restaurant refusing his credit cards today. Martin himself had put a temporary hold on them.

"I can't believe you'd try to use them in the first place," Martin said when Jack finally got through to him on the ship-to-shore phone lines after trying for hours. "With you leaving a paper trail like that, our creditors would know exactly where you are in a matter of hours."

"I didn't think of that," Jack had admitted.

"Well, don't forget it again. Use cash. Only cash."

"Okay. But there's one little problem with that. I forgot to get any before I left. I'm down to my last few dollars."

There was a long silence on the other end of the line. "Jack," Martin finally said, "are you sure—absolutely positive—you want to go through with this takeover attempt of yours? Those guys play hardball. Down and dirty, no holds barred. And speaking frankly—as a friend as well as a business associate—it's not your style."

"I'll *make* it my style! And yes, Martin, I *am* sure. I want to go through with it . . . all the way."

Martin sighed. "Okay. I'll wire you some money right now. And I'll make sure it isn't traced to the company."

"Thanks, Martin."

"Sure. I just wonder if you'll be thanking me for going along with this scheme a few months from now."

Jack frowned as he stood outside the door to Frances's cabin, thinking about Martin's parting remark a short while ago. His top aide had never been as excited about the take-over attempt as Jack was. But he was probably being overly cautious, reacting as an older brother would. The two of them *were* a lot like brothers.

Frances opened the door. She was wearing high heels and stockings—along with the skirt to the blue suit he'd told her he liked—and a short-sleeved blouse in a soft, cream-colored material that he liked, too. He'd be willing to lay odds that she was wearing a bra, as well.

And she was wearing something else—a shy, tentative smile that he found totally endearing.

He automatically responded to that dear smile for a moment before he caught himself. *Watch out for the hormones, Sherrod.*

He didn't want to give her the wrong impression...to make her think he was offering anything more than friendship. He didn't want to hurt someone as sweet and innocent as Frances.

"Ready?" he asked, deliberately keeping his tone light.

"As ready as I'll ever be. Which isn't saying much."

"I think your shoes will make all the difference. Wait and see if I'm not right."

He was. Wearing the dressy shoes—not to mention the bra—gave her the confidence to relax. Soon she was following his every move, every nuance. She was liquid motion itself, graceful and fluid.

Jack was delighted with her.

But not with himself.

While she was making all those graceful, fluid moves in his arms, his body was responding to her in ways that had nothing to do with dancing.

Or even acceptable behavior.

Damnation! He was a thirty-five-year-old grown-up, not a teenager with raging hormones.

Except his hormones *were* raging. Outrageously. In spite of age, maturity, breeding or socially acceptable behavior.

What was wrong with him?

Maybe he was coming down with something. The flu perhaps.

He directed Frances into a turn, a twirl, a deliberate maneuver on his part in order to get away from her sweet fragrance for a moment . . . to regain his perspective. There. That was better.

Then she was back in his arms again. Closer than ever. Her pliant body pressed against his. He tried to think rationally.

Okay. So his male body found her female body attractive and responded accordingly. Like genes calling out to genes. Like a flower opening its blossom to receive pollen, and the pollen fighting toward . . .

Pollen? Jack was dismayed at the direction his thoughts had taken. That was warped. He *was* coming down with something.

Mercifully, the music ended.

Jack walked over to the dresser and turned off the boom box.

"Aren't you going to put on another tape?" Frances asked.

Hearing the disappointment in her voice, Jack revised his plan to leave as soon as the tape ended. "I'm thirsty, aren't you? Let's finish off the champagne first."

He figured that would be harmless enough. They wouldn't be in intimate contact, so he'd have a chance to get himself under control. And he wouldn't run the risk of hurting her feelings by rushing off, as if he were trying to get away from her. Then, after they'd drunk the champagne, he'd make a leisurely, graceful exit.

It was a good plan.

Except things didn't exactly go the way he'd planned.

He poured the champagne, started to hand her a glass . . . and fell into her eyes instead. Warm, liquid pools of brown—not an everyday, ordinary brown, but deep, rich chocolate. He knew he should look away, but couldn't.

She didn't look away, either.

He put the champagne glass back on the serving cart, still keeping his gaze trained on her. He touched the tips of his fingers to her flushed cheek, and found it warm. He smelled the sweet, clean scent of her, and wanted to drown in it. He looked at her pink lips and . . .

Now! he said to himself. *Move away from her now.*

Then it was too late.

She brought up her own hand and lightly brushed her fingers across the scar she'd made on his cheek the night she scratched him. "I'm sorry I did that," she whispered.

It was his undoing. "Don't be," he whispered back, lowering his head to hers, brushing his mouth lightly against hers, finding hers as sweet and soft and giving as it looked.

He closed his eyes then. And kissed her. As he'd been wanting to do for hours.

He'd halfway expected her to pull away immediately. She didn't. Instead, he felt her arms creep up to encircle his neck, felt her kissing him back. He shouldn't be doing this, he thought, slipping his arms around her waist to pull her closer. Again, she didn't resist. Her body seemed to melt against his body, her curves adjusting themselves to his, making him want to pull her even closer, making him want . . .

Damn! Why didn't Frances pull away from him? Didn't she know what all of this could lead to?

No. She didn't know.

But he did.

Jack gave another silent curse and then, drawing on all his willpower, broke off their kiss. He placed his hands on her shoulders to gently push her back until their bodies were no longer touching, and forced a smile. "I guess you're wondering why I kissed you," he said, trying hard to keep his tone light and bantering.

He almost kissed her again when he saw the bewilderment—and hurt?—on her expressive face. "It's because I wanted to be first in line," he explained, hoping he could carry this off and they both could escape unscathed by his weakness in kissing her in the first place.

She frowned. "I don't understand."

"When you're the belle of the ball on the *American Dreamer*, you'll be so much in demand that I won't be able to come within shouting distance."

"Don't be ridiculous."

"Okay. So maybe I was exaggerating...but only a little. What I was trying to say in my usual heavy-handed way was...you're going to be a really good dancer."

Frances rolled her eyes. "Sure. A regular Ginger Rogers."

"I mean it. You have a natural grace and rhythm. And with a few more lessons, you'll be able to trip the light fantastic with the best of them."

"Gee! You mean even with Art Fortuna?"

Her quick quip caught Jack completely off guard and it took a moment to sink in. Then he whooped with delight and hugged her.

Oops, mental lapse. Another one, he thought, quickly releasing her and stepping back a safe distance. "I'm going to ignore your sarcasm," he said, reaching for their champagne glasses again and handing one to her. "This time."

"Thanks."

They both lifted their glasses in a silent toast and Jack breathed a sigh of relief that things were back to normal between them...and that Frances didn't know how close she'd come to having her thirty years of chastity put to the test.

FRANCES WISHED she could think of a way to get Jack to kiss her again.

It was the most enjoyable experience she'd ever had in her life.

She didn't delude herself into thinking it had meant anything special to him. He probably kissed women all the time; it was probably as casual to him as shaking hands.

But it wasn't to her. She hadn't kissed a man—except for her father or brother—since she was seventeen years old. She couldn't even remember how it had felt, but she was positive it hadn't been anything like kissing Jack. If it had been, she would have remembered it, even after all this time.

She tried, but couldn't come up with a single idea on how to encourage Jack to repeat the kiss. She simply wasn't cut out to be a vamp. "Would you like to sit down while you finish your drink?" she said, gesturing to the two chairs by the window.

She saw him hesitate. "Only if you'll join me," he said after a moment.

"Okay." They both sat.

"Here's to belles," Jack said, lifting his glass to her.

"What's the male equivalent of that?" she countered, uncomfortable with his reference because she knew she'd never been a belle and never would be one.

"I'm not sure I understand what you mean."

"You said earlier that every woman wants to be a belle. What do men want in order to consider themselves successful?"

Jack nodded. "Good question."

She waited, hoping he'd tell her something about himself—specifically about where he'd gotten money tonight and whether or not he was a gambler. "And the answer is?" she prodded after several moments.

"I can only speak for myself, of course. And my goals are all related to what happened to my father. It's a long, involved story. And you're probably too tired to listen to it tonight."

"No, I'm not," she said quickly.

"Well-l . . ."

"Really."

"Okay. But stop me any time you get bored."

"I will," she said, knowing she wouldn't because nothing about him would bore her.

"My father was a wonderful man. Kind, gentle, loving. He looked a lot like Lionel Curtis, and had that same kind of Old World charm."

Frances nodded, forming a mental picture of Jack's father.

"He operated a company that manufactured fine furniture—reproductions of antiques, mostly, but some original designs as well. It was a business that had been in the Sherrod family for generations."

"Sherrod?" she asked.

He nodded. "Jack Smith is an alias I'm using on this cruise, but Jackson Sherrod is my real name. I'm telling you this because I trust you, Frances. And I'd appreciate it if you didn't tell anyone else."

"Of course not," she agreed. *An alias!* she thought, flattered and excited that Jack trusted her with his secret.

"Thank you." He picked up his champagne glass, then put it back down again without drinking. "As I said, my father was a gentle man...too gentle for his own good. He couldn't believe it when a consortium started making moves to take over the company. He couldn't believe anybody would be as ruthless as they were, so he didn't do anything about it at first. And by the time he did, it was too late. By then, those heartless bastards had control of the business. My father..."

Jack paused and took a deep breath. "My father held himself totally responsible for the loss of the company that had been in our family for generations. And he couldn't live with that guilt. So...he killed himself."

"Oh, dear Lord!" Frances whispered, covering her mouth with her hand.

"Yes. And that brings us to my answer to your question. I'll consider myself successful when—and only when—I've regained control of my family's company. That's *my* goal, Frances . . . the thing that drives me, my reason for being."

She could understand his reason for feeling the way he did but . . . "Is it possible that you'll be able to do it?"

"Oh, yes. Entirely possible. I've been working on it for ten years now."

"Ten . . . ?"

"Years. Ever since my father's suicide. And things were looking extremely good, up until a short while ago. Then those bastards—excuse my language, I mean the people who stole my father's company—found out about our plans and then planted a spy in my own company to find out even more. That's why I'm on this cruise."

Frances shook her head. "You lost me about halfway through that."

"Sorry. It's pretty complicated, but what it boils down to is that my company still needs additional financing in order to complete the takeover of the company that stole my father's business. We're hoping that some Japanese investors will agree to furnish it. Understand?"

"Yes. So far."

"Good. Then—when the other company, the bad guys—found out what we were planning to do, they tried to stop us by undermining the financing that we already had in place."

"How could they do that?"

"Several ways, including rumors and innuendo—anything to suggest to my company's creditors that we were a bad investment."

"You have a lot of creditors?"

"Enough. But that's not important. The big thing is, we have to stall our own creditors until the rest of the financing is in place. And once that happens, we take over the bad guys' conglomerate and everything's rosy."

"And in the meantime, you're on this cruise because...you're hiding out so your creditors can't find you?"

"Exactly!" Jack said.

Frances tried to make sense of what he'd told her. It was all so complicated. "Did you say you're planning to take over a conglomerate?"

"That's right."

"I thought you said earlier that your father's company was just that—a company, not a conglomerate."

"Yes. But I'm not going to stop with merely regaining my father's company. I'm going to take over their entire conglomerate, as well. I'm going to make them pay and pay again for what they did to my father."

Frances thought about what Jack had just said.

"What?" he said. "You have a problem with that?"

"Why do you ask?" she said, hedging.

"You were frowning."

"Oh." She didn't want to tell him what she was thinking. If she did, it might be the end of their friendship.

"Well?" he asked. "Are you going to tell me?"

She looked at him, unwilling to risk destroying the fragile bond they'd formed between them.

"Friends are supposed to tell each other what's on their minds," he prompted.

Okay, here goes, she thought. "I was wondering about something."

"Tell me."

"If you carry out your plan... If you succeed in taking over the conglomerate that stole your father's business...

If you make them pay and pay again for what they did to him . . ."

"Yes?"

"Won't that make you exactly like them—the people you hate the most?"

Chapter Eight

Their friendship survived.

It was touch and go for a time there, though, Frances later decided. After she'd pointed out to Jack that he was in danger of becoming as ruthless as his enemies, he'd angrily retorted that his actions were justified, while theirs were prompted by pure greed.

"And that makes what you're doing right?" she'd asked. "Because you have a more worthwhile *reason* for doing it?"

"Yes! It makes all the difference in the world."

She'd finally let it drop. She'd said what she had to say—perhaps more than she had a right to say—so what was the point in continuing to argue when his mind was already made up?

After Jack left, Frances forgot about their disagreement and concentrated on more pleasant things—specifically their kiss—replaying it over and over in her mind until she went to sleep. Then she dreamed about him, and in her dream, he didn't stop with merely kissing her. His hands touched her, too, in places where no man ever had. And his touch—by turns hot and demanding, then soft and gentle—aroused a fierce response in her, awakening fires she'd kept buried for years.

She awoke from her dream, breathing hard, feeling weak all over. She sat up in bed, thinking about it. If a dream could leave her so shaken, what would the real thing be like?

I'd like to find out, she decided. She wondered if Jack would be willing to help her. She tried to think of some way she could entice him to help her, but couldn't come up with anything. She went back to sleep still trying.

The *American Dreamer* was at sea the next day, cruising the Gulf of St. Lawrence, and Frances and Jack played a game of shuffleboard on deck with the Curtises after breakfast. Maxine and Mavis walked by while they were playing and Maxine gave Frances a conspiratorial wink. Frances wondered what Maxine would think if she really could read minds and knew what Frances was planning for Jack. She giggled at the thought.

Jack suggested a game of gin rummy after lunch and Frances enthusiastically agreed.

"Are you cheating?" Jack complained after she'd skunked him for the third time.

"That's a terrible thing to say! You're just being a sore loser."

"Look at it from my point of view," he said. "I'm a good card player, always have been. Yet you continue to beat me. How do *you* explain it?"

"Practice. Lots of practice…in games that require only two players."

"You and your father?"

She nodded.

"But…was he *able* to play?"

"For a long time he was. Then later on, when he got worse, we played a lot of chess. He'd tell me where to move his men, and I'd do it for him."

"I would have thought his speech would be impaired, too."

"It was. But I could understand him, and so could Lisa." She frowned, remembering how it had been. "A lot of people *couldn't* understand what he said, though. And when he tried harder to make them understand, he'd become so agitated that it only made his speech worse. That's why we couldn't leave him with strangers. It was much too upsetting to him."

Jack nodded. "I can see how that could be. But one thing occurs to me."

"What's that?"

"Your brother and sister *weren't* strangers."

"Don't start that again . . ."

"Just an observation," he said, holding up his hands in surrender.

THE TWO OF THEM went for a walk on deck after dinner. The moon hadn't come up yet, but there were more than enough stars to make up for it. "Did you ever see so many stars in your life?" Frances asked.

"A couple of times."

"When?" she challenged. "Where?"

"I can't remember." He laughed. "And on second thought, maybe I haven't ever seen this many stars before."

He took her hand in his and they continued to walk. She suppressed a sigh. It wasn't that she didn't enjoy holding hands with Jack—it was actually very pleasant. But she wanted more, much more. And thinking about *that,* she shivered.

"Cold?" he asked.

She started to deny it, but immediately reconsidered. Perhaps this could lead to a step in the right direction—to what she wanted. "A little," she said.

"Would you like to go inside?"

Drat! She hadn't counted on his suggesting that they go inside. "Oh, no," she said quickly. "It's much too nice out here. I mean, with all the beautiful stars and all..."

"Would you like to borrow my jacket, then?"

Hadn't he ever heard of putting his arm around a woman to keep her warm? "Well-l..."

"Here." He took off his jacket and put it around her shoulders. "Is that better?"

"Yes, thank you." It was...sort of. The inside of the jacket was still warm from where it had touched his body, and it was a little like having *him* around her. But it was only a little like it, and she still felt disappointed.

"Frances," he said softly, his warm breath brushing her cheek. "Would you like me to kiss you?"

"What?" she asked, looking up in surprise to find him watching her with something that looked suspiciously like a smile playing around the corner of his mouth. Had she been that obvious?

"I phrased that badly," he said. "What I meant to say was—do you mind if I kiss you?"

She had a sneaking suspicion that he'd said what he meant to say the *first* time, but she wasn't about to argue the point...not now when she might be about to receive what she wanted most on this earth—her Christmas present, Easter surprise and birthday gift all rolled into one.

"I don't mind," she said.

She felt his hand, warm against her cheek, gently tipping her face up toward him. She saw his eyes—deep, dark pools—coming closer as he lowered his head. His lips brushed her, retreated, then returned to settle firmly over hers. She closed her eyes.

She felt his arm wrap around her shoulders, felt his other arm encircle her waist beneath his coat she wore, felt him pulling her close and closer still. She reached up and touched his face, feeling his warm skin beneath her fingers, feeling a delicious shiver race through her body.

Yes. Oh, yes. This was what she'd been wanting all night, all day, all her life.

This was what she'd dreamed about. For years. But never in her dreams had she imagined the pleasure would be this intense, this powerful, this all-encompassing. "Mmm," she heard somebody say. It took her a moment to realize the sound had come from her. Jack must have heard it, too, and she should have been embarrassed, but wasn't. She didn't care. If anything, she *wanted* him to know the pleasure he was giving her.

She felt as if she were floating away on a sea of sensuousness. And when had her arm wound itself around his waist, almost as if it had a will of its own? She moved her hand upward, and delighted in the feel of hard male muscles beneath his crisp dress shirt. She heard another sound, and realized that one must have come from Jack.

Then she felt his hands on her shoulders, and knew he was getting ready to break off their kiss. "I think we should walk some more," he said, his voice husky.

"Why?" she teased. "Are you getting cold without your jacket?"

"No, Frances," he replied with mock severity. "But I think the exercise will do us both good."

She went along with him, mainly because she had no other choice, but would have preferred kissing some more. Then she smiled as she remembered the sound of pleasure he'd made tonight. Maybe if he found kissing her as pleasurable as she found kissing him, he'd do it more often.

EVIDENTLY, JACK DIDN'T find the idea of kissing her completely distasteful because he did a fair amount of it during the next couple of weeks as the *American Dreamer* made its way along the Eastern Seaboard. The trouble was—the more Jack kissed her, the more Frances wanted to be kissed. Not only that, but she was coming to realize that she didn't want them to stop with merely kissing. She wanted more. She wanted everything.

Most of all, she wanted to shed her virginity. But not just with anybody. With Jack. Only Jack.

And that was the problem. He never did anything except kiss her, never even attempted anything. For a man who appeared to be so sophisticated, so worldly, he was surprisingly puritanical. Maybe it was his New England upbringing.

Or maybe the problem was with her. Maybe he simply didn't find her attractive in that way. But if that was the case, why did he continue kissing her, leaving her breathless and bristling with unmet needs, unsatisfied desires?

Sighing, she sent up a wish that things would change for the better after they went shopping in Miami tomorrow. Maybe Jack would find her irresistible in her new cruise clothes.

"I'VE RENTED A CAR," Jack said to Frances as they walked down the gangplank to shore in Miami.

"You have? Why?"

"It's almost a must here, the same way it is in L.A. We'll be able to drive out to Key Biscayne, and over to Miami Beach where you can see what they're doing with all the Art Deco buildings."

"That sounds lovely," she said, remembering what she'd read about recent revitalization there.

"And after that, we'll take the shoreline drive up to Palm Beach to shop for your new cruise clothes."

"All the way up there?"

"It's not that far."

"But couldn't we find what I'll need here in Miami?"

"Possibly," he admitted. "But Palm Beach is something you shouldn't miss. And Worth Avenue is one of the very best places to shop in the entire world. Besides that, I thought we'd drive by my mother's place and say hello to her after we've finished our shopping."

His mother.

Frances gulped. This was something she'd never expected. Never in a million years. *He wants me to meet his mother?*

No, she admonished herself. That wasn't the way it was at all. *He* wanted to see his mother. He was inviting her to come along with him simply because they'd be sightseeing and shopping together. It was as simple as that.

And don't let your imagination—or your daydreams—run away with you again, she cautioned herself.

Still, she couldn't help feeling a lot more nervous about this day than she'd been before.

She loved Miami, especially Cocoanut Grove and Crandon Park, and found Miami Beach totally fascinating, marveling at the difference in architectural styles as the area was developed northward during the decades.

Palm Beach was another world. One she'd never come close to before. *You can almost smell the money in the air,* she thought.

Jack parked the car and they started walking along Worth Avenue. "Which store would be a good place to start?" she asked.

"You can't go wrong with any of them," he replied.

Want to bet? she wondered. She stopped and peered inside a shop window. "I don't see a lot of merchandise," she said. "Only ten or twelve outfits."

"They keep most of their things in back."

"Out of sight? Are they ashamed of them?"

He made a face. "You go into one of their dressing rooms and an attendant brings you things to try on."

"How will I know what I want to try on unless I see it first? Always before, I've bought things I could *see* beforehand."

"From the catalogs?"

"Yes."

"And where did *that* get you?"

He had a point there. They went inside a store.

A saleswoman glided forward to meet them. The woman was tall to begin with, and had the tallest hair Frances had ever seen.

"My friend would like to look at cruise clothes," Jack said to the woman.

"What *kind* of cruise clothes?" she asked, looking down at Frances.

Frances tilted her head back almost as far as it would go. "Day...evening...all kinds," she said.

"Did you have any particular colors in mind?"

"Well-l, no. Not really. What colors do you have?"

The woman glided over to one of the two racks in the store and briefly touched one of the dresses hanging there. Frances didn't blame her for barely touching the thing. It was almost as bad as the garments she already owned.

"This particular number—a direct import from the West Indies—is available in mango, chutney and persimmon."

The saleswoman moved her hand along the rack to another *number.* "And we have this in guava, avocado and apricot."

"Aw, that's too bad," Jack said, clutching Frances's arm and steering her toward the door. "We had our minds set on watermelon and canteloupe."

Once outside the shop, they both collapsed in laughter. "I can't go wrong...anywhere on Worth Avenue?" Frances chided as soon as she caught her breath.

"How was I to know they'd turned that place into a fruit market rather than a dress shop?"

The next place they went was a complete reversal of the last one, and the salesclerk was friendly and helpful. The only problem was—Frances immediately fell in love with everything she saw. And when she saw the price tag on one of the outfits that the salesclerk brought out for her inspection, she almost fainted.

"Jack," she whispered when the saleswoman went to the back room of the store to find a sundress she'd liked, but in a different color, "I can't afford these prices."

"Don't worry," he said. "This is my treat."

She widened her eyes. Then she shook her head. "Don't be silly. Why should you pay for my clothes?"

"Because I want to. It was my idea to come here in the first place, and I'm the one who'll have the pleasure of seeing you wear them."

Frances caught her breath. That was the nicest compliment he'd ever given her...the nicest one anybody had ever given her. She shook her head again. "I can't let you do it."

"Now it's my turn to say it—don't be silly. You said you couldn't afford the prices—"

"That was a figure of speech. Actually, I *can* afford them. I just didn't *want* to pay that much."

"Then let me—"

"No!" she whispered urgently as the pretty blond salesclerk came back into the room.

"Yes, I like that color much better," Frances said.

"I agree. It matches your own coloring," the clerk said. "Would you like to try on some of the things you especially like?"

Frances followed the woman to a spacious dressing room. She stripped down to her underclothes, but hesitated before trying on any of the gorgeous outfits, wondering if it was appropriate to tell the salesclerk what was on her mind.

"Is something the matter?" the young woman asked.

"No. Well . . . I do have sort of a problem, Miss—"

"Please call me Nancy. And I'll be happy to help if I can."

"Thanks, Nancy. The thing is...if I buy anything in your shop today, then Jack—I mean, the man waiting for me outside—might try to pay for it. And I don't want to let him. I want to pay for my purchases myself."

Nancy nodded. "I understand. You don't want to be obligated."

"Something like that." *Only a lot more complicated.*

"It shouldn't be a problem," Nancy said. "I'll tally up your purchases and bring the statement back here to you in the dressing room. I assume you'll be using a credit card?"

"Yes."

"Then, if the gentleman should ask, I'll tell him that you've already taken care of the bill."

"Great." Frances hesitated again. "And there's one more thing. I need a lot of clothes for this cruise we're on. And I love almost everything I've seen in your shop. But the prices . . ."

Nancy grinned. "I know. Stupendous, aren't they?"

"Exactly. Do you have any suggestions?"

"Lots of them. If it were me, I'd go mostly with separates for daytime wear—skirts and slacks with several different tops, so you can create two or three outfits for only a little more than the price of one. Leggings are really popular now, too, and they cost less than half of what you'd pay for slacks.

"And with all those savings, you'll be able to splurge on a couple of knockout dresses for evening wear. How does that sound?"

"Perfect," Frances said. "I knew I was right to confide in you."

The fashion parade began . . . with Nancy bringing back different outfits and combinations of outfits, and Frances modeling them in the main salon for Jack's approval or disapproval. Frances was both relieved and delighted that he approved of most of the selections she and Nancy had chosen.

"That's terrific!" he said of a pair of floral print leggings and coral silk top. "Although I liked that last outfit you had on, too—the one in blue."

Later on in the dressing room Frances turned to Nancy. "He didn't realize it was the same pair of leggings, only with a different top."

"Not many people do. That's the beauty of it—you *can* fool most of the people most of the time."

They saved the best until last, when Frances donned the "knockout" outfits she and Nancy had chosen for evening wear. There were three of them—a shimmering blue silk, an off-white, off-one-shoulder rayon sheath that was Frances's personal favorite, and a low-cut red cotton knit that was probably the sexiest of the lot. She noticed Jack's eyes widening with approval the moment he saw it.

"Which ones should I get?" she asked.

"All three of them. By all means," he said.

She had no intention of doing that. She was sure she could do perfectly well with only two and, since the off-white rayon sheath was the most expensive, she said good-bye to it with a sigh of regret.

"It looked really good on you," Nancy said, correctly interpreting the sigh.

"Are you saying that the other two don't?"

"You know I'm too good a saleswoman to even think something like that."

They both laughed. "I appreciate all the help you've given me today, Nancy."

"Thank you."

"I mean it."

"So do I. And by the way...your friend *did* try to pay for all your purchases. He seemed very upset when I told him you'd already taken care of the bill."

"He'll get over it," Frances said with more conviction than she felt.

"I hope so. He's absolutely gorgeous...if you don't mind my saying so."

"I don't mind."

"I mean—and I hope I'm not out of line in saying this— but he seems like the kind of man that a woman wouldn't *object* to being obligated to."

Frances nodded. "I'll think about what you've said," she said, knowing she was giving Nancy the wrong impression about her relationship with Jack, but not having the heart to disillusion her. And—given any encouragement— wouldn't she harbor some romantic notions of her own?

But Jack never gave her any encouragement. Except for the kisses, he kept things between them completely platonic. Maybe the kisses had been platonic, too, but even with her lack of experience, she couldn't quite accept that. The glorious moments when he kissed her soundly, passionately, certainly didn't seem platonic to her.

She couldn't be wrong about that, could she? She hoped she wasn't. Because it was beginning to seem that kisses were all she'd ever get from him. Still, she shouldn't complain. It wasn't his fault that he wasn't attracted to her the way she was attracted to him.

And she should be grateful to him for what he *did* offer her—friendship, the best one she'd ever known. He was thoughtful, sensitive, intelligent, witty, generous... She frowned. He was *too* generous. He shouldn't be throwing his money around the way he'd tried to do today—buying her expensive clothes at the same time he was hiding out from his creditors.

"A lot of creditors," he'd admitted. "But it's not important."

Not important? How could he think that? How could he be so cavalier about money? Probably because he'd had a lot of it at one time—before his father's tragic disaster—and couldn't get used to *not* having it.

Sighing, Frances followed Nancy out to the main salon, where Jack met them and carried her purchases to the rental car. She halfway expected him to chastise her—or at least say something—about the fact that she'd paid for the new clothes before he had a chance to do so.

He didn't mention it. She wondered why he didn't, and then decided it was because he was secretly relieved but was too proud to talk about it. He refused to discuss the fact that he no longer had money—the kind of money he'd once had. She could understand his pride, and vowed to keep her knowledge of his reduced circumstances a secret. It was the least she could do, considering how nice he'd been to her.

ON THE DRIVE to his mother's cottage, Jack pointed out Donald Trump's mansion, the Kennedy estate and other places he thought Frances would find interesting. She seemed suitably impressed, swiveling around in the car for a last look at the palatial villa of a cereal heiress.

"How far is it to your mother's place?" she asked, settling back down in her seat.

"Not far. And I should warn you—her cottage is nothing at all like these mansions."

"I should hope not!" she said with a nervous laugh that Jack found completely charming. "Even so," she admitted after a moment, "I'm jittery as a Mexican jumping bean at the thought of meeting her. I don't want to embarrass you."

"Embarrass me? How would you do that?"

"By being my usual awkward, self-conscious self. And do you think I did the right thing wearing one of my new outfits? Does it look *too* new?"

"It looks lovely, Frances. And so do you. So relax."

"That's easy for you to say. She's your mother."

"Yes. And she also happens to be a dear, sweet, middle-aged woman . . . who's going to love you on sight."

"Did you tell her about me? I mean . . . that you were bringing a friend you'd met on the boat?"

"Well, no. Not exactly."

"Not exactly?"

"I tried to call her but got no answer, not even a machine."

Frances groaned. "So I'm just going to show up on her doorstep unannounced."

"She won't mind. She'll be so happy to see me that she'll welcome anybody I bring with me."

Jack shot her a sideways glance and was relieved to see her smiling. Then she laughed, relaxing a bit.

"I don't know why I tolerate you as a friend," she said. "Or why you tolerate me."

"It'll probably go down as one of the mysteries of the ages," he agreed, although he knew perfectly well why he tolerated Frances. She delighted him. Surprised him. Angered him. Amused him. He was fascinated by her.

She was a classic study in contradictions.

She was quick to anger, yet totally loyal to those she loved. She'd not only stuck by her invalid father for thirteen long years, but even forgave her sister and brother, who hadn't.

She was shy, but also extremely courageous. Coming on this cruise alone after years of living in a cocoon—and not knowing a soul aboard the ship—was ample proof of that. She'd also demonstrated her courage the night he'd practically forced her to eat caviar for the first time, he remembered with a smile. He'd intended it to be a special treat for her, but had noticed her immediate reaction—suspicion mixed with distaste. He would have understood completely if she had refused to eat it, but she hadn't. Instead, she'd bravely managed to get it down.

She was self-conscious, almost painfully so, but was one of the most beautiful women he'd ever met. At first, he'd mainly been attracted to her fabulous body, but had gradually become aware that her face was equally lovely...with a quiet beauty he never tired of looking at.

He liked her enthusiasm. Even sight-seeing—something he'd always hated and almost never did—was a pleasure with Frances along to infect him with her earnest curiosity about everything.

He liked her fierce independence, although she sometimes carried it to the extreme. He'd almost wanted to throttle her at the dress shop today when she'd insisted on paying for her new clothes instead of allowing him to buy them as he'd intended. Still, even while he'd been angry, he'd admired that spark in her, so he'd dropped the matter. For the time being.

He took another quick sideways glance at her now, seeing her peering eagerly out the window. He couldn't see her eyes because her head was turned but he remembered their warmth, and the way they crinkled at the corners when she laughed.

He liked her eyes. And her quick wit. He liked her mouth. And the occasional sarcasm that came out of it. He liked the way she listened to him with her head tilted to one side when she was *really* listening, paying close attention to what he was saying.

Hearing a slight sound, he looked at her again, this time shifting his gaze to the floor of the car where the sound had originated. He grinned when he saw that she'd kicked off her shoes and was wriggling her toes. The grin faded when he realized he wanted to touch her. His body ached with the need to touch her. He wanted to move his hand along her legs, over her thighs, her breasts...

Was there *anything* about her that he didn't find attractive?

Hell, he even liked her insecurities!

That was the big problem. And the big reason he'd kept his distance except for several lapses when he kissed her. It wasn't easy. It was all he could do to keep his hands off her.

And he couldn't—wouldn't—allow himself to give in to that desire because that's all it was. Desire. Physical need. Sex.

It was tempting, he admitted to himself, painfully so. His body reminded him of that every night, and whenever he allowed himself to come too close to her. He even dreamed of burying himself inside her—again and again—and of hearing, feeling her sweet response. He could make it good for her, too. So good for both of them... he was sure of that.

He was almost sure, too, that she wanted him. And for something more than mere kisses. Her eyes told him that. And her lips. And the way she sometimes breathed a little faster when they were dancing.

He wanted her. She wanted him. They were both adults. So the solution should have been simple.

But it wasn't simple at all.

He liked her too much to simply have sex with her—or even an affair that would last the length of the cruise. She deserved more than that—much more—and he couldn't offer it to her. Not now. Maybe not ever.

He was already committed to the task of regaining his father's company, and taking over the conglomerate that had stolen it. Martin said he was *consumed* by the task, and maybe he was right. At any rate, Jack had no room in his life for anything or anybody else at the moment. And probably not for a long time to come.

So that was that.

Sorry, Frances.

He took another quick glance at her, and wondered whether he was being sorry for her... or for himself.

"This is the street where my mother lives," he said, turning the car around a corner and onto a wide avenue lined with coconut palms. Out of the corner of his eye, he saw Frances scurrying to get back into her shoes. He smiled.

FRANCES'S NERVOUSNESS returned full force the moment Jack announced that they were approaching his mother's house. It swept over her like the pounding surf of the Atlantic Ocean a few hundred yards away, leaving her breathless.

It's only your friend's mother, she told herself. *A nice, middle-aged woman. So don't be intimidated about meeting her.*

That's what Frances told herself. Unfortunately, she didn't seem to be listening.

She hadn't been this nervous—scared to death, she might accurately describe it—since she waltzed out of the bathroom in Jack's room that first night on the ship and encountered *him.* And, of course, he was the reason she was so nervous about meeting his mother. She wanted him to be proud of her, not embarrassed by her. *Please don't let me make a fool of myself.*

"Here it is," Jack said, turning into a winding driveway flanked at the street by two impressive stone pillars.

Frances caught her breath. Then, looking out the car window and seeing the grounds of Jack's mother's house, she continued to hold her breath. She blinked. This looked nothing like the other estates they'd seen today. Nothing at all. All of them had been neatly manicured, carefully landscaped with exotic and expensive tropical trees and shrubs, while this... This place looked like a wild jungle.

An abandoned wild jungle, she corrected herself. *A place where nobody had lived for months. Maybe years.*

Jack chuckled. "I see Mother's been up to her old tricks," he said, wheeling the rental car to a stop in the middle of a concrete turnaround in which weeds were happily proliferating through the many cracks.

Frances turned quickly to look at him. "What do you mean?"

"Obviously, she's not back from vacation yet. She goes to visit friends every summer up in the mountains at Highlands—in your part of the country."

She shook her head. "I live in a working class neighborhood in Charlotte. Highlands might be in the same state, but the people who go there are so rich that the place is nowhere *close* to my part of the country."

"Yes, well... at any rate, Mother goes up there to visit during the summer, and she absolutely refuses to pay for lawn maintenance service while she's gone. I've told her it's false economy—that it takes much more to bring the place back into shape when she returns than it would cost to maintain it while she's gone. But she won't listen to me.

"She says she always *enjoys* bringing the place back to life again after she's been away. She says it gives her something to look forward to doing when she returns from summer vacation."

Frances smiled. Jack's mother sounded like a lovely, lively woman with a mind of her own. She glanced around the grounds again, then at the house. Jack's mother would have plenty to keep her occupied this year. The place probably had been lovely at one time, but was terribly run-down now. *Shabby* was a word her sister Juli might have used to describe it.

The windows and doors were boarded up—which contributed to the overall unkempt look, but was to be expected when a house was closed for the summer. What Frances found extremely sad was the paint peeling from the stucco walls, the tiles missing from the roof, the sagging, mildewed gutters...the overall feeling of a house in distress...and not enough money to keep it up properly.

She wished Jack hadn't brought her here. She wished he would stop trying to impress her with his wealth...which he probably had had at one time, but now seemed to be gone forever. What he had or didn't have wasn't important to her in the first place. She knew that Jack himself was a beautiful, wonderful person...no matter what.

"I'd offer to take you inside and show you around, but I didn't bring a key," Jack said.

"That's okay. Everything's probably covered up anyway." *And maybe a lot of it has been sold off to pay bills.*

"I suppose you're right. But I can't let you get away without seeing the view from the other side of the house—the ocean side." He took her hand and tugged gently.

She followed quietly, allowing him to lead her toward one side of the house, and what appeared to be an impenetrable jungle. "It's pretty grown over," he said, "but I remember the path. I think," he added when they came to a huge thorny bush. "Here, I'll hold this up while you duck under. Wait for me on the other side."

She ducked under the branch he held up, then waited for him.

"Ouch!" he said. He was holding his index finger when he rejoined her.

"Are you all right?"

"Sure. But I'm going to have to talk to that mother of mine. This jungle is ridiculous."

Frances kept quiet, feeling an incredible sadness because he insisted on keeping up this pretense. At last they emerged from the bushes—the jungle—and Jack took her hand again, pulling her along behind him to some crumbling steps that led to a terrace.

"Mother really has her work cut out for her this year," Jack said, repeating the thought she'd had earlier. "But I think you'll agree that the trek was worth it when you see the view."

They climbed three steps up to the trash-littered terrace, and Frances looked out to sea for the first time. She caught her breath.

"Well, what do you think?" he asked after a moment.

"It . . . it's unbelievably beautiful."

"Yes. That's what Barbara always said."

"Barbara?"

"Oh, that's right. You don't know. Barbara's my ex-wife."

Chapter Nine

"That was a pretty casual way to drop an ex-wife on a friend," Frances said after several moments, moments when she was too stunned to speak. But of course, she should have expected that he would have been married before. How could anyone as attractive as he was *not* have been married?

"How would you have had me tell you?" he asked. "With a drum roll and bugles? Tears and violins?"

"How can you be so flippant about it?"

"It happened a long time ago."

"How long is that?"

Jack looked out toward the Atlantic. "We married when I was twenty-three, not long after I graduated from college. We divorced four years later. Eight years ago. On August fifteenth."

He isn't flippant about his failed marriage, after all. He even still remembered the exact date of their divorce. Did that mean he was still in love with his ex-wife?

She didn't dare ask because if she did, he might tell her it was none of her business. And it wasn't.

"What was she like?" she asked instead.

"Barbara?"

"No. Madame Curie."

He shook his head and laughed, but at least he didn't tell her it was none of her business. And he answered her. "She was young, pretty, fun-loving."

"The same as you."

"Me, pretty?"

"Handsome." She saw Jack's face sober then, and saw him run his fingers through his hair the way he had a habit of doing at stressful times.

"We were a lot alike in some ways," he said. "Many ways. We came from the same sort of background, knew a lot of the same people. We both enjoyed parties, sports, having fun."

"So what went wrong?" Frances asked when Jack became silent.

He turned to look at her. "Wrong?"

"Why did you divorce her, when the two of you had so much going for you?" She thought she'd gone too far when she saw the strange, almost-stricken look on Jack's face.

Then he shook his head again. "I didn't divorce her. She divorced me." He took a deep breath and slowly exhaled it. "Another one of my failures."

The woman must have been crazy, Frances thought but didn't say. "It couldn't have been your failure alone. Your ex-wife must have had *something* to do with it. At the very least, she was the one who initiated the divorce."

"I don't blame her. I presented myself to her as one person, and she married that person. And then, after my father died—after he killed himself—I changed into somebody else entirely."

"What . . . what did you do?" she asked.

"Oh, I didn't start drinking . . . or cheating on her . . . or any of those things you read about in the tabloids." He gave a derisive laugh. "What I did was start working—really, actually working—for the very first time in my life."

"And *that* made your ex-wife unhappy?"

"Well, sure. Wouldn't you be unhappy if your husband—a person who'd done absolutely nothing worthwhile his entire life, who'd only lived to play and have fun—all of a sudden wanted to do nothing but *work?*

"Not only that, but my timing was all off, too. I mean . . . I was too late, way too late, to help my father. He was already dead . . . as dead as if I'd pulled that trigger myself. So all I succeeded in doing was wrecking my marriage."

What was he saying? "You . . . you can't mean that you blame yourself for what happened to your father!" she said.

"Why the hell not? He'd given me everything—all my selfish, miserable life—and I gave him nothing in return. Nothing.

"He'd been trying to persuade me to come into the family business for years—in a gentle way, of course, because that was the only way he operated. And for years I'd been putting him off.

"I'd always assumed that I would join the company eventually—and take over my father's job when he decided to retire—but figured there was no hurry. Hell, I was young. And having a helluva lot of fun. Why should I give that up and join the nine-to-five drudges?"

Jack leaned forward, resting his hands on the brick wall surrounding the terrace while he stared out at the pounding surf. Frances knew he was hurting; she could see it in the tense way he held himself, in the tightness of his jaw. She felt instinctively that talking about it would help. Jack needed to talk about it—all of it—even if he didn't want to.

"And then your father died," she said quietly after a moment, prompting him to continue.

"Killed himself," he corrected her.

"Yes."

"After the initial shock wore off—the disbelief and the anger—I started thinking about how things might have been different if I'd joined the company earlier the way he'd wanted me to do. Maybe if I had been more responsible— and a better son to him—I could have prevented it from happening."

"How could you have done that?"

"I don't know. Maybe I would have noticed something, seen something suspicious about the way the company's stock was behaving... Maybe I would have realized that unscrupulous thieves were trying to steal the company and—"

"And maybe you *wouldn't* have noticed anything unusual, the same way your father didn't until it was too late."

"That's possible. But at least I would have been there with him, by his side." Jack's voice broke. He swallowed. "And maybe that would have been enough to change things," he added softly. "Maybe he wouldn't have felt that desperate need to... to take his own life."

Frances felt a tightness in her own throat. She wanted to reach out and touch him, but the distance between them was too great. Although they were standing only a few inches apart, they were separated by miles of painful memories.

Neither of them spoke for a long time.

"I wallowed around in depression and guilt for a while," Jack finally said, "and then decided that my only salvation might be the one thing I'd always avoided—work. Although my father had lost everything he had, I still had a trust fund that my grandfather on my mother's side had left me.

"It wasn't all that big, but it was enough to get me started, and I formed my own company. Then Martin heard about what I was doing, and decided to join me."

"Martin?"

"Martin Armstrong. He'd been with my father for years and had worked his way up from the mail room to administrative assistant. The people who took over my father's company offered him an executive position—at an obscene salary and perks—but he turned them down cold and decided to join me instead. He turned out to be the biggest asset I had."

Frances had noticed the dramatic change that had taken place in Jack as he talked about his work, and the company he'd created. His depression had suddenly vanished, disappeared. He had come alive, and was once again the dynamic, aggressive man she'd come to know.

"What does your company do?" she asked.

"We call ourselves venture capitalists—at least, we did at the beginning—but we're actually much more than that. Our specialty is searching out sick companies—companies on the verge of bankruptcy due to mismanagement, outmoded manufacturing processes or whatever. We acquire them either through majority stock or a complete buyout, do whatever is necessary to make them healthy again, and then sell them off. For a hefty profit, of course."

Frances thought about what he'd told her. "It sounds almost as if you're performing a necessary service."

Jack raised his eyebrows. "That's one way of looking at it."

"And do the companies—the sick ones you take over—agree with what you're doing?"

"A few of them do. And a lot of them don't. As a matter of fact, I've been given a nickname by some of the people who don't, uh, appreciate what I'm doing. They call me 'Jack the Shark.'"

She looked at him and was surprised to see a hint of a smile at the corner of his mouth. "You sound as if you're proud of your nickname."

"Well . . . I can think of worse names to be known by."

She supposed that was true. Still, being known as Jack the Shark didn't sound like something to be proud of. A sudden thought occurred to her. "Your father's company," she said. "What sort of shape was *it* in when those people came in and took it over from him?"

He shook his head, as if disappointed that she would ask such a question. "It was in blue chip condition in every way. Modern plant, state-of-the-art manufacturing equipment, morale, maintenance, management...and it had never failed to return a profit, not in all its years of existence."

"Oh." So much for that possibility. "And what about the company that took over your father's company? What sort of shape is *it* in?"

He narrowed his eyes. "What are you getting at?"

"I mean...if it's foundering, too, then—"

"No. It's in sound shape, Frances. And I wish you'd stop trying to find excuses for their actions...or for mine."

"I was only—"

"I know. And I appreciate what you're trying to do...in a way. But I'm in this thing for revenge, pure and simple. And I won't try to excuse what I'm doing by putting an altruistic motive to it. I happen to think that my own motive is justification enough."

She tried to let it go at that, but couldn't. "You said you have a lot of creditors. You must have put a lot into this takeover attempt..."

"You might say that," he said with a rueful laugh. "I've thought of almost nothing else for years. I've worked on it day and night for almost a year. My social life is nonexistent. And—to go back to what you were too polite to ask outright—I've put everything I've accumulated in ten years into it. Everything I own."

"What...what happens if it fails?" she whispered.

"It won't fail."

"Then what happens if it succeeds? Will it make you happy?"

"Yes. Very happy."

He said it with conviction, but Frances had her doubts. She couldn't believe—or maybe she didn't want to believe—that someone as fine as Jack could be truly happy about destroying someone else, even if they deserved it.

She looked at him and found him watching her, waiting for her reaction. For a moment she didn't know what to say. And then it came to her. She reached up both her hands, capturing his face between them. She gently pulled his head down and kissed him on the lips.

Jack blinked. "What was that for?"

"For luck. For you to get whatever it is you want."

"I thought you didn't agree with my goal."

"That's not the point. I still want you to win."

"Why?"

"Because you're a good person. And because we're friends. I . . . I care about you."

FRANCES SAID LITTLE on the drive back to Miami and Jack wondered if she was thinking about their earlier conversation, the way he couldn't help doing. He had deliberately brought up the subject of his ex-wife in order to warn Frances that he was totally committed to the task he'd set for himself, with no room for anything else in his life.

That was what he had intended. What he *hadn't* intended was spilling his guts to her the way he had—telling her not only about his ex-wife and the reasons they'd broken up, but also about his father. About his own inadequacies. About his own guilt over his father's suicide. Things he'd never before told another living soul.

He wouldn't have blamed her if she'd said she wished she'd never stumbled into his stateroom by mistake . . . and that she wanted nothing more to do with him, ever. But she hadn't done that.

She had kissed him!

In spite of what he'd told her about his selfishness, his irresponsibility. In spite of the fact that she obviously disagreed with the takeover attempt. In spite of everything. She had kissed him . . . for luck, she'd said. "Because we're friends. Because I care about you."

He still couldn't get over that.

But he wasn't going to let it change his determination not to make love to her. If anything, it reinforced his decision. What kind of low-life would he be if he allowed his desires—simple animal lust—to rule his life, causing him to take advantage of someone as sweet and vulnerable as Frances?

He couldn't give her any kind of future because he was already committed, but by damn he wouldn't hurt her, either! He could at least do that for her.

AFTER JACK TURNED in the rental car at the dock, he helped carry Frances's new clothes to her cabin. "Shall I pick you up here for the party?" he asked, referring to Big Bash, the name someone in public relations had given to the dinner dance scheduled to take place tonight.

It would mark the end of the cruise for some, who'd only signed on as far as Miami. For others, it was the beginning of the tropical portion of their voyage, a launching-pad for the delights of the Caribbean and beyond, and the cruise line was building it up as *the* event of the cruise . . . so far. They'd even converted the main dining room into a ballroom for the occasion, with a lavish buffet instead of the usual seated dinner, and a full orchestra for dancing later.

"It might be better if we meet there," she said. "I made an appointment to have my hair done and I'm not sure how long it'll take."

"So you're having your hair done, too, Cinderella?" he said with a smile.

She returned the smile, feeling a little self-conscious. "I figured I might as well go all out."

"By all means. Which of your new dresses are you wearing tonight?"

"I, uh, thought perhaps the red one," she said. Then, seeing the expression on his face, she quickly added, "Do you think it's appropriate?"

"Of course, it's appropriate! All of them are. Its just...I was thinking how terrific you'd look in that off-the-shoulder white dress."

Frances swallowed. "I didn't buy it."

"You didn't? I thought you liked it best of all."

"It was also the most expensive," she said defensively.

"Then why the hell didn't you let me—"

"And I decided that I didn't need three evening dresses in the first place. I can get by perfectly well with two."

She saw him narrow his eyes, and thought he was going to argue about it some more, but he didn't. He took a deep breath instead. "I'll see you at the party then. A little after eight?"

"Yes," she said with relief.

After he'd gone, Frances kicked off her shoes and put away her new purchases, smiling as she touched the sexy red dress on its hanger, imagining how she might look in it...and how Jack might respond to the sight of her in it. Would it be enough to do the trick? She could only hope.

She took a long, leisurely bath, luxuriating in the scented bubbles floating around her, finally forcing herself to get out before she turned into a prune. Glancing at the clock radio, she was surprised at how late it was. She quickly put on one of her granny dresses and hurried off to her appointment at the beauty shop.

Stepping inside the shop, she noticed that almost every woman on board the ship seemed to have had the same idea. The place was packed. Frances gave her name to the woman at the reception desk and was told there would be a short wait.

"Frances," she heard someone call, and turned from the desk to see Angie Curtis patting an empty chair beside her.

Frances walked over and sat down. "Have you been waiting long?"

"Only a few minutes," Angie replied. "But from the looks of things, we might be here for quite a while. Thank goodness the dinner's a buffet, so we don't have to be there at a special time."

With a sinking feeling, Frances thought about Jack, whom she was supposed to meet at the party. What would he think if she didn't show up on time?

"Something wrong?" Angie asked.

"No. I mean . . . I was supposed to meet someone at the party a little after eight."

"Jack?" Angie guessed correctly.

Frances nodded, wondering whether she should try to call him on the house phone and tell him she might be late.

"Don't worry. Men always expect us to be late. Sometimes I think that Lionel is actually disappointed when I show up on time. It means he doesn't have anything to complain about."

Frances smiled, unable to imagine Lionel Curtis complaining about anything his wife did. The two of them were obviously still very much in love. "How long have you two been married?" she asked.

"Fifty years," Angie replied promptly. Then she looked at her wristwatch. "And two hours and seventeen minutes."

Frances's eyes widened. "You mean *today's* your anniversary? Your fiftieth?"

Angie nodded. "It seems much shorter than that...and in another way, much longer."

"Fifty years," Frances repeated. "That's wonderful."

"You think so?"

Seeing the odd look on Angie's face, Frances frowned. "Do you mean...? I mean...the two of you seem to be so much in love...and after all this time..."

"Oh, we are still in love. At least, I'm sure that I am. But as for *wonderful*...I don't know about that."

Frances didn't know what to say. "I'm sorry," she murmured.

"There's nothing for you to be sorry about," Angie said, patting her hand. "You had nothing to do with what went wrong between Lionel and me." She shook her head. "As a matter of fact, the two of us didn't have much to do with it, either. Except maybe..."

Angie shook her head again, then looked at Frances with a wistful smile. "I'm talking to you in riddles, aren't I? An old woman rattling away, and you have no earthly idea what I'm talking about."

"Well..."

The older woman glanced around, as if making sure no one was listening to them, then lowered her voice. "May I tell you something in confidence, Frances? Absolute confidence...and you'll promise never to tell another soul?"

Frances swallowed. "Well, sure...I guess."

"You have to promise."

"I promise."

Angie looked around again before she turned back to Frances. "Lionel is impotent."

Frances simply stared at Angie.

"He wasn't always, of course. And we have four children to prove it." Angie chuckled and shook her head. "And Lord, in the early days...he couldn't keep his hands

off me. But I'm getting away from my point. And that
is . . . *we haven't had sex in more than a year!*''

Frances couldn't believe she was hearing what she was
hearing. She couldn't imagine people Angie's and Lionel's
age *ever* having sex. Or wanting to have it. Or complaining
because they weren't having it.

"It all started with that darn heart attack of his, of
course," Angie said. "He seemed to bounce right back
from it. Everybody said so. All the doctors said so. He
made a complete recovery . . . in every way but one. He was
afraid to have sex anymore."

"Afraid?"

Angie nodded. "The doctor told me it happens to a lot
of men after a heart attack. They become impotent because they're afraid the excitement might bring on another
attack."

"And . . . would it?" Frances asked.

"Usually not. And certainly not in Lionel's case. The
doctor told us there was absolutely no reason for Lionel not
to have sex."

"And, uh . . . what does Lionel say?"

"He says that doctors don't know everything. He says
that his particular doctor is a damn fool who's probably
never had good sex in his life, and doesn't know what it's
like to have your heart start thundering like a herd of buf-
falo when you become aroused."

Frances thought about Angie's predicament. "So, because of that, Lionel won't, uh, do it anymore?"

"Not *won't*," Angie corrected her. "*Can't.* He can't get
it up since his heart attack."

"I'm sorry," Frances said, feeling her cheeks flaming
because she'd just realized that she had the same sort of
problem Angie had . . . with a significant variation. Jack
seemed to have no problem getting *it* up, as Angie had
phrased it; she'd noticed its hot, hard presence many times

when they kissed, exciting her like crazy, driving her almost wild. The thing was...Jack refused to do anything with it once it *was* up.

"That's the main reason I suggested coming on this cruise for our fiftieth anniversary," Angie said, brightening. "I figured that under the right circumstances—a romantic atmosphere, a staff to pamper us twenty-four hours a day, no cares or worries to intrude—Lionel would be able to relax and regain his strength...in a manner of speaking."

"Sounds like a good plan," Frances said. "I'm sorry it didn't work out."

"It *is* a good plan. And don't be sorry. I haven't even put it into operation...yet."

"But I thought—"

"I haven't put any pressure at all on Lionel so far. I've been patient, waiting until he was completely relaxed, sure in his own mind that I *wouldn't* try to seduce him. And *then* I'd planned to bring out the big guns—dress up in a sexy dress, get my hair done, put on the perfume that used to drive him wild, encourage him to have just *one* drink more than his limit... Then I planned to sit back and see what happened."

A slow grin spread over Frances's face as she thought about Angie's plan. "And tonight's the night?" she asked.

"Bingo!"

They both laughed. Then, gathering her courage, Frances said, "I have something to confess, too, Angie."

"What's that, dear?"

"I bought a new dress to wear tonight—a sexy red one."

"Oh?" Angie said, raising one eyebrow.

"And I made this appointment to have my hair done."

Angie opened her mouth to speak, then closed it again without saying anything. Frances wondered if she'd done the wrong thing in confiding in her. After all, their situations were entirely different—Lionel and Angie had been married for fifty years, whereas she—she could be just a woman on the prowl, a promiscuous woman at that.

"Jack again?" Angie finally asked.

Frances nodded, feeling her cheeks flaming with embarrassment. What must Angie think of her?

"I have just one thing to say to you, Frances."

Oh, dear, she thought. "Yes?" she asked.

"Would you like to borrow some of my perfume?"

Chapter Ten

"I'm sorry I'm late," Frances said, breathless not only because she'd been rushing madly ever since she left the beauty parlor, but also because she was nervous about seeing him—or rather, his finally seeing *her*—in her new clothes, makeup and hairdo. And perfume.

By God, she's beautiful! Jack thought, unable to speak for a moment, stunned by the lovely creature standing in front of him—a breathtaking combination of innocence and guile, sincerity and seductiveness. All packaged together in a sexy red dress.

"That's okay. You were worth the wait," he said, meaning it, trying to convey his delight in her.

He grinned, delighted with himself, too, for coming up with the idea of taking her under his protective wing in the first place in order to boost her confidence in herself. He had to admit, though, that he'd never dreamed in his wildest imaginings that she would turn into such a spectacularly beautiful woman as this. Never.

"I think every man in the room is looking at you," he added.

"Is something exposed that shouldn't be?" she asked, horrified that she might have forgotten something in her haste.

"No!" he said with a laugh. "I meant it as a compliment. They're looking at you because you're lovely."

She frowned. "You scared the living daylights out of me with that remark. I thought for sure I was about to be arrested for indecent exposure."

"I'm sorry I scared you. But I still stand by what I said."

She rolled her eyes. "I know what I look like, Jack. And even at my best—which this is—I'm not the type that men all around the room would be watching."

It was Jack's turn to frown. Didn't she realize—didn't she have any idea—of how truly lovely she was? It appeared that his ego-boosting work on Frances wasn't over yet. She still wasn't convinced of her own worth. But he wasn't giving up. Not by a long shot. This night had just begun.

"Would you care for something to drink?" he asked, changing the subject.

"A glass of wine would be nice. Maybe it'll help me relax."

"You'd better come with me. Otherwise, I might lose you in this crowd," he said, placing his hand on her elbow and steering her toward one of several bars set up around the perimeter of the huge room. Interspersed with the bars were lavish buffet tables laden to overflowing. Dining tables had been pushed back and moved closer together for the party, leaving the center of the room clear for dancing, which several couples already were doing to the music of a jazz trio.

Frances said something to Jack but he was unable to hear her because of the noise. "What?" he said, leaning his head closer to her.

"I said...I don't see how they're able to dance. How can they even hear the music?"

He nodded his agreement. It was a little quieter at the edge of the room away from the main stream of people.

Jack ordered their drinks and was just reaching into his pocket to pay for them when he felt a slap on his shoulder.

"Hi there, Jack! I saw you from across the room . . . you and your, uh, *friend.*"

Frances, who was standing beside him, turned her head to look at the newcomer. Even if Jack hadn't immediately recognized the obnoxious voice, he would have known who it was by the look on her face. Jack finished paying for the drinks before he turned around.

"Hello, Art," he said.

"Great party, don't you think?" Art said, almost drooling as he looked at Frances.

"Hmm," Jack said noncommittally, handing her the glass of wine.

"And say, old buddy," Art continued, "don't be so damned selfish. Introduce me to your little friend here."

Frances bristled immediately, from the top of her curly brown hair to the tips of her red shoes. Jack might have done the same thing if he hadn't suddenly recognized the humor in the situation.

"Well-l, Art," he drawled. "I was under the impression that you two *already* knew each other. Frances, you remember Art from our dining table, don't you?"

Swiveling around so Art couldn't see, Jack winked at Frances. She narrowed her eyes.

"Vividly," she said.

Jack turned back around in time to see Art's mouth drop open.

"Frances . . . ? Frances from our dining table?"

"One and the same," she murmured sweetly. "And how are you tonight, Art?"

"Fine. Uh, just fine." Art took out a handkerchief and wiped the sweat from his forehead. "And, uh . . . Say, why don't the two of you join Sharon and me at our table? Yeah. That's a great idea," he added, foundering as he obviously tried to recover from the shock of finding out that Jack's gorgeous friend was none other than Frances, The Timid Mouse from their dining table.

"We can't—" Jack began.

"We've already—" Frances said at the same time. They looked at each other.

"We have other plans," Jack finished.

"That's too bad," Art said. "But listen, Frances, I have to tell you...that red dress is just about the sexiest thing I've ever seen. And I'm counting on you to save me a dance. Several dan—"

"See you later, Art," Jack said, taking Frances's hand and pulling her back out into the milling crowd before she could reply. He didn't trust the combative look he'd seen leap into her eyes the moment Art started his come-on routine.

"I should have slugged him," she said after they'd made their escape. "Can you believe the nerve of that creep?"

"Since it's Art...yes, I can. But he did prove my point—every man in the room is watching you."

"Art Fortuna doesn't count, because he isn't a man. He belongs under a rock."

Jack chuckled. "Come on slugger. Let's see if we can find a seat."

"Angie Curtis was just ahead of me at the beauty shop. She said they'd try to save us a place." She looked around the noisy, crowded room. "If we're able to find them, that is...and if they were able to get a table themselves."

They finally located the Curtises' table. Maxine and Mavis were seated with them, too. "Frances!" Maxine exclaimed. "What have you done to yourself? You look fantastic!"

Hearing a strangled laugh from Jack, who was standing beside her, Frances took a quick glance in his direction. Sure enough, he had an "I told-you-so" expression on his face. Mavis and Lionel also complimented Frances while she and Jack were taking their seats. Angie merely winked at her.

The noise level in the room, already high when Frances and Jack arrived—rose higher still as people continued to pour in, until it was necessary to shout in order to make yourself heard. Frances finally gave up even trying to talk, content to sit back and listen instead.

She was enjoying herself, though, she realized with mild surprise. When she'd first come on board the ship—after living alone with her father for years in a house that was ghostly quiet most of the time—the crowds had made her feel claustrophobic, nervous. But sitting here now—hearing and feeling the noise and excitement around her, but buffeted from it by good friends—she was quite content.

She kept a smile on her face, nodding whenever someone shouted something to her, even if she hadn't understood what they'd said.

She did it again when Jack said something, but he didn't let her get away with it. He shook his head and reached out to pull her head close to his mouth, speaking directly into her ear. "You didn't hear a word I said just now, did you?"

She grimaced at having been found out, but admitted the truth when he leaned back to look at her. "No."

He moved forward to speak directly into her ear again. "I asked if you were having a good time."

She turned her head around to speak directly into his ear this time. "I *am.*"

He started to say something, but stopped and shook his head instead. Then he grinned and leaned over to kiss her on the cheek. Out of the corner of her eye, Frances saw Angie watching them with a sly smile tugging around her mouth.

The noise abated dramatically when a lot of people left the room after dinner. "Whew!" Angie said. "I can finally hear myself think for a change.

"And what are you thinking?" Lionel asked as the orchestra started to play. "That you'd like to dance with your husband on this—the occasion of your fiftieth anniversary?"

"Today?" Maxine asked. "This very day?"

"This very day," Angie said with a becoming blush that only Frances could truly appreciate.

"I think the occasion calls for a bottle of champagne," Frances said, remembering that Angie wanted Lionel in a more relaxed mood for later tonight.

"By all means," Jack said. "I'll order it while you two have your dance."

"Aren't *you* going to dance?" Angie said pointedly, looking from Jack to Frances and back again.

"Sure," he replied. "But later, after I've ordered the champagne."

Angie and Lionel got up to dance. Jack signaled for their waiter and while the two of them were talking, Maxine walked around the table to whisper in Frances's ear. "Did you look at the charts I gave you?"

"Well, sort of," Frances said, remembering the complicated astrological charts that Maxine had given her, not only for herself but also for Jack. "I didn't understand a lot of the symbols and stuff."

"I *told* you that we needed to discuss them," Maxine whispered.

"I'm sorry. It's just that I've been busy lately and—"

"We don't have time to go into that now. Just remember that your Venus tonight is in direct—"

"Frances, I'm here for that dance you promised me."

She jerked her head around and saw Art Fortuna's face over her right shoulder. "Listen—" she began indignantly, getting ready to tell him off once and for all.

"Frances, *listen,*" Maxine whispered urgently.

"What?" she muttered, turning back to Maxine.

"The conjunctions suggest something really important for you and Jack tonight," Maxine said. "You should—"

"I *will.* But I don't have time for it right now and—"

"Had you rather I'd come back for the *next* dance then?" Art asked.

"What?" Frances asked again, looking at him in confusion.

"Okay, I'll be back in time for the next dance," Art said, turning to leave. "Don't forget."

Jack finished his discussion with the waiter and turned to Frances. "What was going on there?"

"I'm not sure," Frances said. "But I think I just agreed to dance with Art Fortuna."

"You did? Why?"

"I'm not sure about that, either."

"Well-l," Jack said with a grin, "he *is* supposed to be a good dancer."

Frances merely rolled her eyes.

"In the meantime, now that the champagne's ordered . . . will you dance with me?"

Frances hesitated. They'd danced together many, many times—more times than she could count, in her cabin or his. But this was different. Scarier.

"I suppose so," she said, still not convinced that she could carry this off, dancing to a live orchestra with hundreds of people around to watch her disgrace not only herself, but Jack, too.

"Just pretend we're dancing in your cabin, to the music from the boom box," Jack said, correctly interpreting her worries. "And try to relax. It'll only hurt for a little while."

To her amazement, it didn't hurt at all. The moment she was in his arms, all the steps and moves they'd practiced for hours immediately came back to her. She forgot her nervousness, her insecurity. She forgot all the people around them, and anybody who might be watching. There were only her...and Jack...and the lovely music surrounding them.

For long, magical moments, nothing else existed... only the two of them, dancing on wings of air.

Then the music ended.

Jack didn't release her immediately. She gazed at the front of his white dress shirt and tuxedo jacket for a moment before lifting her eyes to look at him. "Thank you," she said.

"For the dance?" he asked with a smile. "I'm the one who's supposed to thank you. And I do."

"Not only for the dance," she said. "For much more than that. For everything."

Jack blinked. Then he lifted her hand that he still held in his, raising it to his lips. He focused his eyes on hers while he kissed her hand. "Thank you, too, Frances," he said softly. "For much more than the dance. Thank you for being my friend."

He continued holding her hand, looping it around his arm as he led them back to the table. As they made their way through the crowd, he suddenly realized he was still smiling. *Why was that?* He honestly didn't know. And he really didn't care.

While they were still several feet away from the table, Jack spotted Art Fortuna standing beside it. Waiting to claim his dance with Frances. She must have spotted him about the same time, because she suddenly stopped in her tracks.

"Jack?" she said, turning to look at him.

He saw the consternation in her eyes, the indecision. He quickly weighed the pros and cons and then gave her what he hoped was a comforting smile. "You *did* tell Art that you'd dance with him," he reminded her.

And besides that, Jack knew Art was a really good dancer, much better than he was. Art would show Frances off to her best advantage on the dance floor. Other people would see her. Men might start to flock around her, making her the belle of the ball, as Jack had envisioned her being so long ago.

"And I'll keep an eye on you," he promised by way of encouragement. "You can signal me if he says or does anything really obnoxious."

"And if I signal, what will you do?"

"I'll rescue you, of course ... Cinderella."

"On a white charger?"

"No. In a black tuxedo." He relaxed when he saw her smile. Then he suppressed a frown. He hadn't realized before that he was so anxious that he'd been holding his breath while he awaited her decision. Hell, it wasn't *that* important to him that she was a social success tonight. *Was it?*

Back at the table, Art took Frances off to the dance floor and Jack asked Maxine to dance. While they were dancing, he kept a keen eye peeled on Frances, who seemed to be following Art superbly. The two of them were easily the most accomplished dancers on the floor, Jack thought with a measure of pride as he watched them out of the corner of his eye ... stepping on Maxine's toe while he did so.

"Ouch!" she said.

"Sorry," he said, immediately turning his attention back to Frances again.

After the dance was over, Jack escorted Maxine back to the table and immediately noticed that Frances wasn't there. Scanning the dance floor, he finally spotted her...dancing with a tall, dark-haired man.

Frowning, Jack asked Mavis to dance and she accepted. He tried to steer them close to Frances and her partner, but other people kept getting in the way.

"Why don't you dance with her yourself?" Mavis asked.

"What?" Jack said.

"Frances. You keep watching her. So why don't you go over and cut in? Dance with her."

"In the first place, I am *not* watching her. And in the second place..."

Mavis snorted.

"Why did you do that?" Jack asked.

"Because I don't know which of you is the worst liar— you or Maxine."

They finished the dance in silence.

Jack danced the next dance with Angie, keeping a watchful eye on Frances, who seemed to be enjoying herself enormously with a mustachioed Latin American.

"I'm so happy to see Frances enjoying herself," Angie said. "Aren't you?"

"Me? Uh, yeah. Sure. Of course," Jack replied, trying to sound properly enthusiastic.

"I think that tonight—looking the way she does—she could have her choice of any man on board this ship," Angie said.

"What?"

"As a dancing partner, of course."

"Uh, yes. Of course." Jack took another look in Frances's direction. Wasn't that Latin guy holding Frances just a tad too close for conventional dancing? Did he have other things on his mind besides dancing?

"Is something the matter, Jack?" Angie asked.

"The matter? No! I mean...no, why do you ask?"

"You had such a fierce frown on your face..."

"Me? Oh...uh...sorry. I was just...uh...thinking about some business problems I had back home."

"Nothing serious, I hope."

"What?"

"Your business problems."

"What about them?"

"I hope they aren't all that serious."

Jack blinked. What the hell were they talking about? Who the hell was he trying to delude? This was Angie—a friend. "I told Frances that I'd come and rescue her if some guy got too familiar," he blurted. "And I was thinking...don't you think the one she's dancing with now is..."

Jack and Angie both looked at Frances and her current partner at the same time, just in time to see him move her into a deep dip, then a triple whirl.

"Beautiful!" Angie said. "I've never seen anything so beautiful in my life. And you were saying, Jack...?"

"Yeah," he muttered. "Beautiful." They finished the dance, then he sat with Maxine and Mavis while Angie and Lionel danced together. They'd only completed a small portion of the dance, however, when they came back to the table and excused themselves for the evening.

"Too much champagne, I suppose," Angie said. "I'm feeling a little tired."

She certainly didn't *look* tired, Jack thought, seeing the attractive flush on her cheeks. And neither did Lionel. And then he remembered. Tonight was their fiftieth anniversary. *Fifty years together, and they were still so much in love that they couldn't wait to get away...alone.*

Jack stood up and raised what little was left of the champagne in his glass in a toast to Angie and Lionel. "Happy anniversary," he said, "for the tenth or twelfth time."

"We appreciate your good wishes *however* many times it is," Angie said, waving her hand gaily in the air before reaching out to capture Lionel's. "Come on, Luv."

"Well, ladies," Jack said to Mavis and Maxine as he sat back down at the table, "shall we finish off the champagne before it goes flat?"

Mavis held out her glass but Maxine refused, shaking her head with a thoughtful expression on her face.

Jack filled his glass and took a big gulp, feeling incredibly sad and wondering why he was feeling that way. Frances was a big success tonight, even better than he'd imagined. There was no reason for him to feel sad. He should be elated. *Why wasn't he?*

FRANCES SMILED at her dance partner. The latest one. What was his name? And why was she feeling so sad when she should be elated instead? She had all the dance partners she could handle, and more than she wanted. And maybe that was the problem.

When men had first started paying attention to her tonight, she had enjoyed it—not only because it was what Jack had wanted to happen, and would probably make him proud of her—but also because *she'd* felt flattered, too. She wasn't the belle of the ball, nowhere close, but her success on the dance floor wasn't something to be ashamed of, either. Far from it.

But now that the point had been made, she was becoming increasingly tired of the game. She didn't want to dance with all these strange men. She only wanted to dance with one man. With Jack.

She looked at the table where they'd been sitting, just in time to see Angie and Lionel leaving. She smiled. *Good luck, Angie. God bless.*

She saw Jack pour champagne for himself and Mavis, then saw him take a drink of his. *He doesn't seem all that happy, either,* she thought. Or was that merely something she *wanted* to believe?

She saw Jack put down his glass and look in her direction, the same as he'd been doing all night, just as he promised he would. Suddenly—without even thinking about it beforehand and almost as if her hand and arm had a will of their own—she signaled to him to come and rescue her. He was up from his chair in an instant, making his way across the dance floor, heading in her direction.

Oh, dear. What was she going to say to him when he arrived? What could she possibly say to explain her impulsive signal for him to rescue her from this perfectly nice gentleman with whom she was dancing?

Jack was scowling when he reached them and tapped her dance partner on the shoulder.

The perfectly nice gentleman turned out to be not quite so nice after all. "Go away," he said to Jack.

Jack shook his head. "No. This is my dance with Frances."

"Who says?"

"*I* say," Frances said quickly before things got out of hand. Almost as quickly, she slipped out of the man's embrace and took Jack's hand, leading him a few steps away before she stopped.

"Was he obnoxious?" Jack asked, shooting the man a murderous look before turning back to Frances.

"No."

"Then why...?"

"I wanted to dance with you." *There, she'd said it.* She took a quick breath, horrified at what she'd just said. "Do you mind?"

He looked at her for a long moment. An eternity. Then he shook his head. "No. I don't mind." He took a step closer, sliding his arm around her waist.

They stood that way for several heartbeats before they started moving in time with the music... swaying at first, then taking a couple of steps... pausing... taking several more steps this time. And all the time, Jack was watching her intently, holding her gaze a willing captive with his own.

Finally he closed his eyes for a brief moment, then opened them and pulled her closer, wrapping his other arm around her as well. "I don't mind at all," he whispered.

He was holding her so close that Frances found it hard to breathe, much less dance. But she didn't mind. She didn't mind at all. She smiled against the front of his tuxedo jacket, feeling as if she'd just returned home after a long, long journey. They danced. Sort of. No fancy steps, but a lot of emotion, as far as Frances was concerned.

She'd been uneasy before, but now was content. She'd been sad before, but now was happy.

Jack was the one who'd wanted her to be the belle of the ball, but personally she preferred this. This was where she wanted to be, tucked safely inside his arms. She could be perfectly content here forever.

The music stopped, and Jack and Frances stopped dancing. Neither of them moved away; they simply stood there, motionless but with their arms around each other until the orchestra started playing another song. Then they started dancing again.

They didn't speak, but there was no need for words between them. Simply being together like this, with his arms around her and hers around him was communication enough as far as she was concerned. It was certainly as much as she could handle.

She couldn't imagine trying to carry on a conversation while so many other thoughts and emotions were racing through her the way they were. She heard Jack give a soft sigh, and wondered if he was feeling some of the same things she was. But that was probably too much to hope for, she decided, echoing his sigh.

Jack heard Frances sigh and wondered what she was thinking, feeling right now. Personally, he was feeling pretty good... much better than he had a right to feel under the circumstances. What a jerk he'd been! He'd practically forced Frances to dance with all those other guys... telling himself it was for her benefit, when it was really his own ego he'd been feeding.

"Why should I want to be the belle of the ball?" she'd asked. And she was right. Completely on target. Whether or not she was a social success was totally unimportant; she was still the same beautiful, wonderful person underneath.

He wouldn't have blamed her if she'd never spoken to him again after the way he'd forced her into that other role. But she hadn't held it against him. Instead, she'd signaled for him to come and rescue her. "I wanted to dance with you," she'd said simply.

Jack still couldn't get over that. It was much more than he deserved... and he couldn't help being delighted that she'd had the courage and common sense to call a halt to the fiasco he'd made of the evening so far. He vowed to make it up to her.

In the meantime, he was going to enjoy what was left of the evening... dancing every dance with Frances.

"Enough of that, you two!"

Jack grimaced, recognizing Art Fortuna's voice immediately, even though it was slightly slurred now. A drunken Art Fortuna was just what he needed to complete the mess he'd made of tonight.

Jack stopped dancing, but didn't let go of Frances. He took a deep breath before turning to face the intruder. "Hello again, Art."

"It's time to switch partners, old buddy," Art said with a lopsided grin.

Glancing at Sharon standing beside her brother, Jack saw that her color was unusually high. Had she drunk too much, too? She must have, he decided; otherwise, surely she wouldn't have gone along with Art's clumsy obtrusiveness. He felt a little sorry for her, but not enough so that he'd allow it to change his determination.

"Sorry, *old buddy*," Jack said. "Not now."

"Whatcha mean, not now?" Art said, frowning.

"I mean simply that," Jack said, growing exasperated. "Not now. No."

Art narrowed his eyes. "You sayin' you don't want to dance with my sister?"

"Art, please," Sharon said, touching his arm. He shook her off.

"That wasn't what I said," Jack said, deciding that Art was drunker than he'd thought at first . . . and mean drunk at that. Belligerent, judging by the look in the man's eyes.

"You can't insult my sister that way!" Art said.

"I didn't mean to insult your sister, in any way," Jack said, releasing Frances and moving between her and Art. He hoped he could placate the drunken oaf, but in case he couldn't, he wanted to make sure Frances wasn't hurt. "Did I insult you, Sharon?"

"No," Sharon said.

"You stay out of this!" Art said.

"Art—" Sharon began.

"I said stay out of this!" he said, giving her a rough push on the shoulder.

"Listen . . ." Jack said, so angry at Art's brutish treatment of a woman that he forgot about placating him. "You can't do that . . . not to your own sister."

"What I do to my sister is none of your business, *buster,*" Art said, shoving Jack's shoulder this time.

"And keep your rotten hands off me, too," Jack said, shoving him in return.

"Don't you *dare* hit my brother like that!" Sharon said.

"What?" Jack asked, amazed by Sharon's reaction.

"You heard her," Art said, shoving Jack's shoulder again.

"Stop it!" Frances said. "All of you!"

"You stay out of this," Art said, taking a menacing step toward Frances.

"Don't take another step," Jack said, clenching his fists. "And don't even think about touching her."

"And who'll stop me? You?"

"Yes, me!"

Art took a swing at Jack, missing by a mile. Jack grabbed his arm as it sailed past him, holding on and making a quick move to pull it behind Art's back in what he knew was a painful position. "Aaaoow!" Art shouted, wrenching free, then starting to grapple with Jack.

Jack managed to grab Art's arm again, trying to hold it behind the man's back and stop the fight. And then suddenly, almost from out of nowhere, Jack felt a sharp, searing pain above his left eye.

He heard a woman scream. Frances? He wondered how Art had managed to catch him off guard the way he had. Then he felt himself crumpling to the floor as darkness closed in around him.

Chapter Eleven

"Ouch!" Jack said.

"I don't see how that could have hurt," the doctor said. "We've given you enough novocaine to numb an elephant."

"I'm not an elephant," Jack said. "And it *did* hurt."

"I'm hesitant about giving you any more. If you can manage to sit still for a few more seconds, I'll be finished with this and you can be out of here," the doctor said with a hint of desperation in his voice.

Frances, standing by the operating table in the ship's infirmary and watching the proceedings, would have been tempted to laugh if she hadn't still been so upset. She couldn't help remembering the way Jack had looked when they brought him to the infirmary—groggy, unintelligible, bleeding . . . She'd never seen so much blood in her life.

"How *many* more seconds?" Jack mumbled. "And how many more stitches?"

"Possibly two," the doctor said, leaning closer to look at the gash above Jack's left eye again. "Three at most."

"Seconds?" asked Jack hopefully.

"Stitches," the doctor replied.

"Okay," Jack said, clenching his fists and squinching his eyes. "But hurry and get it over with."

Frances shook her head, wondering how Jack could be such a baby now—when it appeared that he would be okay—when he'd been so brave in the ballroom a short while ago. And remembering that, she felt a fresh wave of guilt wash over her. It was her fault that Jack had gotten into the fracas with Art Fortuna in the first place. If she hadn't danced with the man that first time, none of this would have happened.

"There!" the doctor said a short while later. He reached for a mirror and handed it to Jack. "Would you like to see your stitches?"

Jack took the mirror and examined his face. "Hey, that's good. Really good. You do nice work, Doc. Thanks."

"Don't thank me too soon. It looks a lot better now than it'll look tomorrow...or the next day. There'll be some puffiness, swelling...and a helluva black eye. There shouldn't be any permanent scars, though. That's why I took so many short stitches."

Frances breathed a sigh of relief, thankful that Jack wouldn't be permanently marked.

Jack made a face. "Sorry I was such a bad patient."

"I've seen worse."

"But not often."

"Not lately, at any rate," the doctor admitted. They both laughed and Frances managed a smile.

"Your eye itself seems to be okay," the doctor said. "But I'd like to examine it again tomorrow. In the meantime, I'm going to give you a patch to wear." He tore open a packet and took out a black patch with an elastic band, fitting the patch in place over Jack's eye, then standing back to look at it.

"What do you think?" the doctor said to Frances.

"Very dashing," she said.

"Is it really necessary?" Jack asked.

"It's mainly a precaution. But we don't want to take any chances after that beautiful job of stitchery I did, do we? Oh, and you'll need some painkiller, too."

Jack grimaced. "I will?"

"For when after the novocaine wears off," the doctor said, unlocking a cabinet and handing Jack a packet of pills. "Your whole face will probably start hurting then."

"That's something to look forward to."

"This should take care of the pain, so don't worry. It might make you a little groggy, though, so don't do any driving," the doctor said, laughing at his own little joke.

Gallows humor, Frances thought. "Thank you, Doctor."

"Yes," Jack said, shaking the doctor's hand. "Thank you very much."

Outside the infirmary, Frances looped her arm through Jack's. "What? Are you planning to lead the blind?" he asked.

She winced.

"Bad joke?"

"Yes. But I'm going to lead you directly to your cabin anyway."

"I appreciate the thought, Frances. I really do. But it's not necessary."

"I know it's not necessary, but I want to do it. I insist."

"Why? Because I behaved so cowardly in the infirmary that you thought I might need your protection? If that's true, I don't blame you. I've always been afraid of blood, as far back as I can remember. Then, seeing all that blood tonight... and knowing it was mine... really got to me."

"It's not that! At all. It's because the whole thing was my fault."

"That's crazy."

"If I hadn't encouraged Art by dancing with him the first time—"

"Which wasn't *your* doing . . . it was mine. *I* was the one who insisted—"

"Nobody forced me into dancing with him. It was my own doing, my own vanity."

"It was my vanity, too. I was the one who wanted you to be a big social success, so I could say that *I* was the one who'd created you, I suppose. Like Pygmalion and Galatea . . ."

Frances caught her breath, remembering the myth of how Pygmalion had created Galatea, and then fallen in love with her. She wished it could happen in real life. But she knew it didn't. "Still," she said, "none of it would have happened if it hadn't been for me."

"*And* me. At the very least, the fault is half mine."

She looked at him—at his one good eye, slightly dilated, and the patch over his other eye that was so terribly bruised that it required a patch. "I feel just awful," she said.

Jack sighed. "And it'll make you feel better if I let you walk me to my cabin?"

"Yes. I want to make sure you get to bed safely."

"Okay. I accept your offer."

"Thanks." They had stopped walking while they argued, but now started again.

"What I can't understand," Jack said, stepping onto the escalator beside Frances, "is how Art managed to catch me off guard the way he did. I thought I had him pinned and then . . . wham!"

Frances looked at him, her eyes wide. Then she shook her head. "Art didn't hit you. Sharon did."

"*What?*"

"Sharon's the one who hit you . . . with her little evening bag."

Jack brought up his hand to touch the patch over his eye. "She did all this damage with a tiny purse?"

"She must have had something inside the bag."

"What? A rock?"

Frances shrugged.

"And why would she hit me in the first place?"

"Well ... you know the old saying about hell having no fury like ... whatever."

"But I didn't scorn her," Jack said.

"Maybe she thought you did."

"Did she say so?"

"Uh ... not exactly," Frances said.

They got off the escalator and walked down the corridor to his suite. Jack waited until they were inside before turning to face her. "There's something you're not telling me."

"What makes you think that?" she said, hedging.

"I don't think—I *know*. Does it have something to do with Sharon?"

"Sort of."

"Something she said?"

"No."

"Something else she did—besides hitting me in the eye?"

"No. Uh ... it was more like ... something I did."

"You?" Jack said, surprised. "What did you do?"

"Well ... after she hit you with that deadly purse of hers ... and I saw you lying on the floor with all that blood gushing everywhere ... I didn't know if you were dead or alive.

"Then I looked at Sharon and she didn't seem sorry at all that she'd hit you. She actually seemed proud of it! So I yelled at her ... I don't remember what it was I said. And she yelled back at me. And then—"

"And then ..." Jack repeated, prompting her to continue.

"I socked her."

Jack's mouth fell open. "Frances. You didn't!"

"I did, too! And I'm not sorry. I'd do it again."

Jack shook his head. "I can't get over it. You actually socked her?"

"Yes."

He shook his head again. Then he laughed. "What did Sharon say when you socked her?"

"Nothing."

He frowned as a sudden thought occurred to him. "Did she hit you back?"

"No. Uh, she was on the floor by then."

Jack blinked. "You actually knocked her down?"

"I don't think so. It was more like . . . she took a couple of steps backward after I hit her . . . and then I think she stumbled and fell down."

Until then he hadn't thought about how hard the blow must have been. "Did you hurt yourself?" he asked, lifting her hand to examine it. Sure enough, her knuckles were bruised and slightly swollen. "You *did* hurt yourself!"

"Nothing's broken," she said, flexing her fingers to prove the point. "It's just a little tender."

"Still . . ." He held her hand to his mouth and gently kissed the bruises. To think that she would have done such a thing for him . . . put herself on the line the way she had . . . He swallowed around the huge lump in his throat and focused his one good eye on her dear face. "My protector," he whispered.

"Now you're making fun of me."

"No! Never in a million years." He continued holding her hand in his and brought up his other hand to touch her cheek. "I mean it. You put your own self in danger for me."

"I'm not afraid of Sharon . . ."

"What about Art? As drunk as he was, there's no telling what . . . Did *he* try to hurt you? If he did, I'll—"

"Jack," Frances said, cutting him off. "Art didn't say or do anything to me. He went straight to Sharon. And he started crying."

"Art Fortuna?" Jack said, finding the scene impossible to picture. "Crying?"

"Blubbering like a baby."

"And what did you do then?"

She closed her eyes for a brief moment. "I'm afraid I made as much a fool of myself as Art did of himself. I knelt down beside you and started crying, too."

"You did? Why? I mean—"

"You were so still! And there was all that blood . . . like I told you before. For all I knew, you could have been dead or dying, for God's sake!"

"Shh," he said, putting his arms around her, and feeling her start to tremble. The trembling grew stronger, sending violent shudders through her slender body. He tightened his arms, pulling her closer. She burrowed her head against his chest, almost as if she were trying to hide inside his embrace, and he felt her arms close around his waist.

"It's okay now," he said over and over, stroking her hair while he tried to comfort her.

"I'm so embarrassed," she mumbled against his chest.

"What on earth for?"

"For carrying on this way," she said.

He felt another huge shudder go through her body, and held her still tighter. "It's permitted. And completely understandable after what you went through tonight."

"But—"

"Shh," he said again. "Just relax and let me take care of you."

"I should be taking care of you," she said, shuddering again. "You should be in bed."

"There's no rush," he said, although he had a splitting headache and his face was starting to hurt because the novocaine was wearing off. He continued holding her until her shudders finally ceased . . . he wasn't sure how long it took, but his face was hurting like the very devil by then.

"I'm okay now," she said at last, lifting her head and stepping away from him. "Thank you for..." She stopped and her eyes widened. "Oh, dear Lord!"

"What is it?" Jack said, dropping his arms.

"You're in pain!"

"Not really," he protested.

"Don't lie to me," she said, taking his arm and leading him toward the bedroom in his suite. "I'm so sorry."

"I'm not," he said, attempting a smile. "I enjoyed—"

"And don't try to be flip about it. Your face is white as a ghost . . . you're obviously in pain."

"Maybe a little," he admitted.

Frances raced ahead of him and turned back the covers of his bed. "I'll get you some water to take your painkiller with while you put on your pajamas."

"I don't wear pajamas," he said, watching her face for the telltale blush. It came. He only wished his face didn't hurt so much that he couldn't properly enjoy her blush the way he ordinarily would have.

"Oh," she said, recovering. "I'll get the water while you take off your clothes and get into bed then."

By way of reply, Jack took off his tuxedo jacket and tossed it in the general direction of a nearby chair. His fingers moved to his tie, but Frances was out of the room before he'd even begun to take it off. He smiled. Then he grimaced because the smile hurt.

He undressed in record time and got into bed, sitting with his back propped against the headboard and the bedclothes pulled up to cover his lower body, leaving his bare chest and shoulders exposed. He waited for Frances to come back and give him his painkiller. And waited. And waited. What could be keeping her so long?

"Jack? Are you ready for your pain pill now?" she finally called out from the adjoining living room. It suddenly dawned on him that *she* had been waiting for him to tell her he was decent—or at least covered—and that it was okay for her to come back into the bedroom. *Of course, she'd do that. And how stupid of me not to remember it.*

He took a deep breath. "I'm ready."

She was beside his bed in seconds. "Do you remember what you did with the pain pills?" she asked.

"Yes," he said, holding out his arm and then opening his fist to reveal the packet of pills he'd remembered to take out of his jacket pocket.

"Good," she said, smiling as she took the pills and removed one from the packet. She held the pill between her fingers until he opened his mouth to receive it. Then she held the glass of water to his mouth. He drank the water and swallowed the pill.

"Good," she said again. She stood up straight, smiling at him again as she smoothed the hair back from his forehead with a feather touch, being careful not to come close to his stitches. Her hand was cool where it touched him. And soft. Soothing.

And then it hit him. She'd never asked if he was capable of taking the pill by himself... which he was. It had probably never even occurred to her. She was taking care of him... just as she'd taken care of her father for thirteen years.

"Is there anything else you need? Anything I can get for you?"

"I can't think of anything," he said, resisting the temptation to ask her to stay with him a little longer. It would be comforting to him but unfair to her, especially after what she'd already been through tonight.

"I'll just sit here for a few minutes then," she said, pulling a chair close to his bed. "Long enough for you to go to sleep."

"You don't need to do that," he protested, wondering if she'd been able to read his thoughts.

"I want to do it. It's the least I can do, considering what you've been through tonight."

Was she able to read his thoughts? he wondered, snuggling farther down in the bed, relaxing as he watched her move around the room dimming the lights and finally coming back to sit in the chair beside his bed. "Are we going to argue again..." He had to stop for a yawn, and wondered if the painkiller was already taking effect.

"Argue about what?" she asked pleasantly.

"About whose fault it was...that *what* happened..." He yawned again. "And to whom." He wondered if that had made sense to her. He wasn't sure it had made sense to him, but was too tired to worry about whether it had...or had not... He blinked his eyes, trying to focus on her, and yawned again.

"No," she said, flashing him a great smile that he automatically returned. "We're not going to argue anymore about that, or anything, for tonight."

"Good," he said, closing his eyes, the smile still on his face.

THE POOR DEAR. Frances waited several minutes until she was sure he was sound asleep, then got up and carefully pulled the covers over his bare shoulders. He sighed. She smiled, loving him with her eyes for a moment, then took a step backward because she'd had an almost uncontrollable desire to touch him and knew that would be unfair to do while he was asleep.

She clenched her fists instead. Hard.

Then she kicked off her shoes and went to the linen closet to look for an extra sheet or blanket to wrap around herself while she sat in the chair beside his bed tonight. She had no intention of leaving him—none at all. He might have a concussion, or start bleeding again, or any number of things. There was no way on earth, barring total catastrophe, that she would leave the side of Jack Sherrod, aka Jack Smith, aka Jack the Shark, tonight.

Or ever, for that matter, if she had her choice in the matter.

She was in love with him.

Frances stopped, staring without seeing into the linen closet of Jack's stateroom while she thought about her sudden discovery. Hadn't she thought about him constantly—and dreamed about him—for days now? Weeks, maybe?

Was that the reason—the *real* reason—she'd had such an overwhelming desire to make love with him? Was that the reason she'd been so desperate that she'd even plotted to seduce him tonight? She closed her eyes tight, feeling guiltier than ever when she remembered *that*... and the way she'd confided her plot to Angie in the beauty parlor.

Nobody should try to *trap* someone else into making love with them, even if the trapper was in love with the trappee. It was a shabby thing to do, and Frances was disgusted with herself for attempting such a thing tonight.

For the first time, she began to think that the horrible fight tonight might have been a blessing in disguise. It had made her take a good look at herself and to realize how close she'd come to making a terrible mistake.

She found a light cotton thermal blanket in the closet and carried it back to the chair beside Jack's bed. Settling down into the chair, she pulled the blanket over her. After a moment, she rearranged both herself and the blanket, but still wasn't comfortable.

She shifted again, and was more uncomfortable than ever. She sighed, resigning herself to her fate. After all, wasn't it exactly what she deserved?

JACK WOKE UP in a cold sweat, breathing rapidly, his heart racing furiously. He'd been having a terrible dream . . . a nightmare in which he and Art Fortuna had been fighting over Frances. He reached his hand up to his eye and felt a patch. That part of the dream was true, then. And if so, did that mean the rest of the nightmare was true, as well?

"Frances!" he called out in panic, sitting bolt upright in bed.

And then he saw her in the dim light of a single lamp. She was sitting in a chair beside his bed, huddled under a blanket, her head tilted at an obviously uncomfortable angle. She opened her eyes, blinked, and jumped to her feet . . . all in a matter of seconds.

"What is it?" she asked anxiously, dropping the blanket and rushing to him. "What's wrong?"

"Nothing. I mean . . . I had a nightmare. I dreamed you were in danger. Terrible danger." He combed his fingers through his hair, shaking his head to clear away the lingering memories of the nightmare.

Frances touched his forehead. "You're soaking wet."

"I'm sorry I woke you."

"It's okay. That's the reason I stayed . . . in case you needed me. I'll get a towel."

"Don't bother," he said, but she was already halfway across the room by then.

She was back in seconds with a towel, lotion and a damp cloth. She sat down on the bed beside him without a moment's hesitation, not shy or self-conscious at all, which surprised him. Then he remembered. She'd probably done this sort of thing hundreds of times before for her father. To her—right now—Jack was merely another patient.

He tried to think of her the same way—that she was a nurse or a doctor doing her job—but found it increasingly difficult to do. He felt the slow arousal begin to build as she touched the damp cloth to his face, chest and shoulders. He closed his eyes when she blotted him dry with the fresh towel. And when he felt her soft, lotioned hands touch his bare chest, he jumped, opening his eyes.

Their gazes met, and locked for a long moment.

He saw her blink, swallow. He saw the crimson flush creep into her cheeks, and knew she was no longer thinking of him as her patient. At least not exclusively, he amended as she started applying the lotion to his chest in a slow, circular motion, keeping her eyes focused on what she was doing.

He watched her face as she concentrated on her task, and felt a surge of admiration for her. She was doing a much better job of remaining calm and detached than he was.

She continued smoothing on the lotion with a sure touch that was all the more arousing because it was so gentle. She worked her way over his shoulders, across his chest and downward. Then her hand stopped moving as her gaze fell on the bulge underneath the covers bunched around his hips.

She lifted her head to look at him again, her eyes wide and questioning.

"Yes," he said huskily. "I'm sorry if you're shocked . . . or offended."

"I'm . . . neither," she said, surprising him again.

"Oh?"

"As a matter of fact," she said, taking a deep breath, "I started out tonight . . . with every intention of trying to seduce you."

Jack blinked.

Chapter Twelve

There. She'd finally admitted it. She watched him. Waiting. Holding her breath.

"I...don't quite know what to say," he said after a long moment. "I guess I'd begin by asking *why* you, uh..."

"Because I wanted you, of course," she said impatiently. "And it was obvious that you didn't want me in that way, so—"

"What are you saying? I—"

"This is *my* confession, okay? Will you let me finish?"

He nodded.

"Where was I?" she asked.

"You thought I didn't want you."

"Right. Because you'd kiss me and get me so excited that I thought I couldn't stand it anymore, and then...whoosh! You'd be gone."

"That wasn't exactly the way—"

"So I finally decided to try and *make* you want me. That's why I bought those expensive dresses in Palm Beach...and went to the beauty shop for a new hairdo...and borrowed some of Angie's perfume."

"Angie's perfume?"

"She said it drives Lionel wild."

"Oh."

"But the night didn't work out at all the way I'd planned. So I guess I wound up exactly the way I should have after all that underhanded scheming."

"And how is that, Frances? How *did* you wind up?"

"Frustrated. Still alone. And feeling guilty, to boot."

He took a deep breath. "Is it my turn to speak now?"

She nodded.

"The thing I can't understand is how you'd think I didn't want you in *that* way. You had to know how aroused I became every time we kissed. You must have known—"

"I *didn't* know. I only know you never made a move to touch me . . . the way I wanted to be touched."

"It wasn't because I didn't want to. Lord, how I wanted to! Ever since that first night I found you in my cabin...I've never seen anything as beautiful in my life. I haven't been able to get the memory of the way you looked that night out of my mind, no matter how hard I tried."

"That's my point!" she said. "Why did you even *try*... if it was something we both wanted?"

"Because you're completely innocent. You've never been with a man before."

"I would have thought... I mean I've read that...some men find that desirable."

"I *do* find it desirable!" he said, grabbing both her arms, the grasp of his long fingers almost painful on her tender flesh. "I find *you* desirable. Totally, completely, earth shatteringly desirable." He released her almost as abruptly as he'd touched her, almost as if her skin were burning his fingers. "So much so that it scares me."

"I don't understand," she said.

"I won't take advantage of your innocence, Frances."

Was that what had been holding him back all along? After her initial admission that she'd hoped to seduce him tonight, she'd been horrified that she'd actually said such

191
191

a thing to him, even if it was true. What must he think of her?

But then she'd thought: *What do I have to lose?* If he didn't want her, he was going to have to tell her so. This time—for perhaps the first time in her life, and also perhaps because it was so important to her—she wasn't going to be the one to walk away from a confrontation.

But now, *his* admission—if it could be believed—gave her a new measure of hope. And confidence. She placed her hand flat against the warm, hard surface of his chest and heard his involuntary intake of breath. "Even if it's what I want, too?" she asked softly.

"Yes," he replied, removing her hand from his chest and placing it in her lap. "Because you don't know what you'd be getting into."

"I'd like to know," she said, bringing her hand right back against his chest again, back where it belonged.

"You know what my life is like now, Frances. Chaotic. I'm totally committed to regaining my father's company. I've already told you that—and that I even wrecked my marriage because of it. I can't even think about anything permanent at this point."

"Well . . . yes, you did tell me all that," she said, making tiny circles on his chest with her finger. "But I wasn't thinking about anything permanent, either." *Liar,* she told herself, knowing that she'd like nothing more than spending the rest of her life with Jack. But she'd settle for whatever she could get.

"You deserve more than I can offer you."

"Are you sure?" she asked, deliberately glancing down at the bulge under the covers.

"Frances," he chided, shaking his head. "I'm surprised at you."

"I don't see why. I may have lived a monastic existence for many years, but I'm not a monk."

"Obviously."

"I'm a woman, Jack, in case you hadn't noticed."

"I noticed."

"And I have a woman's desires."

Jack took a deep breath, raking his fingers through his hair. "What are you trying to do to me?"

"I thought it was perfectly clear. I'm trying to get you to make love with me."

Jack closed his eyes, feeling what little was left of his hard-fought resistance start to crumble. At the same time, he felt exhilarated . . . and scared to death. He shouldn't do this. He knew he shouldn't. It was the very worst thing he could do . . . for both of them.

"Damn you," he muttered, seizing her in his arms. "And damn me," he added, crushing his mouth to hers.

Frances closed her eyes, thrilled beyond reason, exhilarated beyond belief. Was it really happening?—the very thing she'd wanted, dreamed about...and almost given up hope would happen?

It wasn't the lovemaking she'd wanted so much. It was making love with Jack, the man she loved. It would never have been the same with anyone else.

Now here he was, kissing her hungrily, greedily. And here she was, kissing him back the same way. One of her hands had been trapped between their bodies when he first took her in his arms, and she let it stay there, stroking the warm skin beneath her fingers. She slid her other hand up his arm, across his shoulder, through the thick dark hair at the back of his neck, getting to know him by touch . . . familiarizing herself with the planes and angles, the different textures of his body.

She sighed with pleasure.

Then she almost cried out with alarm as a horrible thought—a terrifying thought—struck her. She had brazenly and blithely thrown herself at him, almost daring him *not* to make love with her. She'd done so thinking only of her own wants, her own needs, her own pleasure.

But what about Jack? He'd been married before. And most certainly he'd known other women in addition to his wife. Beautiful women. Sexy women. Women who knew how to please a man.

How could she have been so blind—and conceited—as to imagine that she could compete with those women? Given her total lack of experience, how could she possibly please him? Would she even know what to do when the time came?

She worried.

Jack leaned back in the bed, pulling Frances with him and holding their kiss. He snuggled lower, still holding her in his arms, pulling her on top of him, fitting her body to his. His heart was pounding wildly and his loins ached, but he knew he couldn't give in to his need. Not yet. Not for a long time.

He wanted to give Frances pleasure, too. He wanted her to enjoy her first experience at lovemaking—the greatest intimacy two people can share—and knew that in order to make that happen, he first had to make her want him as much as he wanted her.

So he would try to be slow. And gentle.

It wouldn't be easy. He wanted her too much, and had been without a woman too long, for it to be easy. He wasn't even sure he could handle the responsibility.

But he'd try. For her sake. By damn, he would try!

He rolled both of them over in bed until they were side by side facing each other, forgetting that his lower body was under the cover and she was on top of it. Then, realizing what he'd done, he broke off their kiss and shook his head over his own stupidity. Some lover he was!

"I have a problem," he said.

"What's wrong?" Frances asked anxiously. "Is it your head? Or your eye?"

"No. It's the damn cover. I'm hopelessly entangled in it. Would you mind scrunching over a tad so I can get myself free?"

Frances scrambled to the far side of the bed and got to her knees, leaning back to watch him disentangle himself. Then, remembering that Jack had said he didn't wear pajamas, she thought about turning in the other direction. *But that's stupid, really stupid, considering what we're about to do,* she decided.

Jack finally extricated himself from the covers and looked at Frances.

"You're wearing briefs!" she said accusingly.

"What did you think I'd have on? Nothing?" he guessed correctly, getting to his knees, too.

"Yes," she admitted. She didn't tell him that the stark white briefs were even more erotic than nudity would have been, clearly defining the evidence of his arousal.

"But you watched anyway," he teased, walking closer to her on his knees. "Why?"

"Curiosity?"

"Sounds reasonable to me," he said, reaching out to smooth the hair back from her face, then letting his fingers continue their progress around to her back, where they lingered at the top of the zipper on her dress. "I've always suffered from that particular affliction myself."

Frances heard the sound of her zipper being lowered, ever so slowly. "You have?" she whispered.

He nodded, moving his hands to her shoulders, where they lingered for a moment before gently guiding the red dress down to the bed. She lifted one knee, then the other, as he helped her step out of the dress. They followed the same roles in ridding her of her slip. Then Jack got out of bed, taking the dress and slip with him and placing them neatly over the back of a chair.

While he was gone, she quickly stripped out of her pantyhose herself, tossing them onto the floor.

When he came back, he walked across the bed on his knees again to where she was kneeling, stopping just short of touching her. "Now we're almost even," he said.

"Almost?" she whispered hoarsely.

"With one exception." He moved his hands around behind her back again, unfastening the hook of her bra. She held her breath.

He slid the bra straps off her shoulders slowly, one at a time, and held onto the last strap to toss the bra aside. Then he leaned back to look at her. Frances's mouth was dry, but she remained perfectly motionless as she felt his eyes on her, stirring her with their intensity, burning her with their passion, igniting a thousand tiny fires within her.

"Ah," he finally breathed with satisfaction. "Just as I remembered . . . only more lovely."

He pulled her into his arms then and kissed her, feeling her breasts and nipples against his chest, soft again ' hard. He moved up one hand to brush the side of her breast, then slide around it, cupping the treasure inside his hand. He stroked her nipple and delighted in the way it responded to his touch.

Moving his mouth away from hers, he marked a trail with his lips across her cheek, along her neck...down to the treasure he held in his hand. His lips finally found her breast, her nipple, and he opened his mouth wider, feasting on her ripe fullness.

Frances closed her eyes tight, reveling in his touch, not trying to conceal the intense sound of pleasure that came from her throat. She lowered her head, burying her face in his dark hair, feelings its softness against her cheeks, her lips.

Then his lips were on hers again, hotter, more insistent. His tongue was inside her mouth, teasing, tasting, filling her with a sweet longing that started in her stomach and spread in ever-widening circles through her entire body.

Jack slowly lowered them to the bed again, using one arm to guide their progress. They were side by side, facing each other, with no bedclothes to hamper their enjoyment of each other now. He slid one leg between hers, rough against smooth, and lifted his knee until his thigh was touching that softest, sweetest, most intimate part of her. He could feel the heat of her, through the lace panties she wore, through the mat of dark hair that covered his own leg.

Frances felt Jack's leg pressing against her, and wished it was that other, more intimate part of him touching her instead. She clamped both her legs around his, pulling him closer, trying to ease the almost desperate yearning—the emptiness inside her that was crying out to be filled.

Then she felt Jack's hand at her waist, and saw his face when he lifted himself on one elbow to look at her, his expression grave. His fingers slipped inside the waistband of her panties as he slowly, deliberately started to pull them down. She lifted her hips and he slid the panties down off her legs.

"Now it's your turn," Jack said, his voice husky as he stretched out on his back waiting for her.

Frances's pulse raced; her heart pounded. She swallowed. Her fingers were shaking when she reached out to slide them under the waistband of his briefs. She couldn't get much leverage while she was lying down and wondered how Jack had managed with such apparent ease. Practice?

She finally gave up and sat on her knees again, crouched beside him. Taking a deep breath, she reached out for his waistband again, peeling the briefs down slowly until she reached the highest point, then quickly stripping them the rest of the way over his hipbones and down his legs before she tossed them over her shoulder. *There.*

Then she looked at him...really looked at him totally naked for the first time, except for the black patch over his eye. She found herself holding her breath again. He was, quite simply, the most gorgeous person she'd ever seen in her life. He was perfect. Or close enough.

"Frances? Is something wrong?"

She shook her head. "No. Nothing's wrong. At least, as far as I can see...but you know my experience is limited," she added, trying to cover her emotions with a joke.

He reached for her, pulling her down to him and kissing her deeply, lovingly, and she felt herself responding to him, even more fiercely than she had before, so much so that she forgot to worry about whether she would be able to please him...so much so that she forgot about everything except here...now...with Jack's hands all over her...with his lips following his hands...setting her on fire...driving her crazy.

"When, Jack? *When?*" she finally asked, almost begging when she felt she couldn't stand the urgent longing any more.

"Now," he said hoarsely, poising above her for a moment, hesitating, then driving himself deep inside her. He heard the muffled sound she made, and knew he'd hurt her, but also knew it would be much easier on her this way in the long run.

He braced his hands on each side of her, not moving, allowing her time to get used to the idea and feel of a man inside her for the first time in her life. "The worst is over," he whispered into her ear. Then he kissed her ear, licked it with his tongue, and finally nipped it lightly with his teeth.

"I promise," he said. "It gets better from here on out."

Frances hoped so. At the very least, she hoped it didn't get any worse.

"Trust me," Jack whispered into her other ear before kissing it and licking it and nipping it the same as he'd done the other one. "Try to relax."

"I'm not sure I *can.*"

"Do you like this?" he asked, kissing her ear again.

"Yes."

"And this?" He brushed his lips across hers, darting his tongue inside her mouth for a brief moment.

She nodded.

"And how about this?" he asked, taking her breast inside his mouth and teasing her nipple with his tongue.

"Oh, yes!" she said, feeling an exquisite shiver of pleasure. It took her a moment to realize that while he was talking to her and kissing her, he'd started making slow movements inside her again. They didn't feel bad, either. She moved her hips a little, responding to his thrust. That felt even better. She lifted her hips higher.

He thrust deeper and she cried out, not with pain but with pleasure this time.

"Did I hurt you?" Jack asked anxiously, stopping his movements.

"No! No...and don't stop. Please."

He didn't stop. And true to Jack's promise, things only got better. And better.

JACK HELD FRANCES CLOSE, listening to the sound of her rapid breathing and his own, waiting for his racing heart to slow down. Neither of them spoke, and he was grateful for that. What could he say to her? That he'd done the one thing he'd sworn he would never do—make love to her, take advantage of her innocence?

And not only that, but he didn't even feel all that guilty about it. At least not yet. That would undoubtedly come later.

For now, though, he felt strangely happy. Content, almost…certainly more so than he'd been in years. It wasn't making love with a woman that had done it. It was making love with Frances.

He tightened his arms around her, remembering the way she'd responded to him—eagerly, wholeheartedly, holding nothing back. He remembered the little sounds of pleasure she'd made, and the way she cried out with joy and passion during those final, frenzied moments.

Remembering, he smiled. He kissed her cheek tenderly, and her eyelids that were closed. Then he stopped as a thought occurred to him. Was she keeping her eyes closed because she was embarrassed to look at him? Knowing her the way he did, he knew it was entirely possible.

He kept one arm curved possessively over her chest, but slid his other arm out from beneath her and propped up on his elbow to look down at her. "Frances?"

She didn't answer.

"Frances," he repeated. "I know you're not asleep."

Her eyes flew open. "How did you know?"

"I have my ways. Why were you pretending to be asleep?"

"Well…in a lot of books I've read, people always went to sleep after…you know."

"After they'd made love?"

"Yes," she replied in a bare whisper.

"So you pretended you were asleep because you thought it was expected of you?"

"That…and also because I didn't know what to say to you."

That was something he hadn't considered. He'd thought she was enjoying their lovemaking as much as he was when she finally relaxed after the initial penetration, but… Dear heaven! Had he hurt her? If so, he'd never forgive himself.

"Frances . . . are you all right? I mean . . . was it painful for you?"

"Painful?"

"The lovemaking. Was it really awful for you?"

"Oh, no! It was wonderful."

He eyed her. "Would you lie to me?"

"Of course not! Not about something like that."

He allowed himself to breathe again.

He reached up to brush a lock of brown hair back from her forehead. "Then, are you saying that you pretended to be asleep because you were embarrassed to talk to me?" he asked very gently.

She averted her eyes. "Yes."

So his suspicion had been correct. "I'm sorry you felt that way. Personally, I thought that making love with you— sharing what we did—was the most beautiful, incredibly satisfying experience of my life."

She shook her head. "You can't mean that."

"I mean every word of it," he said, meaning every word of it.

She shook her head again. "I was scared silly to begin with, not knowing what to do and all . . ."

"You did fine. Beautiful."

"And then the way I carried on at the end . . . I was like a crazy woman. I don't know what happened to me. You had to be repelled by that."

"*Repelled!* Good grief, woman! You were what every man dreams of—sensuous, passionate, caring. I wasn't repelled. I was thrilled! I still am." He lowered his head and brushed his lips across hers. "You make me very happy, Frances. Thank you for giving me your precious gift."

He kissed her again, so sweetly that she could almost believe he'd meant all the wonderful things he'd said. She wanted to believe them. She returned his kisses, giving herself over to the desire that was building inside her again.

FRANCES PROPPED HERSELF on one elbow and looked down at Jack. His good eye was closed and moisture spiked his long, dark lashes. She didn't think he was asleep, but was grateful that he didn't feel the need to talk right now.

She needed some time herself—time to absorb what had just happened, time to examine the incredible sensations that had swept through her. She needed time to sift and sort, time to savor. One thing was certain—nothing remotely like this had ever happened to her before.

She felt different, somehow. Changed. As if some new, unfamiliar person she neither knew nor understood had climbed inside her skin and taken up residence in her body.

Closing her eyes, Frances let her mind shift from generalities to specifics—Jack's lips on hers, hot and demanding, his touch on her breasts, between her thighs. And her response to him... My, did she respond to him! In his arms, she became a wild woman, wanton...

Remembering *that,* she grew warm all over. She opened her eyes again, and saw Jack watching her, a knowing smile on his face—as if he knew exactly what she'd been thinking and remembering.

"Are you blushing?" he asked.

"Actually, I was flushing."

His smile widened. "I can understand that. That was some workout you just put me through."

She raised an eyebrow. "Me? By myself? I seem to recall having some help."

"Well-l... I didn't want to be ungentlemanly, what with you being a beginner and all."

"That was very gallant of you."

"Yes. That's what I thought, too."

"Wretch," she said, laughing.

"Now, now, Cinderella," he said, pulling her down to kiss her on the lips.

She gave herself over to his kiss for a few moments, then reluctantly drew away with a sigh. "It's time for me to get dressed and go to my own cabin."

"I thought you were going to spend the night with me . . . to make sure the patient was okay."

"Jack, I *have* spent the night with you," she said, pointing to the pale light of dawn visible through the open door to the living room.

Moving quickly, she got out of bed and pulled a sheet along with her. "Don't," he said.

"I have to go. Really."

"I know. But don't hide yourself in the sheet. Let me look at you one last time."

Even though she felt extremely self-conscious, Frances did as he asked, discarding the sheet and standing perfectly still for his long, slow appraisal. Finally, he took a deep breath and sighed. "Thank you."

She didn't know what to say, so she merely gathered up her clothes and headed for the bathroom, feeling his heated gaze on her all the way. Her hands were unsteady as she dressed, which wasn't surprising after the long, emotion-filled night. She would have been surprised if they *had* been steady. She forced herself not to dwell on all that had happened . . . not yet. She'd save that to think about, dissect and savor later.

When she returned to the bedroom, she was surprised to find Jack completely dressed. "It's my turn to walk you home," he explained.

"I'd rather you didn't. Please."

"Afraid someone might see us?"

She lifted her chin and stared directly into his one good eye. "Yes."

He shook his head. "Frances."

"I'm sorry. But—"

"I understand," he said, walking to her and placing both his hands on her shoulders. "You can't change completely in one night." He kissed her forehead. "It's okay."

He stepped back and smiled at her. Then he frowned, and leaned closer to take a better look at the front of her dress. "Is that blood? *My* blood?" he asked.

"Yes," she admitted. "It's a good thing the dress is red anyway," she added, trying to make light of it.

"I owe you a new dress."

"No! I'm sure it will come right out in the laun—"

"And I just happen to have one handy," he said, striding over to a closet and pulling out a big box. He quickly retraced his steps and held out the box to her. "Here."

Looking at the box, Frances saw the name of the dress shop in Palm Beach where they'd shopped the day before. "I don't understand."

"It's for you. Go ahead and open it."

She opened the box, and caught her breath when she saw the off-white dress she'd fallen in love with—the one she hadn't bought because it was too expensive. She looked at him, mouth agape.

"Lucky for me that I happened to have a spare dress to replace the one I ruined by bleeding all over you, wasn't it?"

"How did you get this? And when?"

"I phoned the dress shop when we got back to the ship yesterday...as soon as I learned you hadn't bought the very outfit you obviously loved the most. They delivered it by special messenger shortly before we sailed."

"Jack... I'm touched," she said, meaning it. It was the nicest thing anyone had ever done for her. "Thank you for the thought. I mean it. But I can't accept such a—"

"Of course you'll accept it! We're hundreds of miles from Palm Beach by now, well on our way to Panama. You

can't return it...so give up and accept your gift gra
ciously.''

Frances sighed, giving up. "What would you conside
graciously?"

Jack pretended to think for a moment. "A sweet 'than
you' would be nice.''

"Thank you," Frances said.

"And a little kiss wouldn't be out of order, either."

"You're really pressing. You know that, don't you?"

"Well, it's really a nice dress. And you really wanted it."

She laughed and put her arms around his neck, pulling
his head down to kiss him. "I do thank you, Jack." She
kissed him again. "Thank you very much...and for much
more than the dress."

Chapter Thirteen

Frances awoke slowly, languidly. She yawned and stretched, feeling an unfamiliar soreness in familiar places. Then, remembering the reason for the soreness, she touched her well-kissed lips and smiled.

The smile faded swiftly as soon as she recalled more about last night—her discovery that she was in love with Jack, and his admission that even though he wanted her physically, he couldn't commit to anything more than that. "I can't even think of anything permanent now," he had said.

She frowned, remembering the lie she had told him about not wanting anything permanent, either. So, against Jack's better judgment, they had made love—wonderful, glorious love that had only made her love him more, want him more... leaving her open and vulnerable to terrible pain when they parted, as they surely would when this cruise was over.

Was it worth it?

She thought about that. *Yes,* she finally decided. Loving Jack was worth the risk of pain, every bit of it. And between now and the time they parted, she'd just have to store up enough memories to last a lifetime. Holding onto that thought, she got out of bed and headed for the shower.

Frances encountered Angie Curtis on her way to the dining room for breakfast. "Where's Lionel?" she asked, slightly alarmed because she'd rarely seen one of the Curtises without the other before. What if Angie's plan hadn't worked? Or what if it had worked...and something terrible had happened to Lionel?

"He's sleeping late this morning," Angie replied with a Mona Lisa smile.

Frances breathed a sigh of relief. "Do tell."

"Yes. He decided to skip breakfast."

Frances grinned at her friend. "You look like the kitten who just got the cream."

"I'm not surprised," Angie replied. "It's exactly the way I feel."

"Things went *that* well?"

"Even better than that," Angie said, looping her arm through Frances's as they continued along the corridor. "And what about you? You seem pretty self-satisfied yourself."

"I am, thanks to you. The perfume worked wonders, Angie." They looked at each other. Then they both laughed at the same time.

"You're in love with him, aren't you?" Angie asked.

Frances grimaced. "Is it that obvious?"

"Probably not to everyone. But why should you care whether people know you're in love? Jack's a fine young man...someone you can be proud of loving."

"Yes. Well...the thing is..." Frances hesitated a moment, then plunged ahead. "He's not in love with me."

Angie stopped walking and looked at her in such a way it made Frances feel naked, her deepest, darkest secret exposed.

"I think you're wrong about that," Angie said finally. "I've seen you together. My goodness, the two of you are practically inseparable! I've seen the way he looks at you, too...and it's not the look of a man who doesn't care about you."

"Oh, I think he does care... But as a friend."

"And now as a lover, as well."

"Yes, but..."

"I'm sure Jack has noticed the way you've positively blossomed on this cruise, too, Frances. He couldn't help but notice. And last night while he and I were dancing, he watched you constantly. I could tell he was consumed with jealousy."

"He was?"

"Absolutely. And that's not the attitude of a man who cares about you only as a friend."

Frances hardly dared to hope. Was it possible?

"Believe me," Angie said, as if reading her mind. "Now, let's get some breakfast. I'm starved, aren't you?"

JACK SAT AT THE DINING table nursing his coffee along with a huge hangover of guilt feelings. He'd known last night that it was only a matter of time until his old enemy caught up with him. Sure enough, Guilt finally found him, crushing him like a steamroller in the wee hours this morning after Frances had left.

He hadn't even tried to go back to bed, knowing it would be futile to hope for sleep...or solace. His body desperately needed both, but he knew he deserved neither. Not after what he'd done—making love with Frances, the one thing he'd promised himself he wouldn't do.

What the hell had he been thinking of—or not thinking of—allowing lust to overcome reason the way he had? He cared for her, certainly. But he couldn't allow himself the luxury of falling in love, not until he'd accomplished his mission. Knowing that, taking advantage of the situation by making love to her was indefensible.

To make matters worse, he had a strong suspicion that Frances's feelings for him went beyond merely *caring*... and that made his actions all the more reprehensible.

He sighed. The kindest thing he could do now would be to break things off between them as soon as possible. A clean, fast cut would be less hurtful to her in the long run...even though it would mean giving up her friendship. At the thought of that, a quick, sharp pain shot through him, catching him by surprise, causing him to realize how much he valued that friendship and the times he and Frances spent together.

He looked up and saw Frances coming across the dining room toward him now, as if in response to his thoughts of her. She looked as fresh and beautiful and fragile as a spring flower. Giving her up would be hard; he'd known that for some time now. He just hadn't known exactly *how* hard it would be.

Jack pushed back his chair and stood up, waiting for Frances and Angie to reach the table. "Where is everyone? And what on earth happened to you?" Angie asked, her gaze darting from Jack to Frances, then back to him.

Jack's hand automatically went to the patch over his eye. "I, uh, sort of got into a bit of a fracas last night."

"A fight?" Angie said, looking at Frances again. "With *you?*"

"No!" Jack replied quickly, wondering why Angie would think that he'd gotten into a fight with Frances. "With Art Fortuna."

"You never—" Angie looked at Frances again, not finishing the sentence. Frances shrugged.

Jack wondered what was going on between the two women. Had they been discussing him? "And to answer your other question," he said, "I don't know where Mavis, Maxine and Lionel are. I imagine they're sleeping late. But Art and Sharon have left the cruise ship...for good."

"They have?" Frances said.

"That *is* good!" Angie said. "How did you get rid of them?"

"Sorry, but I can't take credit for it...except indirectly," Jack said with a grin. "The waiter told me they were airlifted off by helicopter early this morning. Urgent business, he said."

"Humph," Frances said.

"Good riddance," Angie said, taking her regular place at the table. "Let's have a big breakfast to celebrate."

"I've already eaten," Jack said. Then, seeing Frances's look of disappointment, he added, "But I'll have some more coffee with you two."

"Wonderful," Angie said. "And later on, after that sleepyhead husband of mine gets up, why don't the four of us play some shuffleboard? Unless you two would rather be alone..."

Jack thought about refusing but glanced at Frances and saw that she was embarrassed by Angie's heavy-handed maneuverings. He immediately changed his mind. "I need to have the doctor check my eye first thing, but shuffleboard afterward sounds good to me. What do you think, Frances?"

"Fine," she murmured.

Jack heard the mingled relief and gratitude in her voice, and saw it in the look she gave him. He changed his mind about making a clean, quick break with her. It would be cruel of him, heartless, and she deserved much better than that. He would take his time instead...let her down gently.

It was the least he could do, considering how very much he cared for her.

IN THE DAYS THAT FOLLOWED Jack spent a lot of time procrastinating. He planned ways to let Frances down gently, but kept postponing the time to put the plans into action, telling himself he was doing it for her benefit . . . but knowing he was merely being cowardly.

Maybe the Japanese financing would suddenly come through—finally—and he could simply leave the ship without telling her at all.

No, dammit! He couldn't—wouldn't—do that to her. So he dithered instead.

He dithered while he and Frances explored lush tropical islands in the Caribbean—St. Martin, St. Thomas and the pastel-colored Dutch houses on Willemstad's waterfront—and while they made their way through the engineering marvel of the Panama Canal, which raised the *American Dreamer* eighty-five feet above sea level . . . then gently lowered it into the Pacific Ocean on the other side.

He dithered while they swam and sunned themselves on exotic beaches, while they laughed and talked and played card games aboard ship, while they danced under the stars . . . and after they'd made love in either his cabin or hers. Yes, he wasn't above that, even.

What was wrong with him? Why couldn't he leave her alone, knowing as he did that he was going to leave her soon? Why didn't he do the honorable thing and get out of her life while there was still time for both of them to survive without serious damage?

He honestly didn't know.

He finally gathered the strength to bring up the subject one night in her cabin when they were lying side by side in her bed. He brushed back a curly lock of brown hair from her cheek, loving the way she always looked after they'd just made love . . . totally relaxed, uninhibited.

At such times as this, there were no barriers between them. They could have told each other anything. Almost.

He kissed her cheek, then marked a trail along it until he found her mouth . . . responsive as always, her lips eagerly seeking his, molding themselves to his. Suddenly, almost as if it came from nowhere, a piercingly painful thought hit him—*how can I bear to leave her?*

He felt a tightness in his throat and around that place in his chest where his heart should have been. *He had to tell her.* He had to prepare her someway, somehow, for what was to come. And he had to do it now.

He pulled away from her abruptly, and she opened her eyes. They were wide and questioning. "You drive me crazy," he whispered, kissing her lightly on the lips once, twice. "It's hard to believe you were a complete beginner only a few weeks ago." He kissed her cheek, her nose, her other cheek.

"I had a good teacher," she said huskily, kissing the tip of his chin.

Clenching his fists with determination, he rolled away from her onto his back, staring up at the ceiling. "God, but I'm going to miss you," he said. He heard her sudden, sharp intake of breath, but she said nothing. He swallowed and blinked his eyes rapidly a couple of times. Then he swallowed again.

"I'm expecting to hear from Martin any day now," he said. "The Japanese financing *has* to come through sometime soon. I can't understand why it's taken this long. Martin says it's because the Japanese are always very deliberate."

Jack held his breath, waiting for Frances to say something, but she remained silent. "I imagine I'll be leaving the ship to fly back to New York fairly soon after the financing does come through." He waited again. She still didn't speak.

Finally he propped himself on one elbow to look at her. Her eyes were closed, and there was a suspicion of a tear at the corner of one of them. Jack felt like crying himself.

"It's something I've worked for for ten years, Frances," he said softly. "Almost all my life, it seems at times.

"The hardest part..." He closed his eyes briefly and took a deep breath. "The hardest part will be leaving you."

He saw a single tear roll along her cheek down to her neck. Then he closed his eyes and gathered her into his arms, feeling her own arms wind themselves around him.

They held each other.

FRANCES LOOKED into the mirror and made a face. The strain was showing. Around her eyes. In the pinched set of her lips.

She'd tried to put on a brave front, especially around Jack, but it was becoming harder to do every day. She kept waiting for the phone to ring—the call to come through that would take him away from her. Forever.

She ran a brush through her hair. Today in Acapulco had been exhausting enough, but then tonight she and Jack, along with the Curtises and Mavis and Maxine, had sampled the nightlife of the Mexican Riviera. She couldn't understand how Lionel and Angie were able to tolerate the pace at their age. Maybe rediscovering sex all over again was what did it.

She'd discovered sex for the first time with Jack, but soon he'd be leaving her...alone and lonely, forever and ever...

"Enough," she said aloud, straightening her shoulders and putting the brush back into her purse. She was here with Jack for the time being, wearing the white dress he'd bought her, and he was outside in the living room of his cabin waiting for her.

She put on her best smile and walked purposefully out to meet him, taking secret delight in the way his eyes sparkled the way they always did the first time he saw her, even if they'd only been away from each other for minutes...like now.

Forget about tomorrow or the next day, she told herself. Think about here...now...

The phone rang.

Jack looked at her.

She held her breath.

With a helpless shrug, he went to answer the phone.

Maybe it was nothing, she thought. But she still held her breath.

"Martin," Jack said with a grin that Frances hadn't seen in a long time. "You haven't called in days. Weeks. What's up?"

Frances saw the grin fade from Jack's lips, then disappear completely. "But I thought—" he said. He stopped and listened to what Martin was telling him over the ship-to-shore phone, nodding his head occasionally, frowning a lot. The call didn't last long, and when Jack hung up, Frances knew the news wasn't good.

He looked at her again and attempted a lopsided grin that nearly broke her heart. Then he shook his head in disbelief. "The Japanese backed out," he said simply.

"Oh, no!"

"Oh, yes." He raked his fingers through his hair. Then he made a fist and slammed it into his other palm, hard. "Dammit to hell!"

Frances wanted to comfort him, but didn't know what to say. "Jack, I'm so sorry."

"So am I, Frances," he said, moving over to the glass doors beyond the sofa and staring into the darkness outside. "So am I."

After a moment's hesitation she walked across the room to stand beside him.

"Martin said they didn't give a specific reason...just that they'd decided this wasn't the right investment for them.

It's possible that our enemies somehow got to them and convinced them not to invest in our project. Or it could simply be what they said...they didn't think the investment was right for them. We'll probably never know for sure.''

Frances touched his arm, resting her hand on his sleeve, trying to absorb some of his pain. Even though she'd never entirely approved of his takeover plans, she still loved him and it hurt her to see him wounded in any way.

"What will you do now?" she asked after a moment.

"I'm not sure," he said, looking down at her hand on his arm. He covered her hand with his. "One thing I *am* sure of is that I'm not giving up." He squeezed her hand. "I'm disappointed, but I'm not defeated."

She smiled at him, admiring his courage and determination, loving him more than ever. "With that kind of attitude, I don't see how you can lose...Jack the Shark."

He grinned back at her and squeezed her hand again. "Damned right. And damn the torpedos, full speed ahead."

"You've just begun to fight."

"I'll fight for truth, freedom and the American Way," he said, starting to laugh.

"Oh, yes," Frances agreed, laughing along with him. "You have nothing to fear but fear itself."

"So I'll fight them on the beaches, in the air, on the streets..."

"But don't shoot until you see the whites of their eyes," she said.

Jack raised an eyebrow. "What does *that* have to do with anything?"

Frances shook her head, still laughing. "I ran out of quotations."

"Ah, Frances," Jack said, wrapping his arms around her and squeezing hard. "Thank you," he added, suddenly serious.

She shrugged.

Jack released her and raked his fingers through his hair again. "It's too late to call Martin back tonight . . . and I'd like to think about it a while longer, too . . . but I imagine the next move would be to have him fly over to Switzerland."

"Switzerland?" she repeated, completely lost.

He nodded. "We might be able to get financing from a European conglomerate based there. They expressed an interest in our project about a year ago. I turned them down then, because they drive such a hard bargain. But now . . . Maybe it's time we approached them again."

Frances frowned. "Will . . . will their terms be more favorable now?"

"I doubt it. They'll probably be even more hard-nosed about it. But our choices are . . . extremely limited, shall we say?"

An idea had been formulating in the back of Frances's mind while Jack talked. She took a deep breath. "Jack, uh . . . there's another possibility."

"There is?" he said, raising an eyebrow.

"I hesitated to mention it because I know how much pride you have. But you shouldn't let it get in the way this time. I mean . . . it would be strictly a business deal, after all. There's nothing to be ashamed of."

He shook his head. "Frances, I have no idea what you're talking about."

She took another deep breath. "When my father died, he left a will naming me as his prime beneficiary. I inherited almost a million dollars. And I'd like you to have it."

JACK STARED AT HER, too stunned to speak.

"It's more money than I'll ever need," Frances said,

speaking rapidly. "And I can't think of a better use to put it to. You can have it all or as much of it as you need and then pay me back after your deal goes through. Like I said, it would be strictly business so you shouldn't—"

"Frances," Jack said, placing his hands on her shoulders and squeezing them to stop her torrent of words. "I can't take your money."

"I knew that was what you'd say. But you shouldn't feel that way."

"What way?"

"Too proud to accept a loan from a friend. That's what friends are for and—"

He silenced her with a kiss. And continued to hold the kiss because he didn't think he was able to talk at the moment. He was too moved, too shocked . . . completely undone by her generous and unselfish offer.

Frances didn't know that what he was attempting involved billions instead of less than a million. She had no way of knowing it. But it didn't matter. She had offered him all her money—everything she owned—with no strings attached.

He still couldn't get over that.

Finally getting himself under a semblance of control, Jack broke off their kiss and smiled down at her tenderly.

"Thank you," he said, kissing the tip of her nose.

"Then you'll take it!" she said, grinning.

"No. I was thanking you for the offer. And for being my friend . . . even though I don't deserve you."

"Jack—"

"No."

"But—"

"No, Frances," he said firmly, ushering her toward the door. "Now I think I'll plead a headache and say goodnight."

"You have a headache?"

"No, but I need to do some thinking . . . and start making plans about what to do next."

"I wish you'd at least think about my offer."

"I will. I'll think that it's the dearest thing anyone's ever done for me in my life. But I won't change my mind about accepting it."

She shook her head. "You're too stubborn by far."

"I know. And that's only one of my lesser failings. See you tomorrow."

AFTER FRANCES HAD GONE, Jack tried to think about plans for his project as he'd told her he was going to do, but his thoughts kept returning to her instead.

And her offer. Nobody in his entire life had ever done such a thing for him . . . or been so open, generous, giving . . . with no questions asked. Only Frances.

He smiled, remembering her impatience when he refused to accept her money. She hadn't merely offered the money; she'd actually *wanted* him to accept it!

He sighed. She was truly a good person . . . not to mention wonderful and adorable. But of course he'd known that for a long time now. It was probably why he'd fallen in love with her in the first place.

Jack caught his breath. He blinked. What was it that he'd just thought? That he was in love with Frances?

Yes.

He was.

And it wasn't something that had happened all of a sudden, either. It had been building deep inside him for some time, so slowly and quietly that he hadn't even known it. Until now. Her unexpected and extraordinary offer tonight had merely caused him to recognize something that he'd kept hidden, especially from himself.

So you're in love with her. And she's probably in love with you, too. What are you going to do about it?

"Nothing," Jack said out loud.

That's really stupid. Why does it have to be all or nothing with you? Why can't you do things in moderation?

"Such as?" Jack asked.

Go ahead with your takeover plans...AND marry Frances. It's possible to do two things at the same time...if you're not a complete idiot.

"I've already botched one marriage."

That was a long time ago. And the woman in that case wasn't Frances. Don't you owe her something? Shouldn't she at least have some say in the matter?

Jack raked his fingers through his hair. He scratched his chin. He rubbed the back of his neck. *Yes!* he finally decided.

"Damn right!" he said, racing for the door.

The corridor was deserted. So was the escalator. Jack looked at his watch. Three-thirty. Pretty late. Maybe he should wait until... "No," he said, knowing himself well enough to know that if he didn't tell Frances now—right now—he might never do it.

At last he was down on Frances's deck, in her corridor, outside the door to her room. Taking a deep breath, he knocked on the door. He waited a couple of seconds, then knocked again, louder this time. After a few more seconds when there was still no answer, he shook the handle of her door. "Frances," he whispered against the door.

Dammit, what was keeping her? Why didn't she wake up and answer the door? "Frances!" he said, knocking again.

"What the hell's going on?"

Jack turned around to see a man's face peering out from the door across the corridor. "Sorry if I woke you," he said sheepishly.

"You'll be sorrier still if you keep up that racket. Do you know what time it is?"

"Yes. It's—" Jack stopped when he heard Frances's door open. He turned around to look at her.

She wore no makeup...only a pair of men's oversize pajamas. Her hair was in wild disarray and her eyes were puffy from sleep. He'd never seen anyone so beautiful in his entire life.

"Frances, I'm in love with you!" Jack said. "Wildly, passionately in love with you. Will you marry me?"

Chapter Fourteen

Frances squinted her eyes and sniffed the air. "Have you been drinking?"

"Certainly not!" Jack said indignantly. "I mean...no, since early this evening."

"So *that's* what all the ruckus was about," the man across the corridor said. "You were waking her up to propose."

"Yes, I—" Jack began.

"Why don't you mind your own business?" Frances said to the man.

"Hey! Your friend here was the one who woke *me* up," the man said. "And things are just now getting interesting."

"Come inside, Jack, before you make even more of a scene than you already have," Frances said, pulling him inside her room and slamming the door shut.

Frances pressed her fingers to her eyes, then to her temples. She'd cried herself to sleep and now she had a throbbing headache. She took a deep breath and turned around to face Jack. "Why are you here in the middle of the night, after you practically threw me out of your room a couple of hours ago?"

"I did not! Throw you out of my room, I mean."

"It seemed close enough to that to me."

"I'm sorry. Really sorry. Especially if I hurt your feelings. But I had to try and sort things out . . . you know, all that had happened with the Japanese and all."

"And did you? Sort things out, I mean?"

"No."

"Then why—"

"I tried to think about the takeover and all that, but all I could think about was you. And it finally dawned on me. I'm in love with you, Frances."

She rubbed her eyes again, wishing this terrible headache would go away so she could think straight. "You're not in love with me."

"Then why does it feel like love?" he said, reaching for her. "Why do I think about you constantly . . . dream about you . . . and want to be with you always? If it's not love, then what is it?"

She stepped back out of his reach. "It's gratitude."

"What?"

"You're feeling grateful because I was there for you tonight. Offering sympathy." She hesitated. "Offering money. You appreciate what I offered, so . . ."

"So in exchange, I'm willing . . . No. Change that. I'm *begging* to spend the rest of my life with you? Come on, Frances. If you don't feel the same way about me, you can come up with a better turndown . . ."

"It wasn't a turndown . . ."

"It sure sounded like one to me."

"I was merely trying to be sensible . . . rational. Pointing out a few things to you that you might have forgotten in the middle of the night."

"You think I won't feel this same way tomorrow?"

"I think it's a distinct possibility."

"You want me to put it in writing?"

"Don't be silly."

"I will!" He looked around the room. "Do you have a pencil and paper?"

"Jack, stop it!"

"Then answer me one thing, Frances. Do you love me?"

She opened her mouth to speak, but immediately closed it again. "That has nothing to do with it," she finally said.

"It has *everything* to do with it. I've already told you I'm in love with you and that's not something I take lightly. I've only said it to one other woman in my life."

"Barbara, your ex-wife," Frances said.

"Yes."

"You've already told me you drove her away by becoming caught up in your work to the exclusion of everything—and everybody—else. Are you asking me to follow the same path to... to heartbreak and divorce?"

"It doesn't have to be the same. Barbara was a child—sweet, but spoiled, too. And selfish. The same as I was at that time in my life. But you're a woman, Frances—strong, generous. And I hope that I've done some growing up these last few years, too."

Frances felt a strange excitement start to build inside her. Was it possible...? *Was it?*

"I'm still committed to my work, and to the takeover attempt. But I think...I honestly believe...that I can handle that responsibility and still be a loving husband to you, Frances."

Frances still had doubts, misgivings. In spite of Jack's denial, she was sure he was grateful for the offer she'd made him. But as he had said, that alone wasn't enough to cause him to ask her to marry him. Was it?

She didn't see his commitment to work as a problem, at least not a serious one. As he'd pointed out in a roundabout way, she wouldn't expect as much attention from him as his first wife had done.

His lack of money didn't bother her, either. She had plenty of money...enough for the two of them to live comfortably for the rest of their lives. And surely he'd allow her to share it with him if they were married.

Married!

The excitement that had been building inside her took a quantum leap at the idea of spending the rest of her life married to Jack.

Mrs. Jackson Sherrod.

Frances swallowed. There was still the matter of her lack of social skills. Jack had boosted her self-confidence a thousandfold on this cruise, but she knew she still had a long way to go in order to become the kind of wife he needed...and deserved.

But social skills could be learned, couldn't they? And with Jack to teach her...guide her...support her...

Did she dare?

"I love you, Frances. It's not gratitude, it's love. It's real. And I think the two of us could have a wonderful life together," Jack said. "But you still haven't answered *my* question. Do you love me?"

She took a deep breath. "You know I do," she mumbled quickly.

Jack grasped her shoulder. "What did you say?"

She lifted her chin and looked him straight in the eye. "Yes," she said, almost defiantly. "Of course I love you...and have for a long time. And you already knew that."

"I suspected. And hoped. But I didn't know for sure until you told me just now." He touched her cheek with the backs of his fingers. "And I won't know for sure that you'll marry me until you tell me that, too. Will you, Frances? Will you marry me...and share the rest of your life with me?"

She felt tears sting her eyes, and overflow. She didn't care. She knew she might be making a big mistake, but she didn't care about that, either. The chance was worth it. And some things you have to do on blind faith... and love.

"Yes, Jack," she said, not trying to disguise the love she felt for him... wanting it to shine through in the look she gave him. "I'll marry you. Happily."

He pulled her into his arms tenderly, brushing away a stray tear from her cheek. "Happily ever after," he whispered, closing his mouth over hers.

Please, let it be true, Frances thought, sliding her arms around his waist and returning his kiss.

"YOU'RE GETTING MARRIED?" Angie said, clapping her hands excitedly. She pushed back her chair and dashed around the dining table to give Frances a big hug. "That's wonderful!"

Frances nodded, feeling her cheeks grow warm, and cursed her lifelong tendency to blush. She'd wanted to postpone telling their dining companions the news—at least for a couple of days—but Jack had insisted they tell them first thing this morning.

"They'd look at you and know right away that something was up," he'd pointed out. "This will save them wondering what it is. Besides, I want the whole world to know the way I feel about you."

"Congratulations," Lionel said, shaking Jack's hand.

"I told you this would happen," Maxine said to Frances.

"Did she?" Jack asked Frances.

"Not in so many words," Frances replied. "She said our signs were compatible, but..."

"Well, what do you think *that* means?" Maxine said huffily.

"Maxine never comes right out and predicts anything," Mavis said. "If something happens, she always *says* she saw it coming."

"You're just jealous," Maxine said to her cousin. "Didn't I say that Art Fortuna would leave this cruise in disgrace?"

"No," Mavis replied. "You said there *might* be trouble in his seventh house."

"Exactly! And—"

"Ladies," Angie interrupted. "Let's not quibble among ourselves. We should be drinking a toast to the happy couple instead," she added, reaching for her glass of orange juice and then holding it up in a toast.

"Hear, hear," Lionel agreed, lifting his orange juice.

Frances felt a lump in her throat and hoped she wouldn't embarrass herself—and Jack—further by breaking into sentimental tears.

"Have you set a date yet?" Lionel asked Frances.

"Maybe you should ask Maxine," Mavis said with a wicked smile.

"Mavis," Angie chided, clucking her tongue.

"I couldn't resist," Mavis said.

"We haven't talked about a date yet," Frances said. "It only, uh, happened last night."

"Early this morning," Jack corrected her. "But I thought we'd pick out the ring when we dock in Los Angeles day after tomorrow."

Frances's mouth fell open. "A . . . a ring?"

Jack smiled at her. "It's customary."

A ring, Frances thought. Last night and this morning, she'd thought she must be dreaming. That she'd wake up at any moment and find she'd imagined the whole thing. But now . . . with everyone crowded around to congratulate them . . . and Jack talking about a *ring* . . . she began to think this might be real, after all.

And if it was real, that made her the luckiest woman on the face of the earth.

"FRANCES!" JACK SAID urgently. "I...I don't think I can..." He shuddered. "I can't hold back much longer."

"Then don't!" she whispered, tightening her arms around his neck, tightening her legs around his hips, raising her own hips to meet his thrusts. "Don't hold back, my darling. Let go...*now!*"

Jack drove himself deep inside her...again...then one final time with a convulsive gasp as he spent himself inside her. He touched his forehead to hers, breathing hard, and shivered. "Sorry," he whispered. "Sorry I couldn't...wait for you."

"Don't worry," she said, turning her head to kiss his cheek, still holding him tightly in her embrace. "There'll be other times...plenty of other times. And I enjoyed it anyway, even though I didn't, uh..."

"Climax?" he said, kissing her neck in a spot she seemed to enjoy being kissed a lot. Sure enough, she shivered. He smiled and kissed the spot again, then raised his head and propped himself on his elbows to gaze down at her. "So you enjoyed it anyway, huh?" he said, teasing her.

"Yes. It was wonderful. Marvelous. Do you suppose I'm becoming a sex addict?"

"Let's hope so," he said with a chuckle. "I know *I* am." He kissed the tip of her nose. "You know...some women *pretend* to have orgasms when they're really not having them at all."

She frowned. "They do? Why?"

"Beats me," he said, kissing her soft, pink lips and thanking his lucky stars all over again that he had been fortunate enough to find such a treasure.

He lifted his head after a moment and rolled over beside her. Then he put his arms around her and pulled her close. "This is where I want you to be," he said. "Always."

"It's where I want to be, too."

They both sighed at the same time. Then, hearing each other's sighs, they both laughed at the same time.

"I talked to my mother this afternoon," Jack said after a moment.

"Oh? How is she?"

"She's finally back from summer vacation. She said she's been working day and night trying to get her house back in order."

Remembering the state of disrepair it was in the last time she'd seen it, Frances didn't envy Jack's mother.

"I told her about us."

Oh, dear. "What did she say?"

"She was delighted. Thrilled. 'It's about time,' I think were her exact words. She wants us to drive up to see her when our ship returns to Miami in a couple of days."

Frances frantically searched her mind for an excuse not to go.

"You'll have to meet her sometime, Frances," Jack said, as if he'd read her mind. "And she's really a very nice person. I think you'll like her."

"I'm sure I would...will. That's not what worries me. What will she think about me?"

"She'll love you," Jack said, kissing her eyes, her lips. "Just as much as I love you...but in a different way, of course."

Jack sounded confident, sure of himself and of his mother's reaction to the strange woman he was bringing home to meet her. Frances only wished she could absorb a little of Jack's confidence.

"WE COULDN'T ASK for a better day, could we?" Jack said, glancing up at the bright blue December sky before opening the door for Frances to get inside the rental car. "The forecast called for temperatures in the high seventies. Do you think we should open the sun roof?"

"Maybe later," Frances mumbled, feeling queasy because she was as nervous as she'd ever been in her life. She'd been nervous the first time she and Jack had driven up to Palm Beach, but she had merely been a friend of his then, someone he'd met on the boat, whereas now...

Frances climbed into the car, feeling much the way she imagined she'd feel if she were climbing into a coffin.

Mercifully, Jack didn't talk much on the drive up to Palm Beach. Maybe he was having second thoughts, too, about introducing her to his mother.

Frances didn't know which was worse—having to make conversation when she was much too nervous to talk...or imagining what Jack must be thinking because he *wasn't* making conversation.

"Here we are," he said, much too quickly for Frances. Tomorrow—or next year—would have been plenty soon as far as she was concerned.

Taking a deep breath, she looked out the car window as they pulled into the driveway of Jack's mother's house. She blinked. And continued holding her breath.

This couldn't be the same place they'd visited before, only a month ago. No way.

That place had been rickety, run-down, with a yard that looked like an overgrown jungle.

This place was lovely. Charming. A sparkling gem of a house, freshly painted with every tile in place, every hinge in order and gleaming, every window shiny-clean. The grounds were manicured, the hedges neatly trimmed, the graveled drive as immaculate as if it had been brushed...and not a single weed in sight. Anywhere.

"I can't believe it," Frances said.

"I told you," Jack said with a chuckle. "It's the way Mother operates. She takes her greatest delight in bringing the place back to life."

A uniformed butler came out to meet them. "Good to see you again, Charles," Jack said, shaking the man's hand. "How's my dear old mum?"

"Feisty as ever."

"Good. And I don't know if she told you—"

"She told me," Charles said, smiling at Frances. "Welcome to the Sherrod family, Ms. Lanier."

Frances blinked. "Thank you."

Charles gathered up their luggage, leading the way inside the house. "You'll have to excuse Charles for his lack of decorum, so to speak," Jack whispered to Frances as they followed the older man. "He's been with the family so long that he thinks he's a part of it. And he is, actually. I don't know what Mother would do without him."

"I understand," Frances whispered back, not understanding at all. Her only experience with servants had been with day help a couple of times each year when her sister had sent her own maid over to "make the house decent for people to live in," according to Juli. Every time, Frances had ended up doing most of the cleaning, with Juli's maid supervising what she did.

The foyer was marble—real marble, not artificial tile—and the chandeliers were crystal. Frances would have bet her life on it. The furniture in the living room hadn't been sold off, either, as she had suspected might be the case on her first visit to Jack's mother's house. It was everywhere, in abundance—eclectic groupings of modern designs and Old World masterpieces, all polished to a high sheen—accented by authentic-looking original paintings and definitely authentic Oriental carpets.

The place was tastefully decorated, not ostentatious in the least, but quietly, discreetly reeking of *money*.

Big bucks.

Frances frowned, confused. If Jack's father had lost everything, and killed himself because of it, then how ... ?

"This cottage wasn't part of my father's estate," Jack whispered to her, again seeming to read her mind. "Mother inherited it from her side of the family after he killed himself."

Frances nodded mutely, but her mind was racing a thousand words a minute. If Jack's mother had inherited a valuable property such as this from her family—and Jack had inherited a trust fund as well ... Approximately how much *had* he inherited?

"Jack! My darling boy!"

Frances watched as a trim, lovely, blond woman in a hot pink exercise outfit ran toward them and hurled herself into Jack's arms. He laughed and caught her in mid-air, whirling her around.

"It's so damn good to see you again," he said.

"It's not my fault that you stayed away so long," she said.

"And it's not my fault that you weren't here the last time we stopped by to visit you."

"Sorry about that. Now put me down so I can give Frances a proper welcome." Jack lowered his mother to the floor and she gave Frances a quick, hard hug. "I'm delighted you're going to be part of our family, Frances. Not just for Jack's sake, but mine as well. I've wanted a daughter for years."

"Thank you. I'm—" Frances tried frantically to think of something to say, but her mind was a complete blank. Naturally, it would desert her at a time like this. "Thank you," she said again, certain that Jack's mother must think her an idiot.

"I wanted to invite some people over to meet you...so I could show you off, but Jack didn't give me enough notice that you two were coming."

"Maybe on our next visit," Jack said. "And we wouldn't have had time for a party this trip, anyway. We have to leave at the crack of dawn tomorrow to get back to our ship."

Mrs. Sherrod frowned. "Must you?"

"Either that, or we miss the boat and you're stuck with us," he said.

"Sounds good to me," his mother replied.

Frances smiled and tried to relax. She really liked Jack's mother, at least what she'd seen of her so far. Ellen Sherrod was open, friendly and unpretentious—marvelous qualities in a person who was obviously as rich as a Vanderbilt or an Astor.

Thinking about that, she wondered once again how much money Jack himself had. And for the first time, she wondered exactly how much was involved in his takeover attempt.

Frances heard a phone ringing in the distance and a few moments later, the butler came into the living room. "Mrs. Littlefield would like to speak with you," he told Jack's mother.

"That's my friend, Candace," Mrs. Sherrod said to Frances. "Will you excuse me? This should only take a moment."

"Please don't rush," Frances said.

"Well, what did I tell you?" Jack said after his mother had left the room. "Isn't she a doll?"

"Yes. She's really lovely, Jack. And nice as can be."

He walked over to sit beside her on the sofa. "She likes you a lot, too. I can tell."

She shook her head. "I don't see how you can tell any such thing in so short a time."

"I *can*," he insisted. "Besides, I know something you don't know."

"What?"

"My mother has wanted me to remarry for so long...and has been so afraid that I wouldn't... that she'd love *anyone* I brought home and introduced as my fiancé."

Frances tried to suppress a snicker but couldn't. "Wretch!"

He smiled, capturing her hand and bringing it to his mouth to kiss. "But you love me anyway."

"That's for sure." Then, remembering her earlier concern about his financial status, she frowned. "Jack, there's something—"

"Good news," Jack's mother said, coming back into the room. "Candace and her husband are going to drop by for cocktails this evening on their way out to dinner. The Rockwells and Dunlaps will be with them, too, so at least you'll be able to meet a few of my friends, Frances. Isn't that grand?"

Yes, grand, she thought, nodding her head. She'd be looking forward to meeting six of Mrs. Sherrod's Palm Beach friends almost as much as she would to having a root canal done.

"IT WASN'T *THAT* BAD," Jack said.

"No, it wasn't that bad," Frances agreed. "It was worse."

The evening was finally over. At last. The cocktails had been drunk, dinner had been served and eaten, after-dinner conversation had been exhausted, and Mrs. Sherrod had gone to bed. Now Frances and Jack were alone on the terrace to rehash what a disaster it had been.

"You're exaggerating, Frances," he said. "Blowing it all out of proportion."

"Am I? *Am I?* Are you saying it was acceptable social behavior to throw red wine all over the front of Mr. Rockwell's white shirt?"

"In this case, *yes.* I saw what caused it all, remember? I saw him come up behind you and put his hand on your...behind. Whirling around the way you did was a perfectly normal reaction. Having the wine slosh out of your glass was normal, too. Of course, having *red* wine in the glass was a fringe benefit."

"It's not funny, Jack."

"You're right. I should have decked the old lecher myself. And I might have done it if he hadn't rushed out the way he did, with his wife right behind him. I think she saw what caused the accident, too, and I'll bet—"

"I've never been so embarrassed in my life."

"It wasn't your fault. My mother knew that, too. She apologized to *you,* not to—"

"It wasn't only that, either. I was totally out of my depth all evening...awkward, inept. I can't carry on a simple conversation, Jack."

"Nonsense. You do fine on the cruise boat, laughing and—"

"That's different. I know the people at our dining table. They're almost like family. But then tonight, with all your mother's friends..."

"The Rockwells aren't really her friends, Frances. They're merely acquaintances. She explained that to you afterward."

"Yes. She couldn't have been nicer...especially after the way I disgraced myself, and you and her..."

"That's not—"

"It is, too. The truth is, I was scared to death tonight. Meeting those people with all their expensive clothes and furs and jewelry..."

"People who have money are still *people*—mortals like the rest of us."

Frances looked at him for several seconds. "That reminds me of something, Jack, something I've been wondering about. How much money do *you* have?"

"What?"

"It's a simple enough question."

"Well, yes... But it's rather difficult to answer... with some cash here, some bonds there... that sort of thing."

"I'll make it easier for you, then. How much is involved in the takeover you're attempting? Roughly." She was watching him closely and although he was partially hidden in the shadows, there was plenty of light for her to see the stricken look that appeared on his face.

"Why, uh... why do you want to know?"

"I just do. How much?"

"It's not important."

"How much?"

He let out a long sigh, one he'd probably been holding. "Several billion dollars."

Frances closed her eyes. Then she opened them and let out a brief, sarcastic laugh, a laugh laced with pain. "And I offered you my inheritance. Less than a million. You must have gotten a laugh out of that."

"Never!" he said, grabbing her shoulder roughly. "I didn't laugh then and I'm not laughing now."

"How stupid of me! How silly... naive. Oh, God! How embarrassing!" She tried to pull away from him, but he held on tighter, his fingers biting into her flesh.

"Listen to me! It was none of those things. It was the dearest, kindest, most unselfish thing anyone has ever done for me in my entire life. You offered me money... everything you owned. I've never been so moved by anything in my life before."

"So out of gratitude, you asked me to marry you."

"No! That wasn't the way it was at all. What you did caused me to take a closer look at you, and at myself... And that made me realize I was already in love with you."

"I can't marry you, Jack," Frances said, feeling her heart shattering into a million tiny pieces.

"You can't mean that!"

"I'm sorry. Truly sorry that—"

"*No!*" He pulled her against him, lowering his mouth to hers, kissing her roughly, harshly.

She didn't resist him... or maybe she did by offering no resistance to his painful assault, she thought. *Oh, Jack! How I wish things could have been different!* He lessened the pressure of his mouth against hers, and his lips became soft, teasing, coaxing. She responded to him, the way she always had, slipping her arms around him, kissing him back, treasuring every detail of this, their final kiss, committing it to memory—a memory she hoped was strong enough to last a lifetime.

He finally lifted his head and gazed at her triumphantly. "You love me. You know you do."

"Yes. I'll never deny that. Ever."

"Then—"

"And that's the most powerful reason of all why I won't marry you."

"That makes no sense to me."

"I love you, Jack. So much it scares me. And my biggest fear is being a drawback to you. I don't belong in this world of yours and your mother's. I'd only embarrass you—"

"*You wouldn't—*"

"And I'd embarrass myself. Both of us. And you'd come to hate me for it. I couldn't bear that," she said, finally running out of steam.

Jack waited a moment. "My turn?"

She nodded.

"In the first place, I couldn't care less about what the kind of people who were here tonight think." He snapped his fingers. "It means less than that to me. And what's more—if it's really important to you—social skills can be learned."

She smiled sadly. "That's what I told myself, too, when I agreed to marry you. But you and I—the two of us—are separated by much more than mere 'social skills.' Our worlds are totally, completely different."

"That's simply not true."

"I offered you what I thought was a vast amount of money, Jack...and it was less than a million dollars. You're not even an ordinary, run-of-the-mill millionaire. You deal in *billions*. And that's not merely being different. That's a whole other *world*."

They argued back and forth some more that night and again the following morning while Jack drove them back to Miami. But Frances didn't budge, because she was sure what she was doing was the right thing.

And in the end, she gave him the ring back, left the cruise and took a plane home to Charlotte, while Jack stayed on board *American Dreamer* for the return trip to Montreal.

"I DON'T DO WINDOWS," the woman said.

Frances looked at the maid Juli had sent over to "help make the house fit for decent people to live in," and tried to hold her temper in check. "Okay," she said in what she thought was a reasonable tone, especially considering the circumstances. "I can understand that. But you not only don't do windows. You don't do floors. You don't clean kitchens. Or bathrooms. Or cabinets. What exactly *do* you do?"

"I—" the woman began indignantly.

"I'll tell you what you do," Frances said. "Nothing. Zilch. And I intend to tell my sister Juli exactly what I've told you. Now get out of here and stop wasting my time."

"But—"

"*Out!* Now!"

Juli called a short while later, just as Frances had expected she would. She was indignant, also as Frances had expected. "My maid said you threw her out of the house!"

"She's lying," Frances said calmly. "That woman must weigh close to three hundred pounds. There's no way I could throw her anywhere."

"Well, *something* happened, and I won't have you insulting—"

"I didn't insult anybody. I told your maid to get out of my house because she refused to do the work I asked her to do."

"Maybe you told her to do something that—"

"Juli," Frances said, interrupting her again. "You might be able to tolerate incompetent help. But I won't."

Juli slammed down the phone and Frances finally released the giggle she'd been holding in. "Way to go, Frances," she said out loud to herself.

Then she sighed, long and loud. And there was nobody in the dark old house to hear it. *About to feel sorry for yourself again?*

"Yes," she said.

Remember how great you've become at standing up to Juli.

"I do. And I'm proud of myself."

But...?

"I miss him. Lord, I miss him!"

"Then why don't you do something about it?"

Hearing the sudden, unexpected voice behind her, Frances caught her throat and wheeled around to face Lisa. "You scared the living daylights out of me."

"Sorry," Lisa said. "But the front door was wide open...and on a nasty day like today...so I thought something might be wrong and came on inside."

"Juli's maid must have deliberately left it open. I ordered her to leave a little while ago."

"What was the problem?"

"She was trying to do her usual number on me—refusing to do any actual work...and then standing around telling *me* what to do. I decided I was perfectly capable of doing the work without her supervision this time."

"Bully for you," Lisa said, grinning. "You're getting really good at standing up to Juli...*and* to her maids."

"Thanks."

"But what was that I heard about missing Jack?"

Frances had confided the whole thing to Lisa, and saw no reason to hold back now. "I thought it would get better with time. But it's been almost two months now...and it only gets worse."

"My suggestion still stands—why don't you do something about it?"

"What's the point? To prolong the pain a little longer? I know I did the right think in breaking off with Jack and..." She took a deep breath. "There's nothing to be gained by seeing him again...except to punish myself. I'm not going to do that, because I happen to think I don't deserve it."

"And you don't," Lisa agreed, walking over to give her a hug. "Although you *might* deserve a couple of lashes with a wet noodle for stubbornness. It's entirely possible that the man really *does* love you, you know."

"I think he thought he did at one time. But he's undoubtedly had time to rethink the matter by now...and come to the same conclusion that I did."

Lisa stepped back, a speculative gleam in her eyes. "Tell me one thing, Frances. When you broke up with Jack did you secretly think—some place way back in a private part of your heart—that he might come after you?''

"No! I—" She stopped and reconsidered the question. "Well . . . maybe yes. I think I hoped he would. Not that it would have made a difference."

"Did you ever stop to consider that he might be hoping the same thing . . . that you'd change your mind and come back to him? After all, you were the one who left."

"And nothing has changed since I did," Frances pointed out. "I was right to do it. And Jack knows that now, even if he didn't want to accept it then."

"So you *think* you were right to break things off with the only man you've ever loved!" Lisa said with exasperation. "And you're determined to hold onto that conviction for the *next* thirty years of your life. Some comfort that will be when you're sixty. And alone. And lonely as hell."

"That's hitting below the belt," Frances said.

"I know. And I should be sorry. But I'm not. I'm deliberately *trying* to shake you up, Frances . . . to make you realize that not everything's perfect in this imperfect world.

"Howie has more faults than I can number on all my fingers and toes...but I still love him in spite of them. Hell, I probably love him *because* of them! And because I'm not perfect, either.

"This is the *real* world, Frances...not the dreamy, fairytale, make-believe place you invented in order to cope with the responsibility of taking care of Pops all those years. I didn't blame you then. I was all for it—anything that would help you survive.

"But now you have a choice. And a chance at the real thing. Don't waste it, Frances! Ignore your insecurity. Forget your pride. Concentrate on—"

"Hello! Anybody home?"

Frances caught her breath at the sound of the familiar voice calling from the hall. A couple of seconds later he was standing in the doorway of the living room. Jack. Looking a little tentative, unsure of himself. Looking wonderful.

Frances simply stared at him. He stared back at her.

Nobody spoke.

Lisa was the first one to recover. She walked across the room to him, holding out her hand. "You must be Jack."

"And you must be Lisa," he said, taking her hand. He looked at Frances again. "I'm sorry to come into your house the way I did, but the front door was wide open. I was afraid something was wrong."

"You didn't close the door?" Frances asked Lisa.

"I'll do it on my way out. And don't forget what I said," Lisa replied, shooting Frances a significant look before turning back to Jack. "It's nice meeting you, Jack. I'm sorry to rush off this way, but I have a horde of hungry kids waiting for me at home. I'm sure you understand."

"Yes. Of course."

With a final flurry of farewells, Lisa was gone.

Frances and Jack were alone. Staring at each other. With nothing to say.

"You're looking well," he said after a long, awkward silence. *Even more beautiful than I remembered.*

"So are you," Frances said. *And that has to be the understatement of the century.* "Did you have a good trip back?"

"To Montreal? Oh, sure." *I've never spent a more miserable time in my life... thinking of you constantly... missing you like crazy...* "How about you? How did you find things in Charlotte when you got back?"

"About the same." *Except I was different and the things that used to matter to me meant nothing without you.* "I did find out that I'm better equipped to stand up to my sister now, thanks to you."

"I didn't do anything."

"Yes, you did. And I'm grateful to you for it."

Is that all that's left between us now? Gratitude? Jack thought. It was a damn poor substitute for what he wanted. He glanced around the room, feeling awkward and ill-at-ease.

Dear Lord! Frances thought. *He looks almost as uncomfortable as I feel.* And no wonder—she realized guiltily. While he was standing in the middle of her living room, the rain dripping from his coat was rapidly forming a puddle at his feet. "Oh, my goodness," she said moving toward him. "You're soaking wet. Here, let me take your—"

"It's okay. I can do it," he said, starting to remove his raincoat at the same time she reached for it.

They collided.

And both of them jumped back immediately from the collision, as if they'd been scorched by fire.

"I'm sorry."

"It's my fault. I should have . . ."

Jack finally removed his raincoat and Frances took it outside to hang on the coatrack in the foyer. "It's really a miserable day outside," she said. "It was this way yesterday, too."

Jack waited until she came back into the living room. "It seems pretty appropriate to me. It's exactly the way I feel—miserable. The same way I've felt ever since you left me, Frances."

"Jack, please—"

"Can't we at least talk about it?"

Frances hesitated. *Don't you owe him that much . . . and yourself, as well?* she could imagine Lisa saying.

"Would you like to sit down?" she said, gesturing toward the most comfortable chair in the living room. "I can make us some hot tea . . ."

"Nothing for me, thanks...except the chance to talk with you," he said, taking her by the hand and leading her over to the rickety sofa, where he pulled her down beside him.

She tried to tug her hand away after they were both seated, but he refused to release it. She saw him rake his other hand through his hair, the way he always did when he was thinking about something...or troubled.

"I know what I want to say to you, but I don't know where to begin," he finally admitted.

She didn't have any idea what he wanted to say, so she kept quiet.

"I'm not a billionaire anymore, Frances...not that I ever was one, actually. I only dealt in billions. But now... I've made an honest man of myself. I don't have to hide out from creditors under an assumed name."

"I don't understand."

"I've abandoned the takeover attempt."

"Oh, no!"

"Why do you say that? I know you disagreed with the idea in the first place."

"It's just...you worked so hard on it. For so long. It was what you wanted."

"Revenge was what I wanted. And to get it, I was willing to sacrifice my scruples...the people I cared about...everything that truly matters.

"After you left, I did some long, hard thinking. I remembered what you'd said early on, when we first became friends and I told you about my plans to take over the conglomerate that had stolen my father's company. You asked me if what I was doing wouldn't make me as bad as them—the people I despised the most."

She shook her head. "I'm sorry I said that."

"I'm not. Because you were right...exactly on target. Once I realized that—admitted it to myself—I knew exactly what I had to do. It's taken me all this time—ever since you left—to put my affairs in order, but now I have.

"I'm a free man, Frances. I'm not only free of financial debt, but I'm also free of that damned emotional baggage I've been carrying around for years.

"So what I'm leading up to is, now that I've abandoned the takeover idea—and rid myself of the pretense and artificial goals... Will you reconsider and have me? Please?"

"Damn you!" she said, jerking her hand away from his grasp and jumping up from the sofa.

"What?" he asked, stunned by her reaction.

"I won't let you do it, understand? I won't have it!"

"What the hell are you talking about?" he said, jumping up to square off with her.

"What you're trying to do—piling all your guilt on me. But I won't let you get away with it. I refuse to accept it."

"Are you crazy?"

"No. You're the one who's crazy if you think I'm going to take all the responsibility for something you did."

Jack reached for her but she pulled her arm away from him. "Will you please tell me what you're talking about?" he said.

"The takeover attempt. You told me you'd not only invested all that time—years and years—but also that you'd invested everything you had in it...everything you owned. And now I'm supposed to feel guilty because you've lost it all."

"No, Frances. That wasn't what I intended. Not—"

"And *I do!* Dammit! I *do* feel guilty. If it hadn't been for me..."

"Frances," he said, finally managing to capture one of her hands and hold onto it. "Ah, Frances. That isn't the way it is at all. Getting rid of that burden is the greatest thing I've ever done for myself. I feel *great* about getting out from under it at last."

"But all that money you lost because—"

"It was worth every cent of it. And more. There's no reason for either of us to feel guilty. Certainly not you. I owe you a debt of gratitude for making me see what I was doing to myself and to the people I loved—especially you."

She squinted her eyes, uncertain whether she could believe him.

"Believe it," he said, reading her thoughts the way he always could. He caught her other hand and laced his fingers through hers, holding on tightly. "And now...now will you change your mind about marrying me?"

She shook her head.

"Why not?" he asked. "Have you decided you don't love me after all?"

"It isn't that. It's just...you've changed, Jack, but I haven't. I'm still the same person—awkward, unable to make proper conversation, a social embarrassment."

"Didn't you hear a word I said? I've given up all that— the pretense...the artificial goals. None of it is important."

"That's what you think now, but—"

"It's what I'll think for the rest of my life...whether you decide to marry me or not."

Frances thought about what he'd said, and what he was saying now, wanting to believe him and not quite daring to.

"I think what we've come down to now," he said, "is whether *you're* willing to give up some of your stubborn ideas and preconceived notions."

"Mine?" she asked, surprised.

"Yes. I think I've proved that I truly do love you. Now it's your turn to do the same, and I think you're scared to death. Isn't that true?"

She worried her bottom lip with her teeth. "Maybe," she said at last.

"If you can gather up your courage to risk it . . . I think you'll find that I'm not as hard to convince as you were. Come on, Frances," he said coaxingly. "Take a chance on me. On us."

She looked at him, still wanting to believe . . . and suddenly she did. That *was* love she saw in his eyes, a deep, abiding love that reflected the same kind of love she felt for him. "Yes," she whispered.

"Yes what?" he said, tenderly touching her cheek with the backs of his fingers.

"Yes, I love you," she said, slipping her arms around his neck. "Yes, I'll marry you. Yes, I believe it's worth the risk. Yes. Yes. Yes."

He kissed her then. Hard.

"I think," he said when he finally lifted his lips from hers, "that it's not quite such a risk we're taking, after all. I think it's almost a sure thing that we're going to live happily ever after."

"I agree," she said, kissing his chin, the corner of his mouth, the other corner.

"And another thing, Frances," Jack said, returning her kisses. "A little while ago I said I wasn't a billionaire. But I didn't say I wasn't an ordinary, run-of-the-mill millionaire."

Epilogue

"Did you really think the party was okay?" Frances asked, kicking off her shoes. "You're not just saying it?"

They'd had a dinner party for eight people tonight—out-of-state buyers in town for the High Point Furniture Mart—and Frances personally thought the evening had gone very well but needed Jack to confirm it.

Also, truth to tell, she wanted a little praise for her efforts. She'd worked like a trojan to get their new home ready in time for the opening of the market, when potential customers for Jack's fledgling furniture manufacturing company streamed into High Point. During this one week, they made decisions on which lines of furniture would be carried—or not carried—in stores throughout the country for the months ahead.

Entertainment during the week was nonstop, with manufacturers vying for the attention, and orders, of influential buyers. Although Frances was aware that the quality and design of Jack's company's furniture was of prime importance, she also knew how vital it was for him to get to know the buyers on a first-name basis. Like tonight.

"I think the party was *great*," Jack said, coming up behind her to kiss her neck. "Fantastic," he added, nuzzling his scratchy chin against the soft skin of her throat and making her giggle.

"And I'm not just saying it," he said, kissing her ear before he nipped it lightly with his teeth. "I think *you're* fantastic, too. As well as gorgeous. And sexy as hell."

She wriggled around in his arms until she was facing him. "I think you're pretty fantastic yourself. And gorgeous and sexy... not to mention the best furniture manufacturer in the whole world."

"I appreciate your confidence in me, dear wife, but it'll be quite a few years before we know whether I can measure up to my father's standards... and his father and his father's father before him."

"Are you sorry, Jack?" she asked anxiously. "I mean, it was a gigantic step for you to leave New York—and all the glamour and excitement—to come down here and start a completely different life in a little town in North Carolina. Maybe—"

"It was the best decision I ever made in my life... next to marrying you."

"Are you sure?"

"Positive. I admit it's a little scary at times. That's why I made that remark about measuring up... but it's exciting, too. Challenging. Exhilarating. And I honestly think the two of us together can make the company a success. We can build it into something our children can be proud of."

"Speaking of which..." she said, deliberately not finishing the sentence. In spite of the demands and uncertainties of forging a new company, they'd talked it over and decided it was time to start creating a family of their own, too. So they'd decided to stop using birth control. Starting tonight.

"I think you'll be a fantastic father, too," she said, looping her arms around his neck.

"You're just saying that to butter me up so I'll kiss you again."

"You bet. Will it work?"

"I'm not above bribery," he murmured, lowering his mouth to hers. The kiss started out light and teasing, but soon turned into something else entirely. She felt herself growing warm and warmer still, wanting him, responding to him the way she always did. And her eager response ignited him, fueling the fires within him that were never extinguished, merely banked, waiting for her to bring them to life again.

Jack was the one who finally pulled away, reluctantly. "I need to cut off the lights downstairs," he whispered. "But don't go away. I'll be right back."

"I'll be waiting for you," she whispered back. "In bed."

"Perfect."

Jack smiled as he made his way down the stairs of their new home, marveling at the job Frances had been able to accomplish in such a short time. They'd only moved in a couple of weeks ago, and already she'd made the place look warm, friendly, inviting—like a home. A home where they could live happily for a long, long time...loving each other, laughing and crying together, growing old together.

He felt a lump in his throat.

Life would be good with Frances always by his side. It already *was* good, and would only grow better when they had kids, if they were fortunate enough to do so. In his heart—and his mind's eye—he knew they *would* have children.

He could almost picture them now—a sweet, beautiful daughter with Frances's brown eyes and her shy smile—and a devil-may-care son who looked like him and would only settle down when he finally met someone as wonderful and loving as his mother.

Jack turned out the lights in the kitchen and living room, then moved to the dining room. He hesitated a moment with his hand on the light switch, remembering Frances as she'd been earlier tonight at one end of the table, opposite him.

He smiled again, recalling how proud of her he'd been. She was lovely, charming, gracious...all the things she wanted to be and still couldn't quite believe she already was. Jack knew her worth—her special magic—and their guests had seen it, too, responded to it.

He took a deep breath, vowing then and there to make it his personal mission to make Frances realize her own worth, as well, to truly believe in herself. It wouldn't be easy, what with her being so stubborn, but he was determined to carry it through. It would be a labor of love.

Jack turned out the lights and went upstairs.

Frances was in bed—dressed in a frilly pink gown that was his personal favorite. She looked absolutely adorable. Then he saw the notepad she held braced against her up-drawn knees, and the pencil she held poised above the pad while she thought.

"What's up?" he asked, taking off his jacket and hanging it on the gentleman's gentleman beside his closet.

"I've finally decided what to do about the money Pops left me in his will," she declared triumphantly.

"It's about time," Jack said. She'd been dithering about the problem for forever, it seemed to him—whether to share her inheritance with her brother and sister or not...and if so, how much to give either or both of them. At one point, Jack had told her to give them the whole thing; that he was perfectly capable of taking care of his own wife.

She'd been indignant at that suggestion...and rightly so. But she still hadn't made a decision about the money. Until now.

"What did you decide?" Jack asked, removing his tie and starting to unbutton his shirt.

"I've decided to split the money three ways," Frances said.

Jack was slightly surprised by that, but kept quiet and continued undressing.

"But I'm only going to do it *after* I've deducted certain expenses," she said.

"What expenses?"

"For one . . . there's the matter of my salary for thirteen years. That's four thousand, seven hundred and forty-five days. And at twenty-four hours a day, it comes to a hundred and thirteen thousand, eight hundred and eighty hours."

Jack finally saw the direction she was headed, and had to clamp his teeth tight together to keep from laughing out loud. When he had himself under control, he turned to look at her and saw the mischievous sparkle in her eyes.

"Do you think that five dollars an hour for a combination nurse-housekeeper-companion is a reasonable amount?" she asked.

"I'd say that's on the low side," he responded, trying to match her businesslike tone of voice. "Ten bucks an hour wouldn't be out of line."

"If I did that, they'd end up owing *me* money."

"So?"

"No wonder they call you Jack the Shark," Frances said, finally laughing. "I'm definitely going with five dollars an hour, not a penny more or a penny less."

Removing the last of his clothing, Jack whooped with delight and jumped into bed beside her. "I'm glad you got that settled," he said, taking the notepad from her hand and flinging it over his shoulder. Frances threw the pencil in the same direction.

"Now it's time to get down to more important matters," he said, pulling her into his arms.

"Such as?"

"Starting our *own* family," he said, kissing her neck and giving a low growl.

"I couldn't agree with you more," she said, tightening her arms around him and growling back.

H A R L E Q U I N

A Calendar of Romance

Our most magical month is here! December—thirty-one days of carolers and snowmen, and thirty-one nights of hot cider and roaring fires. Come in from the cold, get cozy and cuddle with a Christmas cowboy and snuggle with a magic man. Celebrate Christmas and Hanukkah next month with American Romance's four Calendar of Romance titles:

Happy Holidays

DECEMBER

M		W	T	F	S
		2	3	4	5
6		9	10	11	12
13	14	15	16	17	18	19
20	21	22	23	24	25	26
27	28	29	30	31

#465
A CHRISTMAS
MARRIAGE
by Dallas Schulze

#466
A COWBOY
FOR CHRISTMAS
by Anne McAllister

#467
SWEET LIGHT
by Judith Arnold

#468
A COUNTRY
CHRISTMAS
by Jackie Weger

Make the most romantic month even more romantic!

COR12

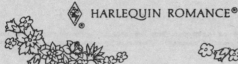

HARLEQUIN ROMANCE®

**Harlequin Romance
has love in
store for you!**

Don't miss next
month's title in

THE BRIDAL COLLECTION

A WHOLESALE ARRANGEMENT
by Day Leclaire

THE BRIDE *needed* the Groom.
THE GROOM *wanted* the Bride.
BUT THE WEDDING was *more* than
a convenient solution!

Available this month in
The Bridal Collection
Only Make-Believe
by Bethany Campbell
Harlequin Romance #3230

HE CROSSED TIME FOR HER

Captain Richard Colter rode the high seas, brandished a sword and pillaged treasure ships. A swashbuckling privateer, he was a man with voracious appetites and a lust for living. And in the eighteenth century, any woman swooned at his feet for the favor of his wild passion. History had it that Captain Richard Colter went down with his ship, the *Black Cutter,* in a dazzling sea battle off the Florida coast in 1792.

Then what was he doing washed ashore on a Key West beach in 1992—alive?

MARGARET ST. GEORGE brings you an extraspecial love story this month, about an extraordinary man who would do anything for the woman he loved:

#462 THE PIRATE AND HIS LADY
by Margaret St. George

When love is meant to be, nothing can stand in its way . . . not even time.

Don't miss American Romance
#462 THE PIRATE AND HIS LADY.
It's a love story you'll never forget.

PAL-A

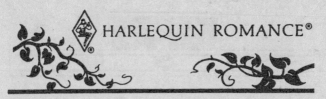

HARLEQUIN ROMANCE®

After her father's heart attack, Stephanie Bloomfield comes home to Orchard Valley, Oregon, to be with him and with her sisters.

Orchard Valley

Steffie learns that many things have changed in her absence—but not her feelings for journalist Charles Tomaselli. He was the reason she left Orchard Valley. Now, three years later, will he give her a reason to stay?

"The Orchard Valley trilogy features three delightful, spirited sisters and a trio of equally fascinating men. The stories are rich with the romance, warmth of heart and humor readers expect, and invariably receive, from Debbie Macomber."

—Linda Lael Miller

Don't miss the Orchard Valley trilogy by Debbie Macomber:

VALERIE   Harlequin Romance #3232 (November 1992)
STEPHANIE   Harlequin Romance #3239 (December 1992)
NORAH   Harlequin Romance #3244 (January 1993)

Look for the special cover flash on each book!

Available wherever Harlequin books are sold.   ORC-2